A FATAL INHERITANCE

A FATAL INHERITANCE

A Burren Mystery

Cora Harrison

severn
House

This first world edition published 2015
in Great Britain and 2016 in the USA by
SEVERN HOUSE PUBLISHERS LTD of
19 Cedar Road, Sutton, Surrey, England, SM2 5DA.
Trade paperback edition first published
in Great Britain and the USA 2016 by
SEVERN HOUSE PUBLISHERS LTD

British Library Cataloguing in Publication Data

Harrison, Cora author.
A fatal inheritance.
1. Mara, Brehon of the Burren (Fictitious character)–
Fiction. 2. Women judges–Ireland–Burren–Fiction.
3. Burren (Ireland)–History–16th century–Fiction.
4. Detective and mystery stories.
I. Title
823.9'2-dc23

ISBN-13: 978-0-7278-8566-1 (cased)
ISBN-13: 978-1-84751-675-6 (trade paper)
ISBN-13: 978-1-78010-732-5 (e-book)

All Severn House titles are printed on acid-free paper.

Severn House Publishers support the Forest Stewardship Council™ [FSC™],
the leading international forest certification organisation.
All our titles that are printed on FSC certified paper carry the FSC logo.

MIX
Paper from
responsible sources
FSC
www.fsc.org   FSC® C013056

Typeset by Palimpsest Book Production Ltd.,
Falkirk, Stirlingshire, Scotland.
Printed and bound in Great Britain by
TJ International, Padstow, Cornwall.

For my friend Cath Thompson who heroically reads each book until she comes to an orange Post-it note, then puts it down and phones me with the name of the killer. The fact that she is so often right has not interfered with a friendship which has lasted for more than thirty years!

Acknowledgements

Many thanks to family and friends who continue to encourage me during the writing of these books; to my agent Peter Buckman who must be the best agent in the world, clever, witty and immensely experienced and hard-working; to my editor Anna Telfer who is always so prompt to praise while pointing out any weakness; to the team at Severn House who turn my typescript into such a wonderfully attractive product (love the cover for this). Once again, I am grateful to the professionals in the field of Brehon law who do all the hard work of translating from medieval Irish and thereby facilitate my weaving of stories about the O'Davorens of Cahermacnaghten.

One

An Seanchas Mór
(The Great Ancient Tradition)

The fine for killing a person is fixed at forty-two séts, twenty-one ounces of silver or twenty-one milch cows.

To this is added the honour price of the victim.

An unacknowledged killing is classified as duinethaoide and this doubles the fine to be paid.

For a moment it looked to Mara as though the figure of the *Fár Breige* had suddenly come to life. A slight breeze from the Atlantic blew into the valley and stirred some strands from the petrified head of the god – not tightly curled filaments of lichen, but something more impossible, more supernatural. Tresses of real hair, iron-grey in colour, were blowing out from the skull. As Mara came nearer she could see arms clasped around the stone torso. And she could see colour and texture: woven wool dyed in various hues. Previously there had been only dark grey stone but now, in some strange way the stone seemed to have been turned into flesh. The mist was thinner here and allowed her to distinguish clothing – the white linen fringe of a *léine*, an over-garment of nettle-green, glimpsed from within a faded, multi-coloured cloak, a real head, bowed down, boots half covered with the coarse winter grass. One of the scholars' ponies gave a high-pitched whinny and even Mara's well-trained horse rose upon its hind legs, its ears laid back, spooked by the weird sight. She dismounted, feeling rather than seeing her eldest scholar, Domhnall, take the reins from her hand, and walked up the slight slope. The breeze faded away and the sea mist swirled down again, for a moment shutting out the two figures, but then it lifted and she could see that this was no apparition.

The woman who, ten days ago, successfully laid claim to

these ancient lands, to *dún, caiseal, cairn* and to the spectre-filled caves in Oughtdara, a valley that from time immemorial had been haunted by the ancient wraiths of the *Tuatha Dé*; now stood in the centre of her property, clasped to the torso of the *Fár Breige*. Mara reached out and touched the clammy flesh of the woman's face. Clodagh O'Lochlainn was as stone-cold as the fearsome god, the *Fár Breige* himself.

'We thought that we should fetch you, we thought that was the best thing to do. We saw that you were up there in the castle.' The voice, tentative and deprecating, came from behind her. Pat, the dead woman's cousin, had said nothing on the way down. Indeed, it would have been hard for him to have entered into any explanations as the sea fog had made their descent so difficult along the narrow stony path from the heights where the Ballinalacken Castle was built above the little valley of Oughtdara. The Atlantic lay only a few hundred yards to the west, but tall cliffs sheltered the place from the wind and the heavy mist had screened sight and sound. It was only when they were quite close that they saw the body.

Mara stood very still for a moment. From behind her she heard a short gasp, the sound of a breath drawn in, but no words from her six scholars. Her position of Brehon of the kingdom of the Burren and her dual role as investigating magistrate, as well as teacher, meant that all of her pupils were used to death.

But not perhaps, to a horror such as this. She cast a swift, worried glance back over her shoulder at them, Domhnall, Slevin, the two eldest would be all right, but there were also thirteen-year-old Art O'Lochlainn, who was a very sensitive boy, her own son, twelve-year-old Cormac, and the MacMahon twins, a year older than Art. But all had their ponies under control and were sitting very straight, gazing directly ahead with inscrutable expressions on their faces. Mara felt proud of them. In all of her almost thirty years in office, she had not seen such an abnormal sight.

Clodagh O'Lochlainn, Pat's cousin, wife of the shepherd Aengus O'Lochlainn, had been bound to the *Fár Breige*, one cheek pressed into the stone, her arms tied around the torso in a ghastly simulation of an embrace. The woman's eyes protruded from the waxy-white face and the mouth was wide open, almost as though it uttered a shrill scream. A rope had been pulled tight in a noose around the neck and then wound around the body and the wrists were tied together on the back of the stone god. From one wrist was suspended a large iron key. Mara gazed at her for a long minute and then beckoned to her scholars to come forward. They were, she reminded herself, all being trained not just in memorizing of legal texts and in the skills of oratory and debate, but also to investigate crimes, and she rarely excluded them from any part of her work as Brehon and investigating magistrate of the kingdom.

'Strangled,' murmured Slevin to Domhnall and he nodded in agreement. In a business-like way they tied the ponies and horses to a willow stump. Cian directed Art's attention to the dangling key with a quick nod of his head and Cormac, Mara's son, leaned over to examine the rope with a knowledgeable air.

Cael, Cian's twin, the only girl present, murmured in Mara's ear, 'May I touch the clothing, Brehon?' and then after a nod of permission, felt, between finger and thumb, a thick fold of the cloak. 'Sopping wet,' she whispered and Mara nodded.

It wouldn't tell them too much about the time of death, she thought. The rain had been so heavy that it would be hard to know whether the body had been out all night in the rain, or just for an hour. After the glorious sunshine of St Patrick's Day, there had been an abrupt change in the weather. Day after day the winds tore up from the Atlantic at gale force and the rain fell without ceasing. Fields were flooded as the limestone gave up its accumulated water from the caves that lay below the grass. Lakes with stately swans sailing across their surface appeared in fields. The sodden trees creaked and their black, bare branches streamed away from the storm winds. The small birds ceased to sing and even the blackbirds skulked beneath bushes. By noon as they rode across to Ballinalacken Castle, the sky was so dark that it felt like twilight and the distant hills were blotted out by a grey and lowering sky. But, on their arrival, the rain had stopped quite abruptly and the deep heavy mist had descended, blanketing out hills and valleys, changing trees into ghostly spectres and imposing a strange silence on the landscape. Mara shivered slightly, wishing she had had time

to change her wet clothes before Pat had come to fetch her.
She turned her eyes from the grotesque sight of the dead
woman pressed flat against the stone god, in a ghastly simulation of an embrace, and began to plan the next steps.

'Slevin, would you go and fetch the physician,' she murmured
in his ear as he bent down towards her and he nodded instantly,
unhitching his pony and leading it back up the steep path that
led to the roadway towards Rathborney. Nuala, once she had
a chance to examine the body, would be able to give a close
approximation of the time of death. It was one of the skills
that the young woman had learned from her studies in Italy.
Hopefully, Nuala's husband, Mara's law assistant, Fachtnan,
would have returned by now. She had lent him for the morning
to the elderly and rather infirm Brehon of Corcomroe, directing
him to go straight home when the case had been heard. Fergus
MacClancy was no longer capable of conducting a day of
judgement without tactful help.

'Who found her?' she asked aloud.

'Pat did,' said Deirdre, and Pat nodded in silent agreement
with his wife's words.

'Saw the crows from the hill,' he said after a minute, finding
that Mara's eyes were fixed upon him.

'And then he came to find me,' put in Deirdre and Pat
nodded again. 'Terrible shock, I got,' she continued. Her eyes
slid over the dead woman for a moment and then came back
to Mara. 'God have mercy on her soul, misfortunate creature,'
she said piously.

'And Pat hollered for me,' said Gobnait with a jerk of the
thumb towards his older brother, 'and I sent the dog for Dinan,
told him it was urgent, and off he ran; and now he's gone for
Finnegas; he's like a human, that dog; he'll do anything you
ask,' he said and the other brothers nodded gravely. All of
them shared his pride in the almost legendary cleverness of the
sheepdog, Ug.

'Bit of a shock for us, all,' said Anu, Gobnait's wife.

'Her being a cousin, when all is said and done,' put in
Deirdre. 'Terrible thing to happen, and after all of her trouble
to get hold of the place; I wouldn't live there, now, if you paid
me thirty pieces of silver,' she added with a vague memory of

a Palm Sunday sermon about the betrayal of Jesus, Mara guessed. She didn't suppose that Deirdre or her husband had ever handled even a single piece of silver. They were poor struggling farmers, desperately trying to make a living from barren rock and salt-soaked grass, and, of course, since the result of the court case a few weeks ago, they were even poorer. Her words, though, brought back the recollection of judgement day only ten days previously.

'She didn't enjoy her property for long, Brehon, did she?' remarked Gobnait.

'Poor misfortunate creature,' repeated Deirdre, but this time there was a slight note of triumph in her voice. The brothers and their wives had been thunderstruck at Mara's verdict giving possession to Clodagh of the property which had been promised to them. They had cared for Clodagh's senile father for years, but before he lost his wits, he had promised them the farm to be divided amongst the four of them after his death. Deirdre's eyes were surveying the property which would now revert to the brothers.

'The gods are not mocked; so they say,' she said after a minute and her eyes moved sideways, half-looking at the woman's body bound to the stone figure.

'Gobnait always said that he never passed *that fellow* without a prayer to St Patrick when he was going in and out of his father's house and Dinan used to make a special sign to keep the evil from touching them all and bringing bad luck,' said Anu, in a whisper. She indicated the *Fár Breige* with a slight lifting of her smallest finger and then looked hastily at her brother-in-law's face. A very interesting man, Dinan, thought Mara. Though unable to read or write he had a huge knowledge of all the old tales about the ancient peoples, the *Fír Bolgs* and the *Tuatha Dé*, who had come to this small valley of Oughtdara in the west of Ireland.

Pat, Dinan and Gobnait who farmed the hilly land around the valley, were brothers and first cousins to the dead woman. There were four boys in the family and the small patrimony of the father had been split into four equal shares. In accordance with Brehon law, the youngest, Finnegas, had made the division and then in order of seniority, the brothers had picked their share, Pat, as the eldest, picking the richer portion of land in Oughtdara valley, Gobnait, the grazing land below Ballynahown Hill, Dinan, the ancient bawns high up on the north-western slope, just above his Uncle Danu's lands of Dunaunmore.

Finnegas, the fourth brother, had been the lucky one. He had picked the barren land of Ballyryan, near to the sea, discovered a rich source of lead there, built a mine and had become rich and prosperous while his brothers struggled to earn a living from rocky pasture in valley and cliffs.

'And Finnegas, where is he?' she enquired aloud and once again the brothers looked at each other, each waiting for the other to answer. Domhnall sank to his knees beside the stone pillar, examining the rope that bound the body. Cael picked an uprooted primrose from the ground, its delicate beauty marred by the smears of wet mud on its pale yellow petals. She held it up towards Mara and then flushed crimson at a frown from Domhnall and replaced the tubular root in the exact position where it had lain. Mara nodded to show that she understood the point that Cael was making. It did appear from the state of the churned-up earth that Clodagh O'Lochlainn could have been still alive when she had been gagged and noosed and tied to the stone pillar; that she had frantically squirmed, twisted and writhed. How long had the terrible agony lasted and was there added to the torture of the body, the anguish of mind, resulting from knowing that a relation had done this terrible deed? In life, Clodagh O'Lochlainn had been greedy and quarrelsome and had shown no feelings for her family, but that did not excuse anyone who had done such a terrible deed. The dead woman must have struggled wildly while the murderer stood and waited for the end to come. Mara repeated her question about Finnegas, the youngest brother, suppressing a note of impatience from her voice.

'We sent the dog for him,' said Gobnait. 'Knowing you'd want to talk to us about what happened. He's the boy who can talk to anyone,' he added and then looked embarrassed. His wife, Anu, glared at him. Pat and Deirdre looked at their feet, while Dinan seemed mesmerized by a solitary crow that circled around their heads.

Mara pondered this statement, ignoring the muttered conversation between Anu and Deirdre from which she only distinguished the words: '*Not a woman to be good to her own,*' until the useful Ug came flying across the cliff, ears flapping and tail wagging with the happiness of a well-trained dog that has successfully followed a tricky command. From time to time he stopped and looked back to make sure of the presence behind of a small, squarely built man who strode in a leisurely fashion across the stone clints, walking with the sure-footed ease of those born in this rocky valley. Why, she wondered, as she watched Finnegas come, had the three older brothers felt they needed a smooth-talker to play the part of advocate between them and the Brehon? Had they something to hide?

And how had the dog, Ug, managed to convey to Finnegas that he was wanted by his brothers and make it sound urgent enough for the man to leave his business and come across the hills? Unless, of course, Finnegas had been awaiting the summons.

Finnegas was, she noted with interest, when he arrived, the only one of the family who did not express horror, pity or even voice a few words of sorrow. He surveyed the body from foot to head, walked around the back of the stone pillar, noted the bound hands and the dangling key and then came back again. Now he spoke, but only a monosyllable came from him: 'Well,' said Finnegas, cousin to the dead woman. And then, after a minute during which no one spoke, he added in a conversational manner, 'What do you make of this, Brehon?'

There was, thought Mara, an almost challenge in his words. She did not reply. The first discovery of the body was a time, she had often found, when the relatives and the friends of the murdered victim often said too much and it was always important to note their words and do nothing to stem the flow of speech. Now she simply looked from brother to brother and waited.

'Nothing to do with any one of us, Brehon,' said Finnegas after a minute. He was quick and sharp, she thought. He was remembering, as she had done, that on St Patrick's Day, on the seventeenth of March, the four brothers had battled with their cousin for the custody of the land where they now stood. And perhaps they, also, were remembering the curses that they had shouted at Clodagh. The words came immediately to her memory: 'May it never bring you a day of luck and may you rot in hell for all eternity!' That had been Pat, she thought, remembering the deep, rough voice. 'And may the land rise up against you and be barren for you and yours.' Gobnait had screamed that after Clodagh as she had brushed past the people standing by the entrance to the field where the dolmen of Poulnabrone stood. 'May the curse of the stone god of the old people take the breath from your body.' Dinan had uttered that last curse.

Mara had a sudden sharp vision of him on that day. He had gone very pale, she remembered, his face in contrast to his brothers' flushed visages, his brown eyes burning with intensity, his mellow, musical voice uttering the virulent words. Did he now feel that his curse had come true? Or had the curse put an idea into his head? She watched him now for a moment, but he wasn't looking at her, or even at his brothers. He seemed to be mesmerized by the solitary crow and so she turned back to the youngest brother.

'How do you know that, Finnegas?'

He was too clever not to see the implication and he came back immediately with: 'You saw me arrive, yourself, Brehon. I haven't been near this place for days, weeks, really, but I know my own family better than you do and I know that none of them could be guilty of an act like this.'

'No accusations have been made, Finnegas,' said Mara mildly.

'But you are bound to think that,' he retorted quickly. 'We all lost what we thought we possessed and we lost it to her.' He jerked his thumb towards the body and then looked at Mara. 'I'm not saying that you should not have given that verdict. The Brehon of Corcomroe being out of his mind, and his memory going was neither your fault nor was it ours. We told you the truth. We told you that our uncle had made a will leaving the land to be divided between the four of us and all four of us saw that will being locked into the chest in the Brehon's house at Corcomroe.'

'The will was not found there, Finnegas.' Mara was determined to keep her temper, though she did not relish the reopening of this argument when she had a murder on her hands. Finnegas, of course, was correct. She was bound to suspect one or all of the four brothers. The land would now come to them, just as they claimed was stated in the will made by their uncle and stored in the chest of the Brehon of Corcomroe.

It had been a painful scene on that morning at Poulnabrone, the place of judgement. Justice under the Brehon law system was a communal matter so the courts were always held in the open in order that all could attend. There were no savage punishments, no prisons; no force was used so the judgements and the fine for any crime committed had to be reinforced by the clan of the guilty person. It made sense, therefore, that all the people of the kingdom should not just be allowed, but encouraged to attend and to express an opinion if they wished. The only practical solution was to hold the courts in the open air – and pray for fine weather, Mara always told her scholars.

And when the matter of Clodagh O'Lochlainn's inheritance was held, on the seventeenth of March 1523, the day promised to remain fine. It had been a beautiful spring morning and everything had a look as though spring-cleaned by an army of servants. The strengthening sunshine of mid-spring brought a gleam from the three limestone slabs that formed the dolmen and the swirling terraces of the mountains that surrounded the Kingdom of the Burren shimmered silver in the strong March sunshine. In the hedgerow beside the road new bright green leaves of the woodbine twined among the black winter twigs and here and there a starry clump of white blossom glowed in the sunlight and formed a perch for a newly returned willow warbler that was singing his appreciation. Mara remembered poor old Fergus, the Brehon of Corcomroe, gazing up at the little songster and gently calling the attention of Fachtnan's little daughter to the pretty bird.

But Fergus, when called to give evidence, remembered nothing. Did not remember making the will, had no idea what had happened to it. Did not even appear to have any memory of Clodagh O'Lochlainn coming to see him.

And yet she must have, thought Mara, and probably at least twice. At the hearing at Poulnabrone, Clodagh had given evidence that she had brought the *taoiseach* of her clan, Ardal

O'Lochlainn, to the Brehon's house to look for the will her cousins claimed would show that the land had been left to them. Ardal O'Lochlainn had verified her claim that there was no will in the strongbox at Brehon MacClancy's house. Clodagh had been astute when she requested the presence of the *taoiseach* when the box was opened and, moreover, had shown an astonishing knowledge of the law when she had asked Ardal to assess her land and to give evidence that the land was no more than a daughter's portion. She had also brought the priest of the parish along to testify to the fact that she had gone through all the correct procedures when she laid claim to her father's lands.

No, Clodagh had won all the battles on that day and she had won them with the unwitting assistance of the Brehon of Corcomroe. Fergus, though vague and forgetful about events that had happened even days ago, had, like many elderly people, retained a sharp memory of what he had learned in his youth. Clodagh, she guessed, had been quick-witted enough to exploit the senile old man.

But now Clodagh was dead and it was the responsibility of the Brehon to find who had done the deed, to enforce public confession and the payment of retribution.

'I will need to ask some questions of you all so that while we are waiting for my scholar to fetch the physician, perhaps we could move into shelter. Is Danu's house open, do you think, Pat?' Deliberately averting her gaze from the stone pillar and the woman tied to it, she glanced down the pathway leading to the gap in the stones that encircled Dunaunmore, the home of Clodagh's father.

'We cleaned the place after the old man moved in with us and we closed it up. After you gave the judgement against us, we handed the key over to Clodagh,' said Deirdre after a minute. Her eyes slid in the direction of the hands tied behind the stone pillar. 'She and Aengus have been living there ever since.'

'And is that the only key?' asked Mara pointing.

'It is.'

Cael gave a brief shudder and Art looked slightly sick.

'In that case,' said Mara decisively, 'we cannot go into

Dunaunmore. I don't want the body touched until the physician arrives.'

She waited for Pat to offer the shelter of his own house. It was only a few hundred yards from where they stood. She could leave Cormac and Cian to guard over the body. However, Pat, after a quick glance at Deirdre, made no such offer. Mara wondered why not. The people of the Burren were, in her experience, unwearyingly hospitable – in fact, she spent most of her days dodging invitations to partake of a mug of ale, a pie, a cake, a cup of blackberry wine – invitations which would take up most of her spare time if she accepted them. Why did Pat and Deirdre not want her in their house? Deirdre was a notable housewife, famous in these regions for having sorted out the terrible mess in Pat's uncle's house, and for keeping the senile old man as neat and presentable as possible. No, Mara could bet that Deirdre was one who was always ready for company.

Did they perhaps have something within the house that might throw suspicion on them? Perhaps a coil of similar rope? Without touching anything, Mara moved a little closer to the body and, averting her eyes from the tortured face, gazed at the rope that was wound around the woman's neck.

'Nettles, ivy and brambles,' said Cormac in her ear and she nodded an acknowledgement. These ropes were all homemade and in this barren region very little flax was grown and no hemp at all, so each householder wove his ropes from whatever was readily available to him. Nettles grew profusely on dumps of household rubbish. Ivy would be plentiful on the hundred-feet high rock faces to the north of Oughtdara, where it grew in immensely long strands and, kept pliable until it dried, would make a good base for a rope, and, of course, brambles colonised the stone heaps where the animals couldn't browse. Any one of the four men facing her could have a rope like that in their possession.

She looked across at them and then said with a sudden shock, 'But where is Aengus?'

It was unforgivable. She had completely forgotten about Clodagh's husband. The fact that most people forgot about him for most of the time did nothing to excuse her. In her exasperation she blamed this ridiculous idea of Turlough's, this elaborate celebration of her fiftieth birthday, for her forgetfulness, but in her heart she knew that was no defence. When she had agreed to marry the king more than twelve years ago, she had sworn never to allow that fact to interfere with her position as Brehon of the Burren and on the whole she thought that she had kept that oath.

'God, I forgot about Aengus,' said Gobnait, his frank admission slightly salving her guilty conscience. Aengus, unlike his tough, energetic wife, was easy to forget. Although he was, in fact, fifty-four and Clodagh was forty-seven, his appearance could have made him twenty years older than she, a small man, prone to rheumatism, with pale blue eyes that blinked continuously and a shy, hesitant voice that he seldom exercised, he was completely overshadowed by his dominant wife.

'I haven't seen him since about dawn,' said Pat. 'I saw him climbing the path to Ballynahown, then.'

'Didn't see sight nor sound of him and I've been up on Ballynahown all day,' said Gobnait. 'And there were none of the *taoiseach*'s sheep there, neither.'

'Doesn't sound as though he would have stayed there, then; surely he'd have gone to where the sheep were, higher up the mountain, I suppose,' said Mara. Ardal O'Lochlainn, the *taoiseach* of the O'Lochlainn clan, employed Aengus as a shepherd and had, Mara remembered, a good estimation of the little man, saying that he understood sheep and was gentle and competent with them. 'I think that the easiest thing would be to send a message to Lissylisheen – either the *taoiseach* or his steward will know where Aengus is. I think that the news should be broken to him before he sees the body, sees Clodagh.' She wondered whether to ask one of the six people in front of her to break the news, but then decided against it. This was law school business, she thought. It was a pity that Fachtnan, her assistant, was not here; she would have to choose one of her scholars.

'Cael, I think that you would be a good person to do this,' she said. 'And I'll send Art with you.' Cael was an intelligent girl and she would keep her wits about her. Aengus would be more at ease with her than with Domhnall who had now grown to man-size and had become a rather redoubtable figure with his quiet self-assurance and formidable intelligence. And, of course, Art was the son of Cliona, a local sheep farmer, someone Aengus knew. He would feel much more at ease with a neighbour's son than he would with Domhnall, who, though the grandson of the Brehon, was born and brought up in the English city of Galway. And certainly a confused old man would be better with a pretty girl, as Cael was beginning to turn into, than a handsome, self-possessed young man, like Domhnall.

It occurred to her that Aengus was actually only about three years or four years older than Mara, Brehon of the Burren, but she swept that thought aside with a new wave of irritation as to the amount of her time that these fiftieth birthday celebrations had taken up. No more wasting of her time, she swore to herself. They can all get on with it as they wish. In any case, there were plenty of barrels of wine sent by her son-in-law, Domhnall's father, and there would surely be enough for everyone to eat. She turned her attention back to the more important things and walked over to stand beside Cael as she mounted her pony.

'Just lead up to it carefully, Cael, give him time to weep and perhaps bring him back to Lissylisheen Castle rather than to here.' Ardal, she reflected, would probably be compassionate to the old man and make things easy for him, would lend a pony for the old man to ride back upon. He had plenty of accommodation for workers in a house behind his barns and Aengus would be better off there with some of the other herdsmen.

And then she turned back to the place where the brothers and their wives stood gazing at the figure of their cousin Clodagh. It was, she reflected, almost like a mirror image of the scene a fortnight ago, on the feast of St Patrick, when she had held court at Poulnabrone, the judgement place of the Kingdom of the Burren.

Except that Clodagh had been vociferously alive on that day.

Two

Críċh Ġablaċ
(Ranks in Society)

Each kingdom in the land must have its Brehon, or judge. The Brehon has an honour price, lóg n-enech, (literally the price of his or her face) of 16 séts, eight pieces of silver or eight milch cows.

The Brehon has the power to judge all cases of law-breaking within the kingdom, to allocate fines and to keep the peace.

To keep the peace within the kingdom, that was something that every Brehon bore in mind. This murder case, thought Mara, this finding of a strangled body tied to the stone god, was going to cause a wave of superstitious horror to sweep through the kingdom. Everyone had heard the words of Dinan on that day, almost two weeks ago. Once the news got out the people of the area would be terrified, would credit Dinan with supernatural powers; would be afraid to anger him. Mara looked across at him. It was odd, but he looked the least worried of the four brothers, almost like a man who has successfully accomplished a difficult task. An interesting man, Mara had often thought. Whenever she had met him on her journeys between the law school at Cahermacnaghten and Ballinalacken Castle, Dinan had always a question for her about some of the ancient legends. The gods in the stories of *Tuatha Dé* seemed almost as real to him as his neighbours in Oughtdara and he chuckled over their exploits and seemed to retain every word that she had dredged up from her readings from books in the library collected by her father, being especially interested in his own father's namesake, Danu, but also fascinated by such powerful beings as Dagda, Lugh and Lir. She wondered whether he had convinced himself that the stone god had actually done this deed, or whether he was just good at concealing his feelings. In any case, it was strangely uncanny that the death of Clodagh had occurred exactly as he had wished for: *May the curse of the stone god of the old people take the breath from your body*, he had said and Clodagh had died almost in the arms of the god, with her breath cut off by the rope around her neck. A guilty man would have feigned shock that his words had been fulfilled; an innocent man would surely have been worried and frightened by the coincidence, but Dinan seemed calm, and, yes, there was a certain air of satisfaction about him as he stood there unconcernedly watching the crow that circled over their heads.

Pat appeared to be the most worried of the brothers and nervously licked his lips every few seconds, but, by contrast, his wife, Deirdre seemed, now that she was recovering from the shock, to be relaxed, slightly bored, gazing cheerfully up the hillside from where the shrill cries of the kids and the deeper toned notes of the nanny goats rose up, undaunted by the rain. Soon the kids would be strong enough to fend for themselves and all of the goats' milk could be churned and then formed into small cheeses that Deirdre would sell at the markets. Her mind had, it appeared, strayed from the dead woman to the living creatures on the rainy hillside and it was with a visible effort that she turned it back and gazed at the body appraisingly.

'It's a terrible thing,' said Deirdre in an undertone to Anu, 'for a body to anger a god.' Did she mean the Almighty in his heaven, or the stone god here, before them, wondered Mara. The latter, she thought.

'Lord have mercy on her,' returned Anu, and both women seemed to look interrogatively at Mara as if in hope of an opinion on this death.

Mara made up her mind. This was ridiculous. They could not all stand around forever in the mist and rain waiting. She had to take a preliminary statement from them all while their morning was fresh in their minds and then organize her lines of enquiry. But there was no possibility of her scholars being able to write in this weather; the rain would soak into the parchment and wash the ink away. She wondered whether they hoped to be invited to Ballinalacken Castle, high up on the hillside. But the castle was part of her private life as wife to King Turlough and played no part ever in the legal affairs of the kingdom and she had no intention of setting a precedent by using it this morning.

'Would it be possible to go to your house while we are waiting for the physician?' she enquired and Pat immediately flushed a dark red, but Deirdre seemed to welcome the idea and cheerfully promised hot ale. Mara took one look at Domhnall, Cian and Cormac and decided to take them also. This was the second time today that they had been soaked with rain and they looked cold and miserable. Pat's house was not too far from the stone god and the road ran past it. The grisly remains of Clodagh should be safe from any interference. Cian and Cormac could take turns at the door, watching for the arrival of Nuala, while Domhnall could write down the statements.

As soon as they entered Pat's house, Mara was struck by how very fine everything was. The house was full to bursting point with furniture, well-built examples of carpenter's craft, chairs, stools, settles, even an elaborate dresser. The walls had hangings woven in well-dyed scarlet and green wool, all of them covering the bare stone. And the well-carved chairs and benches which filled the room were softened by cushions. Very few farmers had anything like this on show. Danu, the father of Clodagh, had the reputation of being a rich man, though mean. Clodagh, herself, had married a poor shepherd with no land of his own and Mara had heard it rumoured that her father had done nothing for them. It looked as though, even if Danu's house itself was in bad repair, its furnishings had ended up here in Pat's house.

'Let's get something warm to drink and something to eat.' Deirdre seemed to be in her element as she bustled off and Anu followed her meekly towards the kitchen. Mara handed her satchel over to Domhnall and he quickly and unobtrusively seated himself on the windowsill and took out the lidded inkhorn, a pen and a large leaf of parchment. Cian had waited at the doorway to keep the first watch and Cormac, with a quick, mischievous grin at his mother, went after the women into the kitchen. He would, thought Mara, probably be more use there than with Domhnall. Cormac, at twelve, had grown tall and strong, a very good-looking boy with red-gold hair and green eyes and he had all of his father's charm and ability to get on well with everyone. And, of course, he was young enough for the women not to guard their tongues while he was around.

'I'll have more questions to ask you when I know from the physician the time of death,' began Mara. She had taken a seat beside the fire and Pat sat opposite to her, while Gobnait, Finnegas and Dinan sat squashed side by side on the long settle facing them. 'However, in the meantime, I would like to know now everything that you can remember about this morning. You found the body of your cousin, Pat. What time was that?'

'Wouldn't have been long before I came for you, Brehon,' said Pat cautiously.

Mara nodded. She had expected that answer, had seen the little group from her bedroom window in the castle. About half an hour before noon, she reckoned.

'So where were you during the rest of the morning?' asked Mara briskly. 'Could you just give me an account of your movements between the time that you got up until the time that you found the body?'

He was a slow-witted man, she thought and yet both his father and his uncle had been reckoned to be shrewd, clever men, and his cousin Clodagh, she had thought a couple of weeks ago, was sharp and intelligent with an excellent memory. Pat spent a long time trying to remember what he had been doing; it seemed to her like a morning used up in meandering around various parts of his land, checking on animals; he appeared to be having difficulty in trying to recollect which task he did first. Only when Mara put in a question about the stone pillar did he show alarm.

'I never looked at it at all, Brehon. I never even seed it. It's something that I take no notice of.' His voice was trembling and his breath came fast. Mara noticed that Finnegas looked at him sharply, appraisingly.

'Yes, of course, I understand that,' she said soothingly. 'It's just part of the landscape for you. It must be visible from almost every part of your property. I can understand that you would not be aware of it . . .' She paused, watching his face carefully as she finished, 'Unless, of course, there was the dead body of your cousin tied to it. Surely you would have noticed that, wouldn't you?'

He looked at her stupidly. 'And then I came to fetch you, Brehon. Gobnait thought it was the right thing to do.'

'Indeed,' said Mara and gave Gobnait a gracious nod. 'Very wise.' She allowed him to bask in this praise for a moment and then said swiftly, 'But what I can't understand, Pat, is how you did not see anyone approach with Clodagh's dead body, or that you did not see a struggle, hear her cries for help before she was strangled. Your land, both your own land and the land that belonged to Clodagh's father, surely is within sight of the stone pillar?' She would not, she resolved firmly, ever refer to it as a god. The idea of the murder being attributed to the *Fár Breige* did not appeal to her, and she would do her best to quench all such talk. 'I'm surprised that you saw nothing – perhaps took no notice at the time, but now, thinking back, you may remember that there was some sort of unusual movements going on down there near the entrance to Dunaunmore.'

This is putting ideas into the head of the witness, she told herself crossly, but the man was beginning to annoy her with his hesitancy.

He stared at her uncomfortably and her heart softened. Better slow, but honest, she told herself reprovingly.

'Let's start from the time that you rose this morning, Pat,' she said encouragingly. 'You got up from your bed . . .'

'I looked out and it was still raining,' he said unexpectedly and then with a slight alarm, he continued, 'I didn't look at the *Fár Breige*. I have no memory of that, at all.'

'No, of course, not,' she said soothingly. 'So you had your breakfast.'

His mind, however, was still on the stone pillar. 'Terrible, dirty weather,' he said.

She nodded. 'That's right.' And then she remembered that 'dirty weather' didn't just mean lots of mud, but was used locally to mean something that you couldn't see through, like a dirty window, perhaps, a day with a thick mist, or rain so dense that it was impossible to see more than a few yards ahead. It hadn't been like that at the law school, but it may have been different in this valley near to the ocean. Cahermacnaghten was very much higher up.

'And when you went out, after breakfast,' she prompted him.

'Me and Deirdre went to the Cave of the One Cow.' He looked at her anxiously to see whether she was following him and she nodded. She had heard of this cave. It was to the north-west of the valley, just where the limestone cliff began to soar up above the random rocks and stones. There was some sort of legend attached to it, she remembered and hoped that she could escape being informed about it. Luckily he went on more cheerfully: 'We had a nanny goat shut in there, away from the foxes—'

'Terrible, the foxes around here,' put in Gobnait.

Pat nodded. 'That's a fact, Brehon. Well, the nanny was just about to give birth so we stayed with it – just as well, as there were a pair of them, in there; a pair of kids and they were all tangled up, the legs twisted around each other and, well, you can ask Deirdre, Brehon, but we had a time of it. Let me tell you . . .'

Pat's brothers were listening with fascinated interest, so Mara felt unwilling to hurry him along. Domhnall, she noticed with amusement, had made a brief note of a few words and now was sitting looking out of the window, his brow creased in thought.

'And after Deirdre had milked the goats and had gone back to the house, what did you do, then, Pat?' It would probably have taken about an hour to help the nanny goat to give birth to her twins, she thought, and then, probably another half hour, or even hour, for the milking. She would ask Deirdre afterwards, any woman who cooked normally had a better idea of how the day was going than farmers who just went by the strength or the weakness of the light.

'Well,' said Pat in a slightly helpless way, 'I had a look around, just checking, like.'

'Checking?'

'Seeing which of the nannies were near her time,' explained Pat.

'And when did you see the body of your cousin?' put in Mara, noticing from the corner of her eye how Domhnall straightened and turned his head towards Pat. Deirdre and Anu came in carrying trays, followed by Cormac, chewing vigorously. The two women went very quietly to the table and placed the hot drinks and cakes on it and Cormac crossed the room to sit beside Domhnall on the window seat.

'It was when I went back up into the Cave of the One Cow,' explained Pat. 'I just wanted to check that the two little kids were feeding and their mammy was happy and so they were, God bless them.'

'So you saw nothing on your way in?' asked Mara. She hoped that no one else, except Domhnall, would notice that Cormac's shoulders were heaving with an effort to control his giggles.

'That's right, Brehon, it was when I came out that I saw something fluttering. I thought first that it was Deirdre, but then when I blinked I saw that it was coming from the *Fár Breige* and I knew that Deirdre wouldn't go within sight or sound of *him*.'

'So the mist had cleared a little, had it?' That would have been about the time that she and her scholars were approaching Ballinalacken Castle.

'That's right, Brehon. The wind had got up. It was blowing nicely. Coming in from the sea.'

'And then you came down, saw your cousin's body, signalled to Gobnait whom you saw on the hill, with his dog . . .' Suddenly Mara turned towards Gobnait.

'Did you see the body?'

Gobnait wasn't as agonisingly slow at giving his evidence as Pat. He and his dog Ug, after they both had their porridge, had gone up onto the hill of Caherdoon to check on his sheep. They found one giving birth and stayed with it as foxes were prowling around. Ug, doing his duty, dispersed them, killing a couple, according to Gobnait, and then came back.

'Did you see anyone when you went up there?' asked Mara, thinking that she should have asked that question of Pat.

'I saw Aengus, Clodagh's husband, same as I see him every morning. He was going up to Ballynahown, and then on to the mountain to see to the *taoiseach's* sheep. That would have been about when the light was coming, the early morning.'

'I see,' said Mara. Of course, both men were climbing, looking ahead to the north of the area and in Gobnait's case, he was looking after Aengus who would have been ahead, to the north-east of him. They would have had little reason to look behind them, but even if they had, the chances were that, around dawn, the valley was filled with mist.

'And you stayed up for the morning?' She was frustrated by not knowing the time of death but any information gathered now while she was waiting for Nuala's arrival would be time saved later on. She was beginning to get a picture of a very lonely valley. Pat and Deirdre had no children. Neither had Gobnait and Anu, and Dinan had never married. Finnegas, the only one of the four to have a family, had moved out of the valley and into Ballyryan, which was on the edge of the sea, and quite near the border with Corcomroe.

'That's right, Brehon. Ug disappeared for a long time and I was mortal afraid that he would have got himself caught in one of the fox traps that we've set among the stones. I was searching everywhere, calling and whistling for him.'

'That's a fact,' confirmed Pat. 'I could hear him and the mountains were giving back the word, like they do.'

It could have been quite a clamour, thought Mara. These hill men had powerful voices and the echoes added to the sound of the wind and the rain might have drowned out any cries from the victim. She tried to remember whether the structure of Dunaunmore would have blocked the view of the *Fár Breige* from the eyes of someone on those north western slopes. She rather thought it would, but that was something that she could check, or that her scholars could find out for her.

Dinan had spent the first part of the morning cutting rods from the sally bushes that grew in the wet openings to the caves that riddled the limestone cliff to the north of Oughtdara. He explained that he needed them to weave baskets for holding the sheared wool in early summer and after he cut them, he had left them to soak in a deep pool beside the Bones Cave. After that, like his two brothers, he went to check on some of his sheep. It was, he explained, important to know which ones are about to lamb as there was a great menace from foxes that built their dens in and around the remains of the ancient fortified duns. Foxes, he told Mara earnestly, were the souls of the evil members of the ancient *Tuatha Dé* people, turned out of hell for their wickedness and doomed to roam the earth and to be hated by man and beast. Cormac, who had sniggered at Pat's sentimentality about mammies and babies, was looking quite interested in this statement, Mara noticed, before signalling him to go and relieve Cian.

There was a little bit of a fuss when Cian came in, with Deirdre, in a motherly fashion, taking his wet cloak to shake the rain from its felted surface and then to hang it by the kitchen fire and leaving Anu to feed him with honey cakes and warmed ale. Domhnall read through his notes and added in a few words here and there. And then he looked across the room attentively at Mara. For an eighteen-year-old he had great patience and great self-control, she thought. These initial hours in an enquiry were always slow where, after the early drama of finding a body, there came hours of meticulous note-taking. Still, these were notes whose significance often was only seen well into the enquiry and she was interested to see how carefully Domhnall had scanned them.

She began to question Deirdre but nothing new emerged, and although she had been working in the kitchen, getting hot drinks and cake for her visitors when her husband, Pat, had given his evidence, she confirmed all that he had said about the early part of his morning. She had come home before he did as she had work to do and so she had left him and had come back to the house by herself. While she was cleaning her beautiful home and making her tasty cheeses, she had been alone except for a visit from Father O'Lochlainn and he had been with them when they discovered the body. He had, she informed Mara, given extreme unction, the last sacrament of anointing with oil, and then had departed for his church to pray for the soul of the dead woman.

'Terrible upset, he was,' said Deirdre comfortably. 'I thought the poor man would faint on me, but he wouldn't even have a drop of ale or anything. Nothing would do him except to go off to the church and to pray for the repose of her soul, poor creature.'

Mara raised an eyebrow at that; she would have thought that a priest would be well used to death, but was just as glad that she did not have to deal with Father O'Lochlainn. She had completely forgotten about sending for him, as she should have done, and so was pleased that he had been on the scene earlier and all had been done for the dead woman's soul. There was, she knew, some sort of belief that the holy oil had to be administered in order for the soul to be able to leave the body, so it was good that all that ritual had been attended to. She dismissed the priest from her thoughts and then she turned her attention to the last of the four brothers.

Finnegas O'Lochlainn had inherited his family's share of brains and drive. Mara's housekeeper, Brigid, had told her how, when a boy, Finnegas had noticed that there was a place on his father's land, just on the boundary with Corcomroe, where little grew and where often a rabbit, or even a fox was found dead for some mysterious reason. According to Brigid, young Finnegas had pestered everyone in the neighbourhood, even the sailors and passengers on ships that pulled into Doolin, asking them all if they knew of any reason for this strange occurrence – and then one day suddenly said no more. Finnegas, sly young fox, Brigid called him, became a model son, seeing to the sheep, selling the wool, but above all, trying out his muscles in breaking up tons of stones, the stones that were lying around the valley and its highlands, and building, seemingly for his own amusement, a pathway. By the time that he was seventeen years old, he had, unaided, built a magnificent road in the poorest part of his father's land, in the townland of Ballyryan. And not a soul nor a sinner, according to Brigid, had realized that this road linked the road to the harbour with that spot of bad land, where nothing would thrive and where unwary animals met their death by drinking the water. All that anyone thought was that it might be handy for the wool, but they wondered why he had bothered. Wool, even large baskets of it, could be easily carried by a man, or a donkey equipped with panniers, across uneven ground. And then had come the death of the father and the dividing of the land. Finnegas had waited while Pat and Gobnait had taken the better areas and then, to everyone's surprise, he had chosen the land at Ballyryan, including the place where nothing grew. A year later, carts were going down that splendid new road, laden with baskets of lead, chipped out from the rock, and burned in fire until the metal ran liquid.

Finnegas, thought Mara, must by now, be a very rich man. There would be no need for him to kill his cousin in order to get hold of those rushy, waterlogged fields that were his portion when Danu's land had been divided amongst them all. That lead mine of his, on the land that had been his father's, must be worth a fortune. He had no need for grazing land. Still she went through the motions of asking him to account for his time this morning when Clodagh was killed.

Finnegas was clear-headed and helpful in his account of his movements. 'I spent most of the morning weighing and checking the loads that the men brought out from the mine, Brehon,' he explained. 'There's a boat going from Doolin to Galway a couple of hours before sunset so I wanted to make sure that everything was right for that. You probably know, Brehon, how almost all of the houses in Galway have window glass and those little diamond-shaped panes all need the strips of lead to hold them in place. And then there are the roofs – no thatch allowed in Galway these days because of the risk of fire, so lead is needed between the slates. We do a great trade in the city with the lead.'

'So you were in sight of your men all of the time.'

'I couldn't tell you that,' he said, with a slight note of impatience. 'I go in and out of the mine, in and out of my house, of the sheds and the storerooms as the case may be and wherever I'm needed. And then I had some dinner when they went to the harbour. But I can tell you one thing I wasn't doing, though, Brehon, I wasn't over here this morning and I wish I wasn't here now, because, to be honest, I have plenty to do. There's nothing that I can help you with, Pat,' he went on, looking impatiently at his eldest brother. 'The unfortunate woman must be buried, but surely you, and the priest, and the others can sort it out between you – and Aengus, of course,' he added and once again Mara realized how much they were all forgetting about the husband of the dead man. 'So if you're finished with me, and if you don't mind, Brehon, I'll be off, now.'

At that moment Cormac thrust his head through the door and announced, 'The physician is coming down the road, Brehon. She's brought a cart for the body. And Fachtnan is with her, and Slevin, of course.'

Mara was conscious of a feeling of relief. It would be good to have Fachtnan at her side. And, of course, Nuala always gave such valuable information.

Nuala O'Davoren, the daughter and the granddaughter of a physician, was a distant cousin of Mara's. From an early age she had wanted to study medicine, had picked up as much as she could from her father, had studied her grandfather's notes. After her father's death, she'd had the best of training from the physician in King Turlough's court and then had furthered her studies by time spent in Italy. She had learned there how to open the body and to find out, not just the reason for the death, but how many hours had elapsed since the victim had died. Nowadays Mara felt that a murder investigation could not properly start before all of this information had been noted down. She rose to her feet and smiled graciously at the brothers and the two women.

'I shall leave you now,' she said. 'I know where to find you if I have any more questions, but it won't be today.' She hesitated in case they would think that she was meddling in what did not concern her, but her conscience made her add, 'And, I hope, in your charity, that you will be kind to Aengus. This will come as a terrible shock to him.'

'Oh, yes, indeed, Brehon, misfortunate man. He's welcome to stay here, if he wishes.' Deirdre was warmly sympathetic and Pat joined in with some inarticulate murmurs while Gobnait nodded energetically and Dinan promised that he would look out for him.

A compassionate family, thought Mara, as she made her way to the door to greet Nuala. Clodagh's father, Danu, had been well-cared for by them and it may be that the dead man's wishes were now being fulfilled, that he preferred his property to go to the nephews who had looked after him, rather than to the daughter who had neglected him and with whom he was at odds. And that, perhaps, there had been a will, made and witnessed by Brehon MacClancy of Corcomroe. And, she admitted to herself, it was likely that the will had been stolen by Clodagh O'Lochlainn.

Nothing, though, she said to herself, justifies murder.

Three

Uraicecht Becc
(Little Primer)

A physician has an honour price of seven séts. He is expected to apply herbs, to supervise diet and to undertake surgery. There will be no penalty for causing bleeding, but if he cuts a joint or a sinew he has to pay a fine and he will be expected to nurse the patient himself.

A banliaig *(woman physician) is a woman of great importance to the kingdom.*

Nuala's black eyebrows met in a frown as she swung herself down from her horse. She tossed her reins to Cormac, strode ahead of Fachtnan and Slevin, and went straight up to the stone pillar. She stood for a moment, touching nothing, her dark eyes intent on the bound and slumped figure, waiting for the cart to come up and, when she spoke, it was to give some practical directions to her servant and her apprentice. Then she stayed them with one hand and moved forward, examining the dead woman's wrists.

'Difficult to know whether she was still alive, or just newly dead when this was done.' The remark was to herself and Mara did not question or interrupt Nuala's concentration. On the whole Nuala preferred to give her report only when she knew all that the body could reveal. But then, uncharacteristically, the physician looked away from the body and at Mara. She moved a step nearer and said in a very low tone to her, 'I warned Dinan that this was a dangerous business. I wish that he would leave all those gods and goddesses alone. If you have to have the supernatural, it's best to stick to Christianity.'

'What do you mean?' Mara was taken aback. Nuala, when confronted with injury or death, seldom spoke of anything except the practical task ahead. It was unusual to see her turn away from a body and take the time to talk.

'Well, a bit of Mass going and chanting of psalms can't hurt,' said Nuala with a shrug. 'But when people start blaming banshees or the Morrigan for deaths and injuries, it all gets very dangerous and bad things like this can happen.' She spoke very quietly, her words barely audible to Mara's ear and Mara nodded silently in return. There was a strong superstition about the presence in local caves of the Morrigan, the great and evil queen of the old gods. All sorts of disasters and crimes were blamed upon her presence.

'Have you been talking to Dinan, then?' she asked. Nuala was rarely seen outside her own home and hospital at Rathborney and she was not a woman with any spare time for gossip. Mara's eyes went to the bystanders, but no one was looking at them. All eyes were drawn to the huge figure of the *Fár Breige* and they watched uneasily while the cart was manoeuvred as close as possible to it. Domhnall and Slevin with the two younger boys had formed a slight barrier and the cluster of people were kept at a distance of about a hundred yards from the body, but there was no doubt about the intensity of atmosphere. No one spoke, even children were hushed into silence, and all gazed intently at their stone god.

'Dinan?' Nuala had turned away towards the body, but then she turned back to Mara. She had a query in her voice as if she had already forgotten what she had said. 'Oh, yes, Dinan. He had a very badly infected fox bite. It had to be cleaned out every day at the hospital; he kept telling me those old tales while I was draining out the pus. He wouldn't believe me when I told him that foxes eat filth; eat dead, decaying bodies and that was why his arm went bad. No, according to Dinan, it had to be the soul of some old god. He loves all of these old stories. I don't like them; they deal too much in pain, mutilation and cruelty. It's dangerous when people take these things seriously. It becomes a screen for evil to hide behind.'

Nuala set her lips firmly and moved forward. She would say no more, but she had already said enough to make Mara feel deeply uneasy. There was no doubt, she thought, that Dinan in particular, but also all of the people within this hidden valley, seemed to dwell rather too intensely on the heroic past and on the suffering and the ugly and terrible deeds that had been performed. Not for a moment did Mara herself believe that this oddly sculpted stone pillar, named as the *Fár Breige*, had anything to do with the death of Clodagh O'Lochlainn; there were only too many ordinary, human reasons for killing the woman, but she feared the effect of wild rumours and superstitious fears and the way that these can screen evil doers. One murder, she thought, often begets another murder. She cast a slightly uneasy look at the cluster of people, which was increasing every minute, and went to stand by Nuala.

Nuala, as always, was quick and practical, her dark eyes focussed and alert as she directed her servant and one of her apprentices to unwind the rope carefully and then to lift the body and to place it upon the cart. Mara, standing beside Fachtnan, watched in silence. It was not something that she enjoyed doing, but she felt that she owed it to the dead person to bear witness to the suffering that they had endured and to the tragedy of their death. Human life, she thought, as she watched, is a very sacred thing and she felt glad and proud that the legal tradition which she had served for over twenty years forbade the shedding of blood and sought always for the compensation to the victim, rather than revenge upon the guilty. Brehon law was above a petty vengefulness and concentrated on re-establishing peace in the community after any violent upheaval such as murder. From now on, until the crime was solved, her whole focus had to be on finding the doer of this deed and to ensure compensation for the family. And the investigation had to start with the victim, respect for the body and a determination to get justice for the dead person.

And so she forced herself to go nearer and to stand beside the cart as Clodagh was laid on it. There was a rough canvas sheet rolled up at the bottom and the apprentice picked it up, getting ready to cover the body with it, but was stilled by a quick motion of Nuala's hand. Mara saw her bend over, looking intently, saw her hand come out and move a fold of the dead woman's cloak aside. Then she straightened herself and looked directly at Mara.

'I can tell you one thing for you to be going on with, Mara,' she said. 'Clodagh wasn't strangled with that noose which was tied around her neck. What killed her was something else. Look at those bruises. These are finger marks. Someone came behind her and squeezed hard – easy to do. She was choked to death by a pair of hands, possibly when she was standing there beside that stone pillar, or perhaps when she was sitting down at a table.' And with a quick nod at her apprentice, Nuala signalled for him to cover the body and then she mounted her horse and rode ahead of the cart back up the hilly road which, after winding through the mountain pass, would bring her back to her house, hospital and farm at Rathborney. She took no leave of Mara or of her husband, Fachtnan; her whole being was now focussed on the task ahead, the scientific procedures that she had learned when studying at a university in Italy, whereby the dead body yielded up its secrets.

Neither Fachtnan nor Mara gazed after her. Their eyes had met, both horror-filled, yet full of surmise. Fachtnan was the first to speak.

'Merciful heaven,' he said. 'Sitting down at a table. Did it happen overnight? Inside her own house? It couldn't have been Aengus, could it?'

'I wouldn't blame him,' said Cormac. 'God, I'd have strangled her if I were he! The way she yelled at him, screamed at him and called him an idiot and every filthy name under the sun.'

'*De mortuis nil nisi bonum*, Cormac,' said Cian loftily, displaying simultaneously both his knowledge of Latin and his superior moral code.

Cormac came back furiously: 'Hypocrite! What's the point of telling lies about a dead person? We're supposed to be finding out the truth and the truth has to start with Clodagh. We have to acknowledge what she was and then decide who hated her enough to kill her.'

Mara thought of hushing him but decided that, too, would be hypocritical. Her son had only voiced what was in her mind and in Fachtnan's also. There was no doubt that Clodagh had treated the nice little man, her husband, Aengus, abominably. Even market traders had sniggered at the names that she called him and the insults that she screamed at him. Mara had silenced the woman once in public, threatening to bring her before the court, assuring her that the law took very seriously the offence of taunting. After that, Clodagh had been careful in her presence, but she had little doubt that the tormenting had gone on when she was absent.

'We should wait for some more evidence, though, shouldn't we, before naming any possibilities, Cormac,' said Domhnall quietly. 'Though I agree with you that he was very badly treated,' he added diplomatically.

'Poor old Aengus! I can't see that he'd ever have got his courage up to do a thing like that, though,' said Cormac regretfully, his eyes on the rope that now lay coiled upon the ground. He leaned over, precariously maintaining his balance, and managed to pick it up and store it into his satchel.

'Evidence,' he said with a grin at Mara and then, quickly: 'But why is the ground all hacked up around here if she were strangled with thumbs and fingers inside her own house. I'd say myself that the murder took place out here. Remember how misty it was until a half-an-hour or so ago.'

'I agree with Cormac,' said Slevin. 'I think it could have happened out here. It would be too risky to bring the body out from the house. And then there are those marks on the ground as though someone struggled violently.'

'Easily done,' said Cian. 'A few hacks with the heel of a boot and you give the appearance of a struggle. The ground is soft after all the rain.'

'That shows that it wasn't Aengus,' said Cormac triumphantly. 'He'd never have the brains to think of that. Anyway, it's not the sort of thing that he would do. He's a very nice fellow.'

'I don't know, though,' said Cian, eyeing the satchel enviously. 'Old Aengus had a temper. I said something to him once, joking-like, and he screamed at me. Took a swipe at me with his stick.' He coloured up when he saw Mara's eye on him and said hastily, 'Ages ago. I was young then.'

Which might, at this age, mean just last Christmas, thought Mara, but she decided to let it pass.

'I don't think that we can do too much more, here, we should talk to Aengus, first,' she said in a low voice to Fachtnan. 'I asked Cael and Art to go and find out from Ardal O'Lochlainn where he might be – Dinan saw him around dawn up in Ballynahown, probably going towards the Knockauns Mountain where Ardal has his sheep.' If Aengus were responsible for the murder then he did run the risk of the body being discovered before he left the valley. But, of course, if he had scaled that steep hillside and had reached Ballynahown by dawn, then he must have left Oughtdara while it was still dark.

It was odd, she thought, that no one, neither Pat, nor Gobnait, nor their wives, nor Dinan had noticed the body tied to the stone pillar.

However, according to Pat, there had been a thick mist in the valley that early morning and that could have cloaked the stone pillar. They probably averted their gaze from it, in any case; it had been, it appeared, an object of fear to all of the brothers from the days of their childhood.

'Yes, we'll go straight to Lissylisheen,' she said aloud and was pleased with her decision. They would have to do without her at Ballinalacken Castle. She had thought to spend the day there making arrangements for the elaborate celebrations for her fiftieth birthday. These had not been her idea. She would have preferred to mark the day quietly with perhaps a special dinner, a choice bottle or two of wine, possibly a few friends to share it. But Turlough had other ideas. She was the wife of a king, he had said solemnly. Her fiftieth birthday was going to be marked in the same way as his fiftieth birthday had been celebrated. He had planned some great celebrations and then went away on a visit to the north of Ireland leaving his staff rudderless and looking for direction. Well, she thought, it could not be helped. Without her presence they would have to make their own decisions and she was glad to be away from the tiresome preparations for a celebration that did not interest her.

She climbed on one of the flat rocks next to where the horses were tethered and mounted. Fachtnan checked the saddle on his horse and then swung a long leg over it. The boys were already on their ponies and they went in a long single line up the small street of Oughtdara and past the tiny church with Father O'Lochlainn's house beside it, and up onto the road leading to Cahermacnaghten.

March was going out like a lion during the week. Day after day the winds tore up from the Atlantic at gale force and the rain fell without ceasing. The limestone gave up its accumulated water from the caves that lay below the grass and lakes had appeared in fields. The sodden trees creaked and their black, bare-branched crowns streamed away from the storm winds. The small birds ceased to sing and even the blackbirds skulked beneath bushes. By noon the sky was so dark that it felt like twilight and the distant hills were blotted out by a grey and lowering sky.

But now the wind had died down and the heavy rain that had drenched them during the earlier part of the morning had turned back to a drizzle, pearling on the stiffly brushed nap of their cloaks, but not soaking them. Small silver raindrops balanced on the sharply pointed spines of the blackthorn bushes and the division between mountain, hills and sky was lost in a soft, grey haze. Mara cast a quick glance at the towering shape of Ballinalacken, high on the hill above them, its crenellated rooftop lost from view and smiled as she saw the illuminated windows and a light moving down the staircase in the old tower, showing first in one loophole, then in the next. All were still busy there, getting ready to celebrate her fiftieth birthday.

'There's nothing too wonderful about living for fifty years when you have shelter from the cold and the rain, and enough to eat,' she said, half to herself and caught her grandson Domhnall grinning at Slevin.

'You don't find it an achievement,' he suggested when he saw that they had been spotted.

'No, I do not,' she said robustly. 'It just reminds me of growing old and dying and after a while no one will remember that I have ever lived.' She thought about that for a moment. Had she achieved anything, other than attaining the age of fifty? Still there was plenty of time ahead of her. She had excellent health and was strong and energetic. An idea flashed through her mind and she savoured it for a minute. She would enjoy a new challenge.

'I'll tell you what we'll do, though, Domhnall, you and I,' she said enthusiastically. 'When I'm about eighty or ninety and too old to work, we'll write a book, together. We'll collect all the judgements from the length and the breadth of Gaelic Ireland, and manuscripts, too; all that has been written down,

all that has been memorized. You can get your scholars to
work on the copying, but you and I will word it and perhaps
if I am gone by the time everything has been collected then
yours will be the ending.'

Domhnall smiled enigmatically and glanced over towards
Cormac who was busy arguing with Cian about the height of
the stone pillar. Mara saw the look, but said nothing. By now,
though, she was fairly certain that Cormac would not want to
inherit the law school that had been first owned by his grandfather and then passed down to Mara. Cormac had little or
no interest in the law and wanted to be a warrior, like his own
father. He had brains and an excellent memory, but he had
no interest in the intricacies that delighted Domhnall. No,
Domhnall – an O'Davoren on his father's side as well as on his
mother's side – was the true heir. He would care for the inheritance of the law school and keep it safe – that was, thought
Mara sadly, if the long arm of England's might and determination had not regained control over the small neighbouring
island of Ireland. King Henry VIII had now been a king for
fourteen years. He had fought France, had laid waste to vast
tracts of that country, was even at this moment marching his
armies north, preparing to overrun Scotland, according to
Turlough's information. Next would come Ireland's time.

'Did either of you pick up anything from the conversation
in the kitchen?' She turned to Cormac and Cian who were
arguing with each other.

'They were talking about Clodagh, just muttering, you know,'
said Cormac instantly abandoning his disagreement and turning
his face towards his mother. 'It's funny but they seemed to
have got the impression that Clodagh was going around hiring
stone workers. What she wanted them for I don't know.'

'Did Deirdre or Anu know?'

'Not them. They thought that she might be doing up the
old house. They kept whispering that Clodagh had said that
she was going to make it splendid, but neither of them knew
why she should be going to employ stone workers. Deirdre
was saying the stone work was the only thing that was good
about the house. "If it were a thatcher or a carpenter now . . ."
That's what she was saying.'

'And Anu?'

'Anu was just agreeing with her. That's always the way when women are gossiping together,' said Cormac impatiently. 'Neither of them could make out why Clodagh would want to hire so many men with sledgehammers.'

'Perhaps she was going to knock down the house,' suggested Cian.

'No, birdbrain, I said they were talking about her boasting that she was going to make it a splendid place.'

Mara turned the conversation over in her head. It was odd, she thought. Why would Clodagh want to hire men who could split stone, men with sledgehammers?

'Brehon, do you think that Aengus might have killed Clodagh? Cian thinks he could, but I don't believe it.' Cormac and Cian had resumed the argument that had been engaging them during her low-voiced argument with Domhnall and now her son turned back and rode beside her, looking intently into her face as he asked his question. 'He's such a terrified little rabbit of a man,' he added. 'I just can't imagine him getting the courage to do something like that. And, I'd say, that Clodagh was definitely bigger than he was.'

'I never really like these sort of discussions, Cormac,' said Mara. 'Everything is just guesswork, at this stage. What we need is to gather all the available evidence, to sift the facts, and only then can we arrive at a working hypothesis.'

It was, she thought, with a moment's compunction, a scholarly answer, but not a very honest one. Her own mind had been dallying with the same thoughts. Would Aengus kill Clodagh? Could Aengus kill Clodagh? Did he have the strength of mind and body? She was not surprised when Cormac gave a shrug of his shoulders and moved back up to resume his conversation with Cian, leaving Mara to her thoughts as they turned off the road and brought their horses onto the sheep-nibbled grass plateau between the hills.

The grass was very wet, but sheep were light-footed animals and had not made the ground as boggy as cows would have done. Mara's horse picked his way with care: stones littered the uneven surface and here and there a puddle formed. Their journey through the mountain pass towards the law school and its nearest neighbour, Ardal O'Lochlainn, would, she reckoned, take about half to three-quarters of an hour. She would stop this useless guessing and employ the time to establish in her mind the facts of the case, she thought repentantly and she allowed her horse to fall back until she was beside Fachtnan.

'I talked with the four brothers: Pat, Gobnait, Finnegas and Dinan, Fachtnan,' she said. 'Three of them: Pat, Gobnait and Dinan were all around this morning – so they could have had an opportunity, depending on when she was killed, of course. I think that there were periods of heavy mist during the morning and also there was a time when Gobnait lost his dog and was, as he said, "hollering" for him, and the hills were echoing the sound. And then, of course, in view of what Nuala said, there is a possibility that Clodagh was murdered elsewhere, perhaps within her own house, and that her dead body was dragged out and then bound to the stone pillar.'

'What about the way that the grass was churned up under her feet?' They had now left the narrow paved road and had turned onto the grass-covered mountain pass where all could ride together. Cormac's sharp ears had overheard their conversation and now he turned back to face them.

'Could be faked by the murderer,' put in Cian.

'We have to think why she was left like that,' said Domhnall. 'Why put the body almost in the arms of the *Fár Breige*, why hang the key from her wrist?'

'Because Aengus was mad at her.' Cian didn't deal in subtleties.

'Or Pat, or Gobnait, or any of them,' argued Cormac. 'Remember the key. The key would be nothing to do with Aengus, but if it was one of them, the key could mean: you have no right to that property.'

'I judged Clodagh to have a right,' said Mara mildly. She was interested to find out what he would say in answer to that. He came straight back at her, the answer flashing like a drawn sword.

'What if you were wrong, and they knew that you were wrong? They knew that there had been a will locked up safely in Brehon MacClancy's chest. They were certain of that. You could tell that. They were flabbergasted when their *taoiseach* said that the will was not there. You'd want to be stupid not to be able to see that in their faces. They weren't lying. They're not like that.'

'You don't think that Ardal O'Lochlainn was lying?' asked Cian in interested fashion.

'Of course not,' said Cormac indignantly. 'He's a friend of the king's. He doesn't lie. Why should he? No, Clodagh took it out of the chest while poor old Brehon MacClancy was—' he hesitated, and then finished diplomatically – 'was feeling a bit dazed. The *taoiseach* couldn't say that there was a will there when he looked if there wasn't, but there was probably a will there a few days earlier.'

'You could be right,' said Mara. 'We can allow it as a possibility.'

'The whole scene, the body tied to the stone pillar, it was set up like a picture, wasn't it?' Domhnall didn't wait for a comment on that, but continued: 'And a picture is painted to make you think, isn't it? The key and the god; it could all be to make you think that Clodagh had been killed by the *Fár Breige* because she had lied and stolen. But on the other hand, the real murderer might have just wanted to throw suspicion on Pat, or on Gobnait, or on all of them.'

'I can't see Aengus being as clever as that,' said Slevin. 'No, that would be out of the question. And we have no more suspects, have we?' He looked sideways at Mara and then added diplomatically, 'But of course, the investigation has not really started. Who knows what we might uncover?'

'I agree with Domhnall about the picture,' said Mara. 'After all, if Clodagh was strangled, why not just try to bury her, or throw her body into the sea, or down a hole in one of the caves.'

'Like the Caves of the Bones that Dinan showed us, do you remember, Cormac?' said Cian. 'That was full of bones. It was a sacred burial place for the old people, Dinan told us. I saw a hand down there, with long, long fingers and loads of skulls,' he added with relish.

'That was a great day! Will you ever forget Cael's face, when he was telling the story about the daughters of Lir and how they turned into swans and had to spend four hundred years buffeted by the storms of the Celtic Sea? She was like in a trance and she slipped over on all that oozy stuff in the Moon Milk Cave.'

He was an interesting character, Dinan, thought Mara. She remembered that day when he had taken four of her scholars around Oughtdara area and taught them about the old people, the legendary *Tuatha Dé*. Even years later they remembered in great detail all that he had told them, almost word for word – 'buffeted by the storms' was not an expression that Cormac would normally use. Yes, it was intriguing that the murderer had not tried to dispose of the body, but had set up this striking picture, to use Domhnall's words, something to make everyone think that it had been an intervention by the gods. Reluctantly she had to come to the conclusion that of the three brothers who had an interest in Clodagh's death, Dinan was the one who was the most likely to have arranged that elaborate scene of the woman apparently in the arms of the stone god and, dangling from her wrist, the key to the ancient fortified place, so connected with all the legends of the *Tuatha Dé*. He was obsessed with these stories. She could see him reason that Clodagh had offended the old people and that she deserved to die, that she should become a victim of the *Fár Breige*, himself.

'It seems to me that whoever did the deed was full of hate,' said Slevin wisely.

'Well, now, that should be easy,' said Cian. 'We'll just look for someone who hated Clodagh and that's your man, or your woman. Only trouble, Slevin, dear boy, is that every single person who knew her just hated her. She was a foul woman.'

'She wouldn't even allow poor old Aengus to keep a dog and he loves dogs. He's the only shepherd in the kingdom that doesn't have a dog. He's always exhausted from doing things himself that a dog could do so easily. I offered to lend him Dullahán, but he just looked at me with those poor old sad eyes of his and said, "A dog like that is too noble for the likes of me, my lord."'

Since Cormac's wolfhound, Dullahán, was the wildest and the most untrained dog that you could ever meet and bound to send a flock of sheep flying in all directions, Mara thought that Aengus had got out of that generous offer rather neatly. Her son's face was pink with emotion, perhaps because of the embarrassment of being addressed as 'my lord' – neither she nor Turlough ever wanted to emphasise his noble descent; he was Cormac to every servant and farm worker – or perhaps because he was so sorry for the old man. It gave her an idea, though.

'Cormac, why don't you and Cian ride on ahead of us? You can get Dullahán out of his kennel and run down the road with him to Lissylisheen. Aengus should be there now and Dullahán is the sort of dog that would cheer anyone up. He'll make the poor man feel more cheerful.'

Cormac's face lit up. He gave her a surprised and almost grateful look. He was devoted to his dog, but was a bit defensive about it in his mother's presence and she was conscious that she seemed to be forever criticizing the animal. There was no doubt, though, that Dullahán was affectionate and above all very funny. It would be hard to be depressed and silent in his presence. With the wolfhound getting up to mischief and bestowing wet licks and muddy paw shakes upon everyone, it would be impossible for the atmosphere to be tense and Mara wanted Aengus to be relaxed. Ever since Nuala had told her that the victim had been strangled, she had a strong intuition that the husband of the dead woman would be found to be responsible. Some final insult, some terrible words spoken, some deeply unpleasant act, might have driven him in despair to that uncharacteristic act of violence.

The sooner he told her the better. Brehon law took into account the state of mind of the offender and also laid emphasis on the mitigating effect of a full and early confession. She wanted to handle Aengus carefully, not drive the poor old man to feelings of despair, but to get him to trust her enough to tell the truth. That enormous, ridiculous dog of Cormac's would lighten the atmosphere and help Aengus to relax.

Four

Do Breathaib Gaire
(Judgements of Maintenance)

The fine (kin group) is obliged to care for those who are handicapped in their minds or their bodies.

The guardian of a drúth *(mentally retarded person) is responsible for his offences in the alehouse.*

Missiles thrown by a drúth *do not require compensation.*

Anyone who incites a drúth *to commit a crime must pay the fine himself.*

Lissylisheen, the home of the *taoiseach* of the O'Lochlainn clan, was only five minutes' walk away from Cahermacnaghten law school. Despite being the most powerful and the richest man in the kingdom of the Burren, Ardal O'Lochlainn's home was modest; his tower house was a single-towered building set a short distance from the road with no elaborate gatehouse or gardens to adorn it. It was three stories high with a guardroom at the bottom, a bedroom in the middle storey, some wall chambers leading off the spiral staircase and a magnificent sitting room or hall on the very top floor where Ardal could sit of an evening, looking over his hundreds of well-cared-for acres, at his cows and their calves, his horses with their foals and at the mountains beyond where the O'Lochlainn sheep grew thick wool which was turned into cloth and blankets and exported to England and Spain. Ardal had so many enterprises going that Mara almost lost count: a mill to grind his tenants' oats and his own corn; a limestone quarry to produce the fertilizer for the fields and the limewash for the stone walls of tower houses, cottages, barns and cowsheds; a ship to export his goods to France, England or Spain; but it was as a breeder of quality horses that he was famous and where, she suspected, the majority of his fortune was earned. A good man, she thought, as they rode up, a man who was kind and caring to his tenants, his workers and his servants. No other clan housed the people so well; no other *taoiseach* was so tireless in his quest to improve the lives of those that he felt responsible for. He would, she was sure, be kind and caring to Aengus and quick to give him practical help.

'Dullahán is here already; listen to him,' said Fachtnan with a smile as they rode their horses into the stable yard beside Lissylisheen Castle. Ardal kept a few small hunting dogs that had set up a series of shrill barks as they came in, but there was no mistaking the deep ringing tone of a wolfhound, announcing new arrivals to the world. The door to the steward's room opened and Ardal came out wearing a slightly harassed expression that Mara recognised. Any sane adult in the company of Cormac's dog for more than a few minutes normally began to look like that. Still a handsome man, though in his mid-fifties, she thought, as he handed her down from her horse. The red-gold hair of his younger days was now a soft shade of silver, but the blue eyes were as keen as ever, the skin was still a smooth, unlined bronze, summer and winter; and the slim, erect figure was as she remembered it from her own girlhood, when she and Mór, Ardal's sister, had teased and tormented the reserved young man.

'Oh, no, here comes the monster!' Domhnall and Slevin groaned in mock despair as the enormous wolfhound burst out through the door, raced towards them, long tail wagging furiously, panting violently with an excess of emotion, jumped up on them and on Fachtnan, leaving the print of his muddy paws on their *léinte* and then turned to Mara, suddenly stopping as he remembered that this member of the human race had some strange, but very strong objections to being jumped upon. He skidded to a halt and, mid-air, endeavoured to turn a riotous leap into a decorous 'sit' and succeeded in producing what looked like an awkward bow. Cormac and his friends screamed with laughter and even Ardal gave a slight smile.

'Take him back inside, Cormac; I want a word with the *taoiseach,*' said Mara trying to look sternly at the ridiculous animal who was now capering around the stable yard, much to the astonishment of several horses who leaned well-bred noses out of their stalls and gazed with amazement at this creature that was the size of one of their own docile foals. The dog was a source of huge embarrassment to Mara. For years she had basked in the consciousness of owning extremely well-trained and perfectly obedient wolfhounds, dogs who instantly obeyed her slightest glance – dear irreplaceable Bran, and Bran's mother, before that. And then she had bought a wolfhound puppy for Cormac, taking him up to Cahercommaun, where Murrough of the Wolfhounds bred his magnificent hounds, and allowing him to pick out his favourite. She should never have agreed to the choice of a nine-year-old child. From the first moment that she had seen the small puppy she had realized that this was a bad idea. She remembered her thoughts clearly. One of these wild dogs, she had said to herself, her heart sinking, a puppy who would undoubtedly be a handful, would need a huge amount of exercise and training, would probably cause trouble with neighbours. And so it had turned out. The dog was wildly excitable from the start and Cormac and his friends, though spasmodically embarking on training sessions, had just made him worse.

'I used to think that he would grow out of it, that it was just puppyhood, but he's nearly three years old now and he doesn't seem to be getting much better,' she said ruefully to Ardal.

'You go back in, lads, and he'll follow,' said Ardal's steward, Danann. He was a decisive, quick-thinking young man, but it was, Mara noticed with interest, Aengus, his red-rimmed old eyes looking fondly at the dog, who clicked his tongue, held out his hand, and by some miracle managed to distract Dullahán from a friendly desire to make closer acquaintance with a strawberry roan horse. Cormac grabbed his dog's collar then and Dullahán was hauled back into the steward's room.

'Fine dog,' said Ardal politely. 'Very large, very . . .' His voice tailed away and then he gave a grin.

'Never a dull moment when he's around,' agreed Mara.

'You'll take a cup of wine?'

'Just a few minutes of your time.' Mara walked across to the well-built wall that enclosed the meadow where the young horses grazed. Despite the drizzle they seemed to be enjoying their freedom, tossing their heads and racing around the lone hawthorn bush that stood in the centre of the field, still winter-dark and hung with grey-green lichen. Even as she watched she saw brown patches appear on the green grass and the burnished legs and flanks were flecked with mud.

'Two hours, and we'll have to take them back out of there or they'll plough up the field. What we need now is some hot sun to get the grass growing again. What a terrible March we've had, haven't we? Still, April is on the way.'

Ardal, Mara realized with amusement, was making conversa-tion, talking about the weather just like any farmer. He so seldom did that. He must have sensed that she was slightly reluctant to come to the point. However, she had no excuse to waste a busy man's time so she plunged in.

'I wanted your opinion of Aengus?' she said.

'A good worker. Very reliable. Nice man. Very gentle fellow. Wouldn't hurt a fly.' He looked at her searchingly.

'And Clodagh.'

'She didn't work for me. I know little of her except hearsay.' He folded his lips firmly and looked away from her and back at his horses.

Hearsay was not something that Ardal O'Lochlainn, who seldom spoke an unnecessary word, would deal in. Mara real-ized that she would have to take him into her confidence. She had known him a long time – they had grown up as neighbours and his younger sister, Mór, Nuala's mother, had been her best friend. Ardal was the second of two brothers and there was, she remembered, a lot of excited gossip when his father had put forward his younger, not his elder, son for the position of *tánaiste* (heir). The clan had agreed to the father's choice, and had, she knew, never regretted it. Most of the people in the kingdom of the Burren belonged to one of four major clans: O'Lochlainn, O'Brien, MacNamara or O'Connor. Of these Ardal's clan had grown to be the largest and the most impor-tant, but he himself lived in a simple style, a good landlord, trusted and respected by his people and by his king. There was no one in the kingdom whose discretion Mara trusted more. She decided to probe a little.

'How did Aengus take the news of his wife's death?'

'Wept a little. Poor old fellow. Danann gave him something to drink, some hot ale; that did him good and then he had something to eat. Your girl Cael was very kind to him, and young Art. They broke the news very gently to him and Art looked so upset that Aengus seemed to want to comfort him, more than to make too much of his loss. He was delighted when Cormac and his wolfhound arrived; he loves dogs. Dullahán the Large, was a great distraction.'

Ardal was uneasy, Mara sensed. It wasn't like him to try to make a joke. *Nice fellow, one of the best, trust him with my life, but too serious*, was her husband, King Turlough's verdict on his principal vassal in the Burren. Ardal, she guessed, knew that Aengus would be under suspicion and he was protective towards him, anxious, also, she thought.

'Could you gauge his reaction to the news of his wife's death?' This was a question that she would ask of Cael and Art afterwards, but she was interested in the opinion of a man who had employed Aengus for well over thirty years. He took a long time to answer, and when the reply came, it was unexpected.

'I think that he felt frightened, worried,' said Ardal.

'Frightened of accusation? Frightened of retribution?'

He looked at her closely and did not answer that question but substituted one of his own.

'Should he be?' asked Aengus's employer and his clan *taoiseach*.

'You know that is not a question that I can answer, Ardal,' said Mara trying to suppress a note of irritation. Surely he should know that she could not openly divulge any suspicions to him. And then when he didn't respond, she substituted another question.

'Would you consider that Aengus is simple-minded, Ardal?' She watched him closely and saw a look of genuine surprise on his face.

'No, no, what put that in your mind?' After a minute, when she said no more, he added, 'These men of the hills, they're slow to talk. They spend most of their lives up there in the quiet, nothing but the sound of the larks to listen to and the flight of the eagles to watch. If you want quick wits, clever answers, go to a carpenter's shop or a blacksmith's forge, but if you want the truth go to the men on the hills; that's what my father used to say. He thought a lot of his shepherds and his herdsmen. Aengus used to live up there, on Slieve Elva, all of the year around, you know, in one of those booley huts, before he married Clodagh and, to be honest, I think that he still spends lots of his time up there. It's his own affair; I am the gainer by it so I don't object. Anything else was between himself and his wife.'

'I wonder what put it into his head to marry her,' said Mara. 'Do you remember the marriage, Ardal? You're older than I am and I suppose your father may have been involved, may have spoken to you about it.'

A slight look of distaste crossed Ardal's face, but it disappeared almost instantly. 'No, I've no memory of it,' he said shortly. 'Seventeen-year-old boys are not interested in such affairs.'

'How did the marriage work out?' Mara wished that he would not be so cautious. Surely he knew that she was not engaging in idle gossip but was trying to probe possible motives for this killing of the elderly wife of one of his shepherds. Murder, she thought, was like a sore. Allowed to remain closed up beneath the surface the poison grew and made the whole body sick. Once opened up and the evil substance drained and the sore exposed to the air, then recovery would come. She looked enquiringly at him when he did not respond immediately.

'I'm no expert on marriage, Brehon,' he said with the air of a man who measures his words. 'I've never been too tempted to dip my own toe in the water, though, of course, I know that it works well in many cases,' he added politely. 'As for Aengus and Clodagh, I'd say that you could find others who would guess the reason for the marriage better than I. Neither my father nor myself ever felt that it was any business of ours to interfere in the marriage plans of our tenants or our workers.'

'I suspect that she may have been the one that asked him. What do you think?' But he said nothing, just nodded, whether in agreement or in acknowledgement of her words, she didn't know and so she went back to the subject of Aengus.

'The law,' she said carefully not looking in his face, but, while she marshalled her thoughts, bending down to pick a tiny fragrant violet from the large clump that had seeded itself in a conveniently shady place on the north side of the wall. 'The law,' she continued, her eyes on the exquisite flower as she inhaled the faint sweet scent, 'makes it clear that a *drúth* is someone who is perhaps not insane, but does not have the full reasoning powers of a man, is not responsible for his actions. He must be cared for, watched, so that he does not commit a crime, but not punished for an action that may not have been deliberate on his part.' She looked hopefully into his face, but it was impossible to read Ardal O'Lochlainn. 'Your evidence, as a man of good repute, as *taoiseach*, would be taken very seriously by the court, as it was when you gave evidence about the land fit to graze seven cows,' she could not resist adding.

'I would certainly give evidence that Aengus was a good-tempered gentle man during all the years that I had known him,' said Ardal evenly.

'But what about his understanding, his mind?'

'I would have to say, if questioned on the matter, that his understanding was as good as that of the other herdsmen or shepherds.'

Mara nodded her head. This was integrity and integrity was something that she valued. She had no right to complain if it did not go the way that she had intended. She would have to trust him and to go back to where Ardal felt comfortable.

'There is,' she admitted, 'the possibility that Clodagh was killed by someone close to her. Would Aengus be capable of that?'

He took his time over his answer, gazing thoughtfully at his young horses, but when it came it was quick and decisive. 'I've learned through sad experience, Brehon, never to judge the guilt or innocence of anyone except myself.'

Mara swallowed this. She guessed what sad experience that he referred to, but she was finding this noble attitude intensely irritating. However, she knew how stubborn he was, so she veered away from the question of Aengus and his capability for crime.

'And the brothers?'

Ardal hesitated. He was always the soul of discretion, never presumed on his status as chieftain of the most numerous clan in the kingdom of the Burren. He said no more, allowing her to ignore his silence, or to pursue the matter.

'You would know them better than I,' she said frankly. 'They are so nearly out of this kingdom and into Corcomroe, well, you know yourself. They went to Fergus, not to me, when it was a question of their uncle making a will in their favour.'

'Unfortunately,' said Ardal.

'As you say,' she said wryly. And then she decided to ask the question. 'Did you believe them?'

'Of course.' The response was instant so she decided to move onto the next question.

'But you helped to ensure that Clodagh got all the land. Without your evidence I would have given her only the house and a portion of land. The law is quite clear on that. A female can only inherit land for her lifetime and that land can only be enough to graze seven cows.' There was, of course, the proviso that if the land was gained by a man's endeavours, rather than through inheritance, this could be passed on to a daughter for ever. Mara, personally, had benefited from this as her father, a Brehon, had been given the land by the king of Thomond, Corcomroe and Burren in order to found a law school. Now she looked enquiringly at Ardal.

'I spoke the truth,' he said rather stiffly. 'I surveyed the land. It's full of rocks and stones. I wouldn't put cattle on that land. They would break their legs. To my mind it's fit only for sheep and goats. Pat uses it for goats and I think that is the best use for it.'

'I understand,' said Mara. Ask an honest man a question and you get an honest answer, she thought. 'Neither of us could have said, neither of us could have done anything different on that day,' she said firmly, 'but . . .'

The fact remains, she thought, that a woman died and died in horrible circumstances soon after that day at Poulnabrone.

'It was strange, though, was it not,' he said suddenly, 'that Clodagh knew of all the procedure for laying claim to the land. I was surprised, at any rate. I can't seem to remember a case when this was quoted before. I presume that she was right in all of her details. I had a word with the priest after the judgement day and he told me that he just went because requested, but he had never heard of such a procedure before. All this business about . . .'

Mara smiled. 'It's something that the scholars learn in law school,' she said. 'It's called *Din Techtugad* meaning "On Legal Entry" and it dictates that: "In the case of a dispute over the inheritance of property, the claimant should cross the boundary and should formally enter the land to which he lays claim, taking with him two horses and two male witnesses. He should kindle a fire and then withdraw asking for arbitration within seven days." But,' she went on, 'according to the female judge, Brig, a woman may also evoke this process and may take with her such livestock or articles which are precious to women and in this case the witnesses may be female. The interesting thing, Ardal, is that it almost appeared as if Clodagh O'Lochlainn had studied the law books and had done everything according to the ancient law of Brig, the first female Brehon. Do you remember what she said, Ardal? I remember it very clearly, perhaps because it echoed something that I had studied as a child.' She paused for a moment, remembering Clodagh's rough voice and then quoted: 'This, as far as I can remember, is what she said: "I, Clodagh O'Lochlainn, claim the land of my father and of his father, and back through the generations for time out of mind. And as the law commands . . ."'

'I remember that,' said Ardal. 'Yes, I remember her saying it and I remember how she said it. Her voice was very forcible, I remember it echoing off the cliff. I don't remember the rest of it, though.'

'I remember it,' said Mara. 'And I remember it because it was one of the first things that I learned when I entered my father's law school, when I was five years old.' She thought for a moment, remembering that far off day, standing there in her snowy white *léine,* starched and washed by Brigid the night before her darling started school. 'I could quote it to you, word for word, as Clodagh said it: "I entered my property, crossing the boundary line, tethering two ewes, leaving my kneading trough and my spindle as a token of my presence and kindling a fire on the hearth. I took with me two witnesses."

That was what she said, and her two witnesses were Father Eoin O'Lochlainn and his sacristan, Padraic. Do you remember that, Ardal?'

'Not as clearly as you do,' he said, 'but it was something along those lines.'

Mara waited for a moment, expecting the obvious question and then prompted him: 'How did she know what to say? How could she have used the exact words that every law school scholar learns?'

'I don't know,' he said sombrely. This business, she thought, was troubling him. He was worried about the implications to his widespread clan, the O'Lochlainns.

'I do,' she said robustly. 'I suspect that she got the procedure from Fergus MacClancy.'

'But could he . . .? Fergus MacClancy? Was he . . .?' Ardal stopped and looked at her. The picture of Fergus MacClancy, once the sharp-witted Brehon of Corcomroe, but now reduced to a doddering old man was before both of their eyes. Mara, however, shook her head.

'I thought like you, initially. I discounted Fergus. But then where else had she got that information? Where, on earth, I said to myself, had Clodagh got the idea to leave two ewes and a kneading trough? It was almost word for word what was given as an example in a law case heard by the legendary female Brehon, Brig, when she scolded a young male judge because he had refused a woman's case on the grounds that she had not obeyed instructions that were intended for men, that she had brought ewes instead of horses, and a kneading trough for bread-making instead of a valuable weapon or sword. And then, of course, I realized that Fergus, although he might be vague and hesitant about something that he had heard three minutes previously, has an amazingly good memory for the laws that he had learned so thoroughly at his father's law school seventy years ago. Fergus told her what to do; that was obvious to me then. It was obvious that she had gone to see him before the time when she asked you to accompany her to verify whether there really was, as her cousins stated, a will in their favour.'

Mara stopped there. She did not want to share her thoughts

any further, but she knew that it had crossed her mind on that day that Clodagh, paying a visit to the senile Brehon, had taken the opportunity, perhaps sending him out of the room on some errand, to steal the will giving her father's property to be divided amongst her four cousins. That there had been such a will, she did not doubt. The brothers had an honest air. They were kind people, but they were unlikely to have gone to that much trouble over Danu's land and person without the bribe of some sort of return. And, of course, Fergus, ten years ago, had been perfectly capable of drawing it up and suggesting, as she would have done herself, that it would be safer locked away in his chest than taken back into an over-crowded cottage.

Aloud, she said to him, 'I had to give a verdict based on facts, rather than on surmise.'

'And now you're worrying about whether that judgement led to murder,' he said.

'I am,' she said briefly and then said no more. Hers was the responsibility. This, after all, was her profession, her task in life. It brought her many joys, was interesting and challenging and she would not change places with anyone else in the world. This murder had to be solved, the culprit named in public at Poulnabrone and the fine paid. After that, life in the kingdom of the Burren could settle down again to its normal easy rhythm. But until then, she could spare no one in her efforts to seek the truth. She decided to go back to questioning him.

'You've met Clodagh, of course, Ardal,' she said in a conversational tone. 'How would you have estimated her, bodily and mentally?'

He looked a little startled at the question, but after a minute of self-communion, decided to answer it. 'Bodily, she was a strong, active woman,' he said. 'And, mentally . . .' He paused and then, unexpectedly he smiled. 'You, of course, were lucky, Brehon,' he said. 'You were born the daughter of a man who fostered your brains, gave you opportunities to shine, to develop. Perhaps not all women are equally lucky.'

'And morally?'

'That's certainly not something that I could judge,' he said stiffly.

'I see,' said Mara. She would question him no more. A picture of the dead woman had risen in her mind. Clodagh O'Lochlainn had been strong, active and with brains. She had, probably in a matter of minutes, assimilated enough law from poor old bemused Fergus in order to see her successfully through a complex legal procedure, and that seemed to show her capabilities.

What had her life been like with nothing to do, married to a man whom she despised, a man that spent most of his time on the mountain with his beloved sheep, even slept up there?

And had she received any legal information from Fergus that would have enabled her to change that life?

Cormac's dog was unusually quiet when Mara entered the steward's room. He was lying on the floor, stretched out, with an ecstatic appearance on his hairy face as Aengus gently scratched under his whiskery chin.

'If you'll excuse me, Brehon, I'll go and see about a few tasks,' said the steward and with a quick glance around to make sure that there were still plenty of refreshments available, he slipped out. Fachtnan vacated the chair next to Aengus and Mara sat down, avoiding the dog's gaze in case he felt bound to celebrate her arrival.

'How are you, Aengus?' she asked.

'I'm very sad, Brehon,' he said and tears came again to his red-rimmed eyes.

It could be true, she thought. Probably he was quite shocked that someone, who had been so very much alive, was now dead – perhaps his tears were for her, rather than for himself. The chances were, though, that Aengus wept because he thought that it was expected of him. He could not truly miss a woman who had made him a laughing stock in the market places.

'When did you see her last?' asked Mara. There was, she recognised, a slightly crisp note in her voice and he responded to it, wiping his eyes on what looked like one of the law school's well-laundered, snowy white, linen handkerchiefs, probably belonging to Cael, and then sitting up very straight, plaiting his fingers nervously.

'This morning, Brehon, before I went to work; I saw her this morning. I made the porridge and I had some and then she came in and I went out.' So the poor old fellow made his own breakfast. There was a neglected look about him. His cloak was threadbare and inexpertly patched and his *léine* was filthy, not just with the mud of the present day, but with the deeply engrained dirt of years. He was very thin, his skin scaly and there were patches of some white powder around his mouth.

'And did she say anything to you before you left?'

'Not a thing, Brehon, not a thing?' There was an uneasy note to his voice and Dullahán lifted his great head and looked at him. Aengus averted his eyes from Mara and began to run the dog's floppy right ear through his fingers and Dullahán licked his boot.

'She didn't tell you her plans for the day, did she?'

He looked astonished and bewildered at this question and the thought came back to Mara that he might be slightly simple-minded, despite Ardal's opinion. However, there was the beginning of a grin on Cian's face and a look of sympathy on his sister's. No doubt the twins shared the same thought – that Clodagh was most unlikely to discuss her day with Aengus.

If he were telling the truth, then the chances were that he had sidled out through the door as soon as she appeared.

If, on the other hand, she had sat down at the table, uttered some insult, made some threat, then that could be the moment when he had turned back, put his hands around her neck, while her face was averted, and squeezed as tightly as he could. Nuala's report would be of interest. She could usually tell the hour of death and also the length of time that had elapsed since the last meal.

'So you make the porridge,' Mara said chattily. 'My house-keeper, Brigid, makes great porridge. Can you make porridge, Cormac?'

'Easy,' scoffed Cormac. 'All you do to make porridge is to put the oats and the milk into the pot and let it cook through the night. And then put loads of honey on it in the morning. I can cook better than that. You didn't know, but that pie you had the other night, well, I cooked the pastry. Brigit said it was as good as her own.'

'Boys are quite good at cooking,' said Cael in a lofty tone that indicated that an ambitious young woman law scholar, such as herself, had better things to do.

Aengus muttered some protest about the little lordling doing women's work, but Mara talked him down.

'So did you get the supper yesterday evening, Aengus, when you came down from the mountain? What did you and Clodagh eat?' Did he resent being forced to do 'woman's work', she wondered.

'Potage,' he said after a minute.

The traditional fallback of the poor – a mix of vegetables and herbs from the hedgerows, boiled up afresh every day, with the occasional rabbit thrown in from time to time.

'And you didn't see Clodagh alive after you went to work this morning?'

He shook his head, wordlessly.

Mara waited for a moment and then asked gently, 'Do you have any idea who might have killed her, Aengus? It must have been someone who hated her very badly.'

Once again he shook his head. He didn't appear to consider the question with any interest. 'She was a very clever woman, Brehon,' he proffered hopefully, looking at her with his mild blue eyes. 'I didn't know half the plans that she had. I'm not good with that sort of thing. Don't know anything much about stone.'

'Clodagh had plans, what sort of plans?' Mara tried to give her voice a note of friendly, relaxed interest, but he shook his head sadly.

'She didn't talk to me about her plans, Brehon.'

'I see,' said Mara and then she glanced across at her son. 'Cormac, you'd better wake up Dullahán, time for his dinner. Come along all of you, we'd better be going.' She cast a quick glance at Fachtnan and he ushered the others out, managing to close the door unobtrusively during the excitement when Dullahán raced, barking wildly, across the stable yard, no doubt trying to resume his friendship with the strawberry roan horse. Mara waited for a moment until the shouts and barks began to die down and then she looked across at Aengus with interest.

Aengus hardly seemed to notice that she had stayed. He didn't look worried. He didn't even look enquiringly at her as if he wondered what she wanted from him. He was gazing sleepily into the fire. He looked, she thought, rather ill. She could not let the occasion pass, though. The question had to be asked sooner or later, and sooner would be better for him.

'Aengus,' she said as gently as she could, 'there is a question that I must ask you. Did you kill Clodagh?' If he confessed to it now it would be within the statutory twenty-four-hour period and that would mean that the fine would be half of that payable for a secret murder. The fine was payable to the dead woman's nearest relations, and would be divided between the four brothers. She was hopeful that she could induce them to be compassionate, nevertheless they were poor men and they might argue that most of the fine would come from the clan, rather than from Aengus who had very little of his own. Ardal, she was sure, would not grudge paying the fine for his shepherd, knowing how greatly he had been goaded into that action. She looked keenly at Aengus, willing him to have the courage to confess now within the twenty-four-hour period and save his clan the expense of twenty-one ounces of silver, or twenty-one milch cows. However, he just gave a quick and almost indifferent shake of the head and continued to gaze into the fire. He seemed, she thought, like a man who has had a terrible shock and whose mind has stopped working, leaving the body to carry on, just as a ball will roll down a slope without guidance or propulsion.

'It would be best if you told me now, Aengus,' she said. 'Just tell me what happened and I'll sort things out. You were, perhaps, very angry.'

He looked at her in puzzled fashion, as though he did not know what she was saying, as though her words were just drifting past him like the clouds on a blue September sky.

'Tell you what, Brehon?'

'About the killing of Clodagh,' she said.

He still looked puzzled. 'But I don't know about that at all, Brehon; I was up the mountain all day,' he said. When she said nothing he added, 'It was your own young scholars who told me all about it.'

'And you got a surprise,' she said, looking closely at him but he responded very naturally.

'It was a terrible shock to me, Brehon. I would never believe that such a thing could really happen.'

'Who do you think killed her?'

She had thought that he would immediately deny all knowledge, but he looked at her in a puzzled way, almost as though he didn't want to be rude, but felt that she should have known the answer to the question. After a minute, he said tentatively, 'I understood that it was the *Fár Breige* that did it, Brehon, strangled her, that's what young Art said.'

'I think that Art told you how she was found, that's right, isn't it?' Art, whatever his private beliefs and superstitions, was a well-trained law scholar, and would not have given any opinion on the cause of a murder without direct sanction from the Brehon. 'Art told you that Clodagh's body was found tied to the stone pillar, the *Fár Breige*, is that what he said?'

He nodded readily. He did not shudder, but then the whole thing might well have lost reality for him by now. 'That's right, Brehon. Strangled, she was. Strangled with a rope around her neck.'

'I wonder where the rope came from?' Mara did not look at him, but uttered the question in a meditative way.

'He'd be having all these sort of things.' He was presumably referring to the god and she thought she should steer him away from this fantasy.

'You can't think of anyone else who might have strangled Clodagh, someone, man or woman, who hated her, or who wanted something that she had, can you?' she asked and saw him look at her sharply. She had an impression, although he drew his brows together, as in puzzlement, something had changed in those pale blue eyes, almost as though some unwelcome idea had come to him. He licked his lips and she saw that the white powder seemed to come from his mouth: his tongue was coated with it.

She gave him a long moment, but he seemed to have forgotten about her and had turned back to staring into the fire.

'Well, I'll leave you now, Aengus,' she said moving towards the door. She had gone as far as she could; too far, perhaps, said her legal conscience. Her duty now was to solve the question of who had killed a woman of the kingdom, to judge the case impartially, to allocate blame, to ensure that the culprit made full and open confession in front of the people of the kingdom, and to fix the fine.

Five

Bꞧecha Oéin Chéchc
(The Laws of the Physician Déin Chécht)

All physicians must know these matters:
1. *The twelve doors of the soul where a blow can cause death.*
2. *The seven most serious bone breakings.*
3. *The classification of teeth.*

Brigid, Mara's housekeeper, was at the gate when they came riding down the road towards the law school at Cahermacnaghten. They could hear her voice calling instructions to the two girls who helped her in the kitchen and to the stable boys, and she was there when they dismounted, words pouring out volubly, as usual.

'Holy Mary, Mother of God, what a terrible thing to happen, what's the world coming to at all?'

'Cormac and Cian told you the news,' said Mara resignedly. It would, she acknowledged, be a difficult story for the boys to have kept to themselves. Brigid did not even bother to nod, just addressed herself to the scholars.

'Come in and get warm, and get some food inside of you all; go on, go straight into the kitchen. Nessa's got some pork roasting in a pot on top of some roots. She'll dish up for you. Now, Brehon, I've got something tasty ready for you over in your own house, so just you come over and have a rest. Cormac, don't you take that dog into my clean kitchen. No good you looking all innocent! I know what you're up to, young man! Cael, I've hung up all of your clean *léinte*, so just you keep them tidy now. Art, you're looking tired, go straight in and get some food inside yourself. Now, Brehon, leave that horse to Dathi and come straight over with me.'

Mara followed her with a smile. Brigid had been her nurse – her mother, after the death of her own mother – and, while

showing the utmost respect and always insisting on calling her
by the formal title of Brehon, she still treated Mara as if she
were her nursling. She would, of course, also be intrigued to
know all the details of the spine-chilling murder.

Everything was ready when she went into her house. The
Brehon at Cahermacnaghten Law School did not live within
the wall of the old fortified enclosure, but separately from the
scholars' houses and the law school. Set a good one hundred
yards down the road from the noise and tumult of the law
school and the farm buildings, the Brehon's house was spacious
and comfortable, two storeys high and built of stone. There
was a fire blazing; the room was illuminated by its flames and
by one tall candle, its light golden against the blue-white of
the limewashed wall. The scent from the apple logs filled the
whole room. The table was spread with a snowy white linen
cloth and one of Mara's precious crystal glasses sparkled in the
light. Cumhal, Brigid's husband, and the farm manager,
emerged from the cellar with a jug of wine and carefully filled
the glass. From the small kitchen at the back of the house
came a delicious smell and a minute later, Efan, one of Brigid's
assistants, came in bearing a dish of venison in a wine sauce.

'Goodness, is this a celebration?' The question was drowned
in the bustle of orders to the girl and Mara did not repeat it.
She knew the reason for it, anyway. Brigid was deeply jealous
of the luxury at Ballinalacken Castle with its many servants
and always, when Mara returned from there, endeavoured to
show how much better things were at home. So Mara ate,
sipped, praised and paid compliments and then when a perfect
goat's cheese, toasted on a griddle to a delicious perfection and
garnished with the first watercress of the season, had been
consumed, she said, 'Did you know them at all, Brigid; Clodagh
and Aengus?'

'I knew Clodagh a bit, a long time ago. I used to see her
when I went over to visit my mother, Lord have mercy on
her. Clodagh was a good-looking girl, then, clever, too. Full
of herself, she was. Wove the wool for that cloak of hers. She
used every kind of dye that she could make, borrow or buy
at the markets so that it was all the colours of the rainbow. It
was beautiful when it was new. You'd see her coming down

the mountain path from a mile away. Lovely hair she had, then, fox-red it was. She went grey early and she seemed to lose her looks then, got heavy and old-looking, but she was a lovely girl when she was young. She was the priest's housekeeper when I knew her, very puffed up about it, too.'

'I didn't know that.'

'Well, why would you? You weren't much more than a child, yourself, at that time. She didn't last too long as the priest's housekeeper. There was a bit of scandal about it, him being a young man and she a young girl. The bishop didn't like the talk and he came and had a word with Clodagh's father and the next thing that we knew was that she and Aengus were married. I'd say that the bishop had a word with the O'Lochlainn; Aengus was working for him even away back then. Myself, I think that it was all fixed up between the pair of them and that neither Aengus nor Clodagh had a word to say in the matter. Not suited to each other, they were. Not in a million years, that's what people said, you know, at the time, and I'd say that they had the rights of it.'

'They didn't ever have a child, did they, Clodagh and Aengus?'

Brigid's eyes met Mara's meaningfully. 'There was talk of a child, in the early months after they married, but it came to nothing.'

'I see.'

And, of course, she did see. The probability was that the child was not fathered by Aengus, but by the priest. It would have been strange, otherwise, if the marriage had borne no other fruit, apart from that one early bud of promise. Sad that the child died, leaving Clodagh with nothing in her life to love. A feeling of anger against the bishop overcame Mara. Why interfere? Surely it was more natural that a priest, if he wished, had a companion, a mate. There were many married priests around; and many others who used the euphemism of 'housekeeper'. Who cared? And surely a man who knew about women, knew about relationships, had children of his own, was a better human being and much more able to advise and sympathize with his parishioners.

And of course, mused Mara, after Brigid had gone back to check on affairs in her kitchen house, Father O'Lochlainn had been around when the body was found. And, she remembered, he had quickly left the scene before the Brehon had arrived, as if he wanted to disassociate himself from the killing? Perhaps, however, it was natural for him to go to the church to pray after he had received a shock.

Nevertheless, Father O'Lochlainn's name should definitely go onto the list of suspects. Clodagh had paraded him in public on judgement day, acting as though he were under her command. Had she blackmailed him into allowing his name to be, once again, in some sort of way, publicly linked to hers?

Restlessly she finished the last of her wine and stood up. She needed someone to sharpen her brain against, someone who would argue with her. Fachtnan had gone back to his wife's house in Rathborney with the promise, according to Brigid, that he would bring news from Nuala as soon as she had finished. But the scholars would now have finished their meal, so she would go across and talk it over with them.

Unusually, they were not playing hurling – the sticks and the balls were still standing under the shelter of the stable roof and there was light coming from the window of the school-house and the sound of voices arguing vociferously.

Mara pushed open the door and there was a sudden silence until they saw who it was, and even then they waited until the door was shut before they resumed. So they were using their free time to talk about the case. Mara felt pleased and proud of them.

There was a piece of board against one of the walls, lime-washed by Cumhal during each of the three school holidays: after the Michaelmas Term, the Hilary Term and the Trinity Term. On it someone had written, with a piece of charcoal, the word: MOTIVE and a space away from that: OPPORTUNITY. Dullahán was snoozing in front of the fire, Cian and Cormac stood, one on each side of the chimneybreast, and Domhnall, who had been sitting on her chair, sprang to his feet, looking somewhat confused, and hastily putting a scroll back on the shelf of the press behind him.

'We're doing a judgement day, Brehon, and Cian is *aigne* for the prosecution and Cormac is *aigne* for the defence; Domhnall is the Brehon and Slevin and I are the people,' said Cael in her most grown-up voice.

'What a good idea, well, I'll join the people.' Mara sat on a stool beside Cael feeling genuinely pleased and half-sorry that she had come in and perhaps destroyed the atmosphere. It had been a long time since anyone in the Burren had bothered with finding an *aigne*, a junior lawyer to state the case, and she herself had never used one for the prosecution, but, of course, there were plenty of examples of this court procedure among the judgement texts that the scholars had studied.

'They kept arguing about Aengus and then they started shouting; you know what boys are like so I thought this would calm them down,' Cael whispered in an elderly fashion and Mara nodded understandingly and settled back to listen as Cian took a step forward.

'This,' he said impressively, 'is not a crime motivated by fear, or indeed, by greed, but by anger, sheer and simple. This man, Brehon,' he said, arranging an imaginary gown on his shoulders, with a courteous nod of his head towards Domhnall, 'this man, Aengus, was tied hand and foot to a woman who made his life a misery, who continually disgraced him in the eyes of the people of the kingdom. Even the sheep on the mountains heard his shame. And for all that he appeared to be meek and submissive, he's a man with a man's feelings, a man who can be overwhelmed by anger. I, my lord,' said Cian blandly, with his eyes fixed on a point above Domhnall's head, 'have seen this man, mad with rage, threaten to bring down his crook on the innocent and vulnerable head of a child who had just made a joke. And moreover, my lord,' he went on quickly, 'who could have had such ideal means of killing the victim as the man who lived in the same house. It is possible that the victim lay there all night, and then on a mist-filled dawn, with his anger still unquenched, the man decided on the ultimate revenge. He took the body of the victim, a woman who had perhaps denied her body to him, her lawful husband—' Cian gave a quick glance at Mara's impassive face and went on bravely, though his cheeks went scarlet – 'and he placed her in the arms of the *Fár Breige* and bound her to the god's stony breast and dangled from her wrist the key to the property.'

And then Cian looked solemnly around all of his friends. There was a slightly scared look in his eye, Mara thought, as if he had suddenly realized how good his arguments were and that an old man whom he had laughed at and regarded as a fool had, perhaps, really killed his nagging wife. Cian, she thought, might not be quite as clever as his twin sister, but he had made his points well for the prosecution.

'I call on the lawyer for the defence,' said Domhnall.

Cormac didn't make at all as good a case as Cian had done. His arguments were built on the premise that Aengus was a nice fellow and would not murder anyone, even someone as nasty as his wife. He was clever enough to read the verdict of the court in Domhnall's eyes as he wound to an uncertain finish, and then, typically Cormac, decided to play the fool and he said quickly, 'I call on my witness for the defence: the law school dog. Come into the court, Dullahán.'

On hearing his name, Dullahán dragged himself to his feet and went to sit obediently at his master's feet. His mouth dropped open in a wide yawn and his eyes were fixed on the leather pouch that hung from Cormac's belt, expecting that some tasty morsel, salvaged from the breakfast table, was lurking there.

'Dullahán,' said Cormac solemnly, inserting his hand into his pouch, 'bark if you believe that Aengus is innocent.'

Since this was the latest of Dullahán's tricks, he barked vigorously and was rewarded with a piece of honey bread.

'I rest my case,' said Cormac.

'There can, I think, be no verdict from the court before the facts are established,' said Mara, rising to her feet. 'I propose that we ride down to Nuala's place and save Fachtnan the journey. I'd like to hear what she has to say before I do any more thinking. Cormac, put Dullahán back into his kennel before we go. You know that Nuala doesn't want him trampling on her herb garden with those enormous feet of his.' And then as Cormac hauled the dog out, she said, 'I was very impressed by your performance, Cian. We'll do this again, perhaps make a performance with an imaginary murder case and argue it out in front of the king. I'm sure that he would enjoy giving his verdict.'

That was a popular suggestion and the scholars all chatted about it as they went down towards Rathborney. Cian and Cormac seemed to be best of friends and were laughing over the wolfhound's evidence, but Mara was not deceived. Cian was sharp and clever, no cleverer than Cormac, but Cian saw his future as a lawyer, perhaps at the king's court at Bunratty, or perhaps as a wandering legal adviser for the defence or the prosecution of cases in Brehon law courts throughout the west and north of Ireland. Cormac, she guessed, had no such plans so he didn't care how well, or how badly, he could argue a case. Quite soon now, Cormac would force upon his parents a decision about his future. The law that was ever fresh and intriguing to his mother bored him. As the horses made their slow way down the path that circled around the stony hill, she meditated on the parting that would have to come sooner or later.

Nuala was at the door when they arrived. 'I heard that you were sighted on the hill,' she said. 'Come in all of you. Come into my room.'

Nuala's room was a business-like place. She had a large quantity of medical texts that she had purchased in Italy, thanks to the substantial legacy left to her by the former owner of the property at Rathborney, and the printed books, ranged on shelves by the fire, were interspersed by handwritten scrolls. There were shelves filled with surgical instruments on one side of the room, and on the other side, where the light would not fall, there were flasks of medicines, all neatly labelled. In one corner of the floor sprawled Saoirse, carefully gluing leaves of dried herbs to a large scroll of parchment, held open with two weights from the scales that stood on a table. The child was writing in the names and the medical use of each herb and all watched her for a moment until the quill was back in the inkhorn, waiting for the eight-year-old to leave the room before the question of cutting open dead bodies would arise.

Nuala, however, ignored the presence of her daughter. She appeared to Mara to be over-compensating for the grievance that she bore about the way she had been excluded from medical matters by her own father who had been unsympathetic to her ambitions. Fachtnan, when he came in, looked rather uneasily at his elder daughter, but said nothing, just taking a seat close to her, as though to shield her from harsh realities.

'Well, I opened the body of Clodagh O'Lochlainn,' began Nuala, glancing once only at some notes on the table beside her and then fixing her eyes on Mara. 'She had been a healthy woman – eaten well all of her life, I would say. The cause of death was manual strangulation, someone with quite strong hands, I would say, and who was standing or sitting behind her. The bruises on the throat definitely come from fingers, not thumbs.'

From the corner of her eye, Mara saw little Saoirse surreptitiously place her hands on her own neck and then nod wisely. Her mother gave her an approving look and then went on with her exposition.

'The victim's last meal was porridge and she would probably have died about three hours after it.'

'Porridge!' exclaimed Mara. 'Not pottage?'

'Definitely not,' said Nuala. 'There's no possible resemblance between the two, even after they have been in the stomach for some time.'

Mara passed over this quickly, for her own sake as well as that of the child at her feet.

'So when did she die?' she asked.

Nuala referred to her notes again. 'About two hours before she got here. About half an hour before noon, I should say.'

'What?' The word escaped Mara's lips before she could stop it.

'I knew it; I just knew it.' Cormac was blazing with triumph, turning around to his fellow scholars in the absence of his dog, Dullahán, with whom he could have done a triumphant dance.

'Did you?' Nuala was looking at Cormac with interest. 'Well done,' she said. 'Of course, there are certain subtle signs, the skin colour. The body, as you can guess, Cormac, would have cooled rapidly in the heavy rain, but there are other indications. It was clever of you to notice.'

'I just knew it,' said Cormac, with a slight grin. He had realized the reason for Nuala's praise. 'I am your godson, after all,' he ended modestly, but with a flash of his green eyes at Cian.

'Anything else that you want to know, Mara?' Nuala turned her attention away from Cormac and his friend.

Mara yearned to say, 'Are you sure?' but she resisted the temptation. Nuala never spoke unless she was sure. She got to her feet, thinking ruefully that it was a good lesson to her personally about the dangers of speculation before all the facts were established. It now appeared sure that Aengus could have had no hand in Clodagh's murder. He had been seen by Gobnait going up Ballynahown towards the Knockauns Mountain in the early morning soon after dawn. He had made no appearance near Oughtdara during the whole morning while the three brothers were on the foothills, checking their sheep and their goats. And he had been discovered on Knockauns by one of Ardal O'Lochlainn's men after Cael had arrived with the message seeking help.

No, although the crime looked as though it were committed by an angry husband, driven to his limits by an overbearing and foul-mouthed wife, Mara had to admit that it did not seem possible that Aengus had done the deed.

So, thought Mara, as they rode back up the hill, since Aengus is struck off my list of suspects, now I have to fall back on Pat, with, or without Deirdre; I have Gobnait, also, and Dinan; Finnegas, the fourth brother was probably not a suspect. It had taken him a good half hour, she reckoned, to get from his mine to Oughtdara and during the morning he had been under the eye of his workers for most of the time. But what if Finnegas was the mastermind behind the crime? There was no doubt that he was the sharpest of the brothers and would be the best organiser. What if he had planned the scene of the corpse in the embrace of the *Fár Breige* in order to lay suspicion on the husband of the dead woman? Or else to hint at supernatural involvement? He had, she reckoned, little to gain personally. The land that was his allocation from his uncle's property was poor land, as each of the brothers had agreed to take the portion of his uncle's land closest to their present holdings. Finnegas's riches came from under the ground, not from the grass that grew on top of it. And would any man risk involving himself in a murder that might take from him all that he possessed for the sake of enriching his brothers? Somehow Mara could not see a clever business-like man, such as Finnegas, doing this. And for what; for some barren, mountainous acres, strewn with rocks? Land fit to graze only seven cows, Ardal had deemed the whole four parcels to be worth only that and Ardal was a person who knew about grazing land. So, if Aengus were not the killer, who was the most likely suspect?

She turned towards Fachtnan. 'Who could it be?' she asked. 'I suppose that of the four brothers, Pat probably had the most to gain as he has a lot of goats, but I'm not sure that he's the type. I'd say that he is cautious and basically a kind man. Would he choke the life out of a woman just for the sake of some acres of ground? And don't say that it was the *Fár Breige*,' she added hastily as she saw a tentative, uneasy expression cross his face as though he were about to say something that he knew she would not like.

Fachtnan laughed, but still slightly uneasily. 'I was thinking about little Orla, I must confess. You could see for yourself what it's like. You know how Nuala is. From the time she was a child, as far back as I can remember, medicine has been Nuala's life. And now she has one daughter who is just like her mother. Saoirse is so dedicated, so involved in her work that Nuala has no time for Orla, who is just not interested. I'm worried about her. I was wondering whether you might rethink your decision about waiting for her eighth year before admitting her to law school.'

'I said that I would wait until she turned eight years before I would assess her,' said Mara shortly. 'My own daughter, Sorcha, Domhnall's mother, was quite unsuitable for the degree of study and application. It may well be that Orla, also, is not suited to this life and if that were the case then it would be sheer cruelty to your daughter to try to make her fit the mould. We'll see in another few years.' What a time to bring this up when he knows that I am busy with this murder case, was her thought before she continued, 'Who, in your opinion, is the most likely suspect, now, since it looks to be impossible that Aengus could have returned from the mountain unseen and killed his wife about half an hour before midday. You remember how the brothers recounted seeing him on the hillside in Ballynahown just at dawn.'

'I can't tell at the moment, Brehon,' said Fachtnan. He looked around at the cheerfully arguing boys and said, rather poignantly, 'Those days of being a scholar here, were the happiest in my life. I wonder whether they realize how lucky they are.'

'What do you think about Dinan?' Mara's thoughts went to Nuala's words earlier this morning when she had come to collect the body. 'Nuala thinks that he is dangerous.'

'I think that she is talking nonsense,' said Nuala's husband in an irritated fashion. 'What harm can those old stories do? Orla loves them. She's quite a talented child, you know, Brehon. She listens to these stories and draws little pictures about them and they are very clever for her age.'

'How lovely,' said Mara. It was, she thought, a good way of putting a stop to this conversation without hurting Fachtnan's feelings. 'I understand what Nuala meant, though. She thinks that Dinan's stories might provide a cover for the murderer, who might hope that this murder would be laid at the door of one of the gods of evil.'

'Perhaps,' said Fachtnan indifferently.

'I think that it is also just about possible that if a man truly believed in one of those gods of the *Tuatha Dé*, that he might persuade himself that one of them had sanctioned, and even required of him, that he should murder one who had blasphemed them and made a mockery of them.'

But even as she said the words she could hear a lack of conviction in her own voice and Fachtnan received her idea in a discouraging silence.

But as they turned their horses and ponies into the enclosure at Cahermacnaghten and Brigid popped out of the kitchen house to greet them, Mara suddenly thought back to Father Eoin O'Lochlainn. Now he, she thought, might be a more likely murderer than the essentially sane, though imaginative Dinan.

There had been, she acknowledged, at the back of her mind, the feeling that there was a sexual element tangled within this crime. Cian had been correct in his reading of the scene.

If Brigid were right, that there had been some sort of relationship between the priest and Clodagh when both were
young, then perhaps she had blackmailed him, tried to insert
herself into his bed again, threatened to betray him to the
bishop.

A priest was a man like other men.

And there are, she thought, probably few feelings as strong
as when sexual love turns into disgust and hatred.

Six

Uraichecht Becc
(Little Primer)

There are seven orders of clerics: lector; usher; exorcist; sub deacon; deacon; priest and bishop.

The wife of a priest must never be seen in church with an uncovered head.

Father Eoin O'Lochlainn must have been a very good-looking man thirty years ago, thought Mara when he opened the door to her himself the following morning and invited her to come within. He had a pair of very large, very blue eyes, a broad brow and a delicately chiselled nose. There was nothing effeminate about the face; the chin was firm and the mouth well-cut and the thick iron-grey hair was clipped closely, in the English fashion.

Mara was alone. This, she knew, was a delicate matter. She hoped to induce him to confide in her, but knew that there was no prospect of that if her scholars, or even just Fachtnan, were witnesses to the conversation.

'You wanted to speak to me, Brehon.' He was eyeing her in a slightly apprehensive manner.

Mara nodded her head as though confirming the hint of fear in the blue eyes.

'I'm afraid so,' she said. She wouldn't, she decided rapidly, call him 'Father' if she could help it. The less he was reminded of his priestly vocation, of the expectations of the very old and very fanatical bishop, the easier it would be to talk about Clodagh.

'As you can guess, I came to talk to you about the secret and unlawful killing of Clodagh O'Lochlainn, less than twenty-four hours ago.' She wasn't sure whether he grasped the significance of the time lapse and so explained to him that it existed in order to give the killer a chance to make a confession and to show remorse for something that might have been merely a momentarily overwhelming impulse. She had seen Pat, Deirdre, Gobnait and Dinan this morning and had explained the same matter to them, but it had not resulted in any new facts about the previous morning.

'Jesus,' said Father O'Lochlainn, unexpectedly, 'placed no such limits on his forgiveness.'

'Ah, but we Brehons do not have his divine powers. We do not presume to offer forgiveness or condemnation for an offence. We exist purely to keep the peace between neighbours. If loss is incurred, whether the loss of a life, or the loss of goods, or, indeed, even the loss of face because of satire or mocking taunts, then the Brehon calculates the remuneration needed to endeavour to compensate for that loss. That is our function in the affairs of the kingdom.'

'The church, of course, has always disagreed with you on this. The Bible says that there should be an eye for an eye; a tooth for a tooth; and a life for a life.'

'It doesn't sound very Christ-like.' Mara was getting tired of this and she could see from the triumphant expression in the man's eyes that he was pleased to have engaged her in debate. A cross of swords, she thought and then, before he could throw another argument at her, she said briskly, 'As I mentioned, I've come to talk to you about Clodagh O'Lochlainn.'

There was a few moments' silence. He didn't, she noticed, utter any of the usual and conventional, priest-like, holy comments. There was no '*Lord have mercy on her*' or '*May she rest in peace*'. He just sat very still and let the silence elapse, until eventually he said, 'Yes?' and the slightly interrogative note in his voice irritated her.

'I understand that you knew her very well,' she said and watched his response.

He had great control over his features or else he had anticipated and was prepared for the question.

'You are mistaken.'

'She was your housekeeper.'

'A very, very long time ago, too long to remember anything about her.'

Mara's patience snapped. 'That's ridiculous,' she said forcibly. 'Of course you must remember. She was your housekeeper. There was some scandal. The bishop intervened and she was married off to Aengus O'Lochlainn, still here in Oughtdara. You probably saw her almost every day of your life afterwards. Don't tell me that you remember nothing about her. A lie like that will only serve to make me disbelieve everything that you say.'

He went very white. She saw a flash of panic in the blue eyes. For a moment she was sorry for him. These priests were being forced by Rome to lead unnatural lives. The Celtic church did not enforce celibacy, so why allow Rome to inflict its alien laws on Ireland?

'Tell me about how Clodagh persuaded you to be her witness when she laid claim to possess her father's house and land.' It might, she thought, be easier for him to begin with that, though she had every intention of probing more deeply.

He rose from his seat, almost shot out of it, and went across the room in two long strides. He stood by the window; for a moment the noon sunlight shone on his white face and then the next moment he had jerked the curtains closed.

'I have weak eyes,' he said, when she looked at him with surprise, 'the light hurts them.'

'Too much study,' she said affably, though that was not something she believed to be true. Her own eyes were still excellent and, goodness knows, there had been no lack of studying on her part. 'But, you were just going to tell me what induced you to stand out in public, side by side with Clodagh, and to bear witness for her. Weren't you afraid that it might set tongues wagging again?'

She thought that he would deny it, but somehow he seemed to be suddenly weary of this sparring.

'She forced me,' he said with a half groan. 'She was always able to make me do what she wanted. The Lord knows, I tried to escape from her often enough.'

Mara sat very still. This had been easier than she had expected. The priest was resting his forehead on his linked hands. His eyes were shut and his mouth compressed.

'I asked and asked the bishop to give me another parish,

but he always refused. He disliked me and he liked to torture me. Or perhaps he thought that it would strengthen me. I don't know.'

'So you continued to be lovers?' Mara felt a certain amount of surprise. Clodagh had not acted like a woman who was having a love affair. She was an angry, bitter, abusive woman. She dressed badly, her hair went uncombed and her cloak, according to Brigid, was more than thirty years old and was stained and threadbare in places. It looked as though no attempt to clean or to mend it had ever been made.

For a moment it seemed as though she had not been heard. He still held his head within his hands. Now his splayed fingers grasped his head as though in an effort to avoid it splitting open. His eyes were opened very widely, but they were dead and blank, almost as though his internal thoughts blotted out anything that was happening outside of his own head. And then suddenly life came back into them and he swivelled around to face Mara.

'What did you say?' He muttered the words and she felt impatient with him.

'So why did you do her bidding?' And then her conscience made her add, more gently, 'Was she blackmailing you? Did she threaten to go to the bishop?'

He shook his head. 'That would not have troubled me. I told the bishop about her. I went to confess to him again and again, and I begged him to spare me this trial, to allow me to go away, to have pity on me.'

Mara knew a moment's astonishment. So this man had confessed to the bishop, confessed his guilty passion. She had not expected that. It was all very well for Brigid to say that Clodagh had been a fine-looking girl in the past; the fact was that she was certainly not 'fine-looking' for many a long year and nothing but the eye of true love would have discerned anything that would arouse a man. And yet, he was still quite an attractive-looking man, himself. If he found it difficult to keep his passions under control there were probably plenty of women who would not have minded a love affair with him. Still, she told herself, there was no accounting for tastes. Perhaps to him, she was still aged eighteen, still had a head of glorious red hair, still had the slimness of youth and her cloak of many colours was still as resplendent as ever. She had a moment's compassionate thought for the girl who had gone out into the lanes and the market places for dye and who had soaked and boiled the wool, dying the different sections, spun it on her spindle, woven the brightly-coloured squares and then stitched them to make a cloak that would stand out among the cream and grey cloaks of her neighbours.

'But if you loved her, why didn't you defy the bishop and take her into your house? Aengus would have given her a divorce if she had applied for it. And even if he refused, the fact that she was childless after thirty years of marriage would have guaranteed it.'

Though she would have been past the days of bearing a child for quite a number of years, thought Mara, nevertheless, the law set no date and upheld the right of a woman to have a child, no matter whether she had to leave her husband and go to another man in order to become pregnant. Moreover, once pregnant, the woman could then choose to return to her husband and no reproaches could be made. 'Why not take her into your house if you loved her still?' She repeated her words because he was staring at her as though she were speaking some foreign tongue, unknown to him.

'Are you mad?' he demanded with an intensity that almost made her recoil from him. 'Are you mad? Loved her! I loathed and hated her.'

Mara concealed her exasperation. 'So why do her bidding?'

'Because she threatened to force herself into my bed, if I didn't.' The words came out in an explosion, something between a sob and a grunt of pain. The man, thought Mara, seemed nearing a breakdown.

'She was always coming to me, talking about the splendid house she was going to have, fit for a king, it would be, she said.'

'When did she say that, was it after her father died?' asked Mara.

'I suppose so,' he said after a short pause. 'Yes, I suppose it must have been. I didn't take any notice of her. I didn't care what she did or where she went as long as she would just leave me alone.'

'But she wouldn't leave you alone, was that the problem?'
Mara held her breath. Was he going to confess to the murder?

'She even forced herself on me in the confessional box,
saying foul things . . .'

'What things?' asked Mara bluntly; more to stem the rising
tide of hysteria than because she really wanted to know. Even
the tough boys of the law school seemed shy of actually
repeating Clodagh's words of abuse.

'She said . . .' Now the priest's face was totally drained of
colour and he stared ahead as though seeing a strange and
terrible sight. 'She said that I was denying her what she wanted
and there was only one man left who could satisfy her, only
one man in whose embrace she could find release and that
. . . and she screamed with laughter when she said this, she
said that the only man in the place, the only real man, was no
man but was the god of evil, the *Fár Breige*. Whenever I passed
the place she would glue herself to it, pretend . . .'

Mara sat very still. The priest wore a haunted look on his
face, the look of someone who has awoken in the grip of
a terrible nightmare, afraid to move, gulping for air. He was a
simple sort of man, like many priests. It almost seemed as though
the life they led, isolated in every real sense from the concerns
of adult men and women, made them childlike. Did that, Mara
wondered, make them childlike in their desires, also; made their
concerns or wishes to be of overwhelming importance to them,
of such importance, that nothing else could interfere.

Such men, she thought, could kill.

'And so you killed her,' she said aloud. She spoke softly and
felt sorry for him, but murder could not be justified. This man
was not insane, not simple in any way. A clever and well-read
man; a Caxton copy of Chaucer's *Canterbury Tales* lay open
upon his desk and there were copies of Virgil's great poem,
The Aeneid, upon the shelf by the fire. Father O'Lochlainn had
choices that he could have made, but weakness and cowardice
had prevented him from decisive action.

There had been no answer to her question and for a moment
she thought that he had not heard her, but then he lifted his
head, looked across at her and shook his head.

'No,' he said, quite simply, almost as though he corrected her on some simple fact, 'no, that's not right. I didn't kill her. Her own lusts killed her. The *Fár Breige* took his terrible revenge. He was like me; he could take no more.'

Aw, teach dar! thought Mara. This was a favourite expression on the lips of her younger scholars, expressing scorn and disbelief. It was, she thought, the only appropriate response to the last utterance. He must think her totally weak-minded and credulous if he expected her to believe that.

Or else, he was, in fact, insane.

That would be the defence, no doubt, if the bishop, as she expected, engaged a young lawyer to defend his underling. His lordship could be relied upon to do that. He would have been better off moving the tormented man to another parish, before any crime was committed.

She looked closely at the priest. He sat listlessly, his eyes blankly staring ahead, his hands dangling loosely. And then, quite suddenly, there was a complete change. He jumped to his feet, jerked back the curtain from the window, replaced a book on the shelf, poked the fire and added a few more sods of black turf and then went swiftly to the door.

'It's Deirdre,' he said and to Mara's amazement, she saw that a half-smile had come to his lips and the large blue eyes were shining with pleasure. Before she could say anything, he had gone to the door and opened it.

'Come in, come in,' he said. 'I thought I knew your step. Come in, you are welcome.'

'I had just baked a few griddlecakes so I thought I'd run across with one while it was still hot; I know how you like it.' Deirdre's voice was soft and affectionate. She had not noticed the visitor and Mara remained seated in the dark corner beside the window, watching with interest as Deirdre removed the square of linen from the platter and revealed her gift. Not just a griddlecake, but a knife, a large pat of butter and a few spoonfuls of honey were on the plate. In a motherly fashion, with a smile on her lips, Deirdre had cut a generous slice, spread it with butter and honey, before she noticed Mara and then she gasped dramatically.

'Oh, Brehon, oh, I'm sorry; I didn't see you. I just came across to give . . .'

'Looks delicious,' said Mara. She watched with interest as Deirdre put the griddlecake aside. Her presence had spoiled a cosy little interlude. Deirdre, she thought, would have been a cosier armful for the amorous Father O'Lochlainn than the wild and harsh Clodagh O'Lochlainn. However, she was not to be deterred from her interview with a suspect by this neighbourly visit, so she said firmly, 'I'll be dropping in to see you in a while, Deirdre, but in the meantime . . .' She left her sentence unfinished, hoping that her meaning was plain and Deirdre immediately moved towards the door.

'You'll be very welcome, Brehon. Now I must be off. So much to do in this season! Terrible weather, isn't it?'

Father O'Lochlainn half-rose as though to detain her, and then sank back onto his chair. Petulantly he pushed the untouched cake aside and glowered at Mara, reminding her rather of a resentful three-year-old who didn't have the spirit to make a more vigorous protest. It surely would not be too difficult a task to get out of such a man whatever he knew about the death of Clodagh O'Lochlainn. She got up, went to the window and peered through the rain. It was almost impossible in this weather to imagine the valley and its hills as it would be on a sunny day – fifty shades of green and the cliffs sparkling silver. Today the hills were screened from her view by low clouds like mounds of grey fleece and the rain-washed valley grass was dull and monochrome.

But even through the veil of mist, Mara could see the towering figure of the *Fár Breige*, the stone god. She knew now why the priest wanted to keep the curtains of his room closed.

'Did you notice at what time the figure of Clodagh appeared in front of the stone pillar?' She asked the question in conversational manner and without looking back at him.

'I've told you, Brehon, she was always there. She would look in the window, or tap at the window as she passed, and then when I looked, I would see her, right up next . . .'

'I see,' said Mara. And she did see. There was something rather wicked about the way in which Clodagh had taunted this stupid man. It would certainly be something that she could have dealt with if he had brought a complaint to her. And yet, she had to admit, a complaint of that nature, heard in public, would have caused a lot of sniggering and probably made his position of parish priest almost untenable.

'But yesterday morning,' she went on, hardening her heart and now looking back at him, eyeing him keenly, 'yesterday morning, Clodagh was dead. That made a difference, didn't it? If you looked out yesterday morning you would have seen a dead figure tied to the pillar, not moving, like a live figure.'

He gulped hard and suddenly she could see his eyes sharpen. An apprehension of danger had restored them to normal appearance. Was that mystical appearance feigned or did he, as she suspected, withdraw into a world of his own when reality threatened?

'I did not look out of that window yesterday morning, Brehon. I was busy at my desk preparing my sermon.'

'But your desk faces the window,' she pointed out.

'I did not look up from my work.' His tone was curt and decisive and slightly disdainful. He might, thought Mara, when he had his wits about him, be a difficult man to shift in a court of law. Even a confession, unless witnessed, might be challenged by whatever lawyer the bishop managed to find. There was a strong conviction among the followers of Rome that a cleric should be above the law. It was not, however, something that Mara felt like tolerating, and she knew that King Turlough would back her on that.

If this man was guilty of murder then she was determined that he would face the people of the kingdom, confess his crime and pay retribution. The fine, unlike Clodagh's land which had to revert to the near kin group, would be paid out to poor old Aengus and would keep him comfortable in his old age when his joints became too stiff to roam the mountainside with his beloved sheep.

'I feel that you are not telling me the whole truth about what happened yesterday morning,' she said as she rose to her feet. 'I want you to think it over very carefully, to think of the consequences of not telling the truth to the king's representative.'

In the meantime, she thought, she would just go across the road and sample one of Deirdre's freshly baked griddlecakes, if possible without honey; but if it had to be with honey, she hoped that her sense of duty and devotion to the law would enable her to swallow the nauseating stuff. She looked at him keenly, but he had bowed his head, staring down at the wood of his desk, his face a mask of pain, and his hands joined as though in prayer.

Deirdre was certainly a much more appetising prospect for a man looking for affection than Clodagh. In her forties, Mara reckoned, but fresh-faced with clear skin, still-brown hair and eyes as darkly blue as the May-flowering gentian flowers, she was also still slim and active. She seemed to live her life in a whirl of activity. While Mara sampled the bread, she energetic-ally churned some goats' milk, rapidly ladling out the lumps that would be turned into the small round cheeses, chopped some cloves of wild garlic, mixing them in deftly, then drained the skim milk into a bucket and scoured out the churn. Mara munched as slowly as she could, noticing the longer that she took, the more relaxed the woman was becoming. It was, she thought, excellent bread, with a nutty flavour and a light texture. And Deirdre had been flattered by the statement, hastily attributed to Brigid, a notable housewife in the area, that only poorly baked bread needed to be spread with honey.

'You must have got a terrible shock yesterday morning when Father O'Lochlainn told you about Clodagh,' said Mara, while Deirdre poured fresh water into the huge black pot suspended from the iron crane in the chimney place. Purposely she spoke with her mouth half-full of cake, something that she would reprimand her scholars for, but which she felt would lend her question a more informal air. For a moment the flow of water seemed to stop and then it continued on, but there was no doubt that Deirdre started at the question.

'Oh, but, Brehon, it was Pat that told me about Clodagh,' she said after a moment.

'But the priest had come to you first.' Mara purposely made this a statement, not a question, and heard with satisfaction how firm her voice sounded. 'He was telling me about looking out of the window and seeing Clodagh beside the stone pillar.'

There was another moment's silence. Deirdre spread a well-laundered linen cloth over what remained of the fresh water in the bucket. Mara said nothing more. She could see that the woman was thinking hard.

'Well, to tell you the truth, Brehon,' she said eventually, 'I never take too much notice of what the poor misfortunate man says to me. He suffers with his nerves, something terrible,' she added.

'So he came babbling to you about Clodagh and the *Fár Breige*; is that right?'

There was a reluctant nod. Deirdre had given up all pretence of busying herself with her household tasks. Her eyes were wide and very nervous, and the colour had gone from her cheeks. There was no doubt that the woman was fearful about something; fearful for someone, Mara corrected her first thought. But was this fear for the odd, and slightly child-like priest? If that were so, then she would lie to protect him. Still, her memory of Pat and Deirdre, together made her feel that their relationship was a good one. Pat was a nice fellow – it was sad that they had no children, but they had the satisfaction of building up a prosperous farm of goats, one of the biggest in the kingdom, she thought, and remembered Brigid saying that they had been lucky with them. 'Lucky' was Brigid's way of saying 'successful', a common saying; it was a slightly oblique way of propitiating the gods of the *Tuatha Dé*, the *sidhe*. The belief in the presence of 'the old people' was very strong in this part of the kingdom; even she, the most sceptical of persons, almost felt aware of their presence here amongst the ancient walls and bawns, presided over by the immense stone figure.

I must, Mara decided, trust that the relationship between husband and wife was stronger than that between woman and priest. Deirdre should realize that her husband was in danger of being named as the killer of his cousin Clodagh.

'The trouble is, Deirdre,' she said, in a confidential, woman-to-woman fashion, 'it is easy for someone like me to suspect that the killer is the person that has the most to gain. I always try not to take the easy way out, but I need to know everything. That's why I ask so many questions. Only when I understand everything, know where everyone concerned was at the time of the death, know what everyone said and did; well, only then can I solve the mystery. If I don't get the

information, then I have to start guessing and I don't want to
do that, don't want to take any easy way.' She watched Deirdre
as she spoke. There was intelligence in those darkly blue eyes
and then came a reluctant nod. Pat, of course, as the eldest of
the three brothers, the one who could choose first, would
benefit most from the distribution of the property that had
belonged to Clodagh's father.

'So what time was it that the priest came into you?' Mara
decided to ask the routine question first.

Deirdre answered that promptly. 'I'd say that it would have
been about a quarter of an hour before the Angelus bell.'

So Clodagh, according to Nuala's estimate, would have been
dead by that stage.

'Try to remember exactly what the priest said, Deirdre, will
you. I know he is an odd man; so don't worry about me.'

'Well, it's not something I would like to say to anyone else,
Brehon, but he comes in here gabbling about Clodagh and
the *Fár Breige* . . .'

'Often?' It was always good to fill an awkward silence with
an inserted word or two.

'Once a week, or so.' Deirdre was more assured now. 'She
was a wicked woman, Brehon. Lord forgive me for speaking
ill of the dead, but she tormented him, tried to tempt him,
to make him . . . as if he would . . . her looking like that
. . . you wouldn't believe it, but she tried to make him
jealous . . . as if . . . she nearly drove him mad . . . saying
things . . . things about the *Fár Breige* . . . I just can't bring
myself to repeat it, Brehon.'

'No, no,' said Mara soothingly. 'But yesterday morning,
when Father O'Lochlainn came into this house to see you,
well, things were different, weren't they? You know that, now,
don't you? Clodagh was not alive, though of course you didn't
know that at the time. So, think hard, Deirdre, what was it
that he actually said?' She forced herself to lift the slice of
cake to her mouth in a casual fashion. She nibbled a crumb
from the crust, watching Deirdre's face and wishing that the
light were better.

'I believe,' said Deirdre slowly, 'that what he said was: "The
Fár Breige has a hold of her now!"'

'I see,' said Mara after waiting a moment to see whether any more was forthcoming. 'And how did you answer him?'

'I took no notice; I never do. I just gave him a sup of ale and a slice of my bread, and then I told him that poor old Máire had been asking for him. Poor soul, she hasn't much more days left in her, that's what I told him, so I got him out the door and then I went back to my work.'

'And you didn't think of going out of the house and looking up the valley to see the stone pillar?'

'No, I didn't, Brehon. I had my work to do. The kids are being weaned and the nannies are giving lots of milk. I have the churning to do and the skim milk to bring to the kids – we give them that and they eat the ivy and the other herbs. We try to get them good and fat over the next six months so that they are ready for the winter.'

'So you didn't take much notice of what Father O'Lochlainn said, did you?'

'I didn't, and that's a fact, Brehon. And, to be sure, it wasn't the first time that I'd heard that kind of *ráméish* from him, poor man.' There was a guarded look in Deirdre's eyes and she turned, rather ostentatiously, back to her cheeses, remodelling their perfectly circular shapes. 'Of course when Pat came to tell me about her being dead, well, I fetched the priest then. I didn't think it would do any harm if she was really dead.'

'I'd like to see where you keep the kids, some time when it's convenient,' said Mara, rising to her feet and speaking lightly. She thought that she had obtained as much as she was going to get from Deirdre. Whether it was the whole truth, she was unsure, but people have different reasons to lie. Defensiveness and prudery can sometimes be as potent as guilt.

'You'd be very welcome, Brehon. Himself would love to show you them. When the weather takes a turn for the good, perhaps; merciful God; we can't have rain for ever, can we?'

There was no doubt that there was a great note of relief in Deirdre's voice. And yet, anxiety shone from her eyes as she ushered Mara to the door.

Anxiety for the strange priest?

Or was it for her husband, Pat?

As she walked up the road, Mara was conscious that she, also, was feeling anxious.

There was, she thought, a strong chance that Father O'Lochlainn was the murderer. But there was an even stronger chance that if he were not the murderer himself, he knew the identity of the person who had strangled Clodagh O'Lochlainn. Despite the heavy mist that morning, he surely would have been able to see from his window if someone had dragged the dead body to that place and lashed it to the stone pillar. And, in that case, he could be in grave danger. At the time, he might not have realized what he was seeing, but now; now, strange and all as he was, there could be little doubt in his mind that he had witnessed a murder.

Seven

Críth Gablach
(Ranks in Society)

If a lord gives to a tenant the gift of a buck goat and a female goat, the tenant must repay him a year later with the gift of a tub, twelve inches high and full of sweet cheese. In the second year he must give the same amount of butter and in the third year he must give two tubs, one five inches high of man-butter and one four inches high of woman-butter.

Mara's scholars arrived just as the Angelus bell was sounding for midday. Despite Deirdre's prediction, the rain still poured down as heavily as ever. Low black clouds still covered the sky and the westerly wind even penetrated the sheltered valley of Oughtdara. Up on the hillside Mara could see Ballinalacken Castle, like a beacon, its windows glowing through the storm. Her six young scholars were dripping and Fachtnan had six-year-old Orla in front of him, swathed in his cloak, but her small nose looked pink and her eyes were miserable. Mara frowned slightly at the appearance of the child. From the time of the birth of her first child, Saoirse, Nuala had employed a woman to care for her children. There was no real need for Fachtnan to take Orla out in the cold and the wet.

She understood why, though. He was keeping up the pressure on her. He had decided that the best thing for Orla would be to become a law scholar. About a year ago he had, for the first time, asked whether Orla might be admitted to the law school as a scholar and Mara had refused, saying that she had decided not to admit anyone younger than the age of eight years due to the strenuous study required. It was, also, far easier to judge ability at the age of eight than five, she told him, but already she had reckoned that Orla had not inherited her parents' brains. And in addition, she seemed to have her father's poor memory, without his intelligence. She was an ordinary, sweet-natured, quite artistic little girl who was finding the task of learning to read and to write was taking all the efforts of which she was capable.

Fachtnan, though, was quietly persistent and took Orla around with him as often as possible. Mara worried a little about him; worried whether the marriage between him and Nuala was a satisfactory one. From the time when she was thirteen years old, Nuala had worshipped Fachtnan, while he, treating her more like a younger sister, had fallen desperately in love with Fiona, the Scottish law scholar, who had no interest in Fachtnan. Eventually after Fiona had gone back to her native country, Fachtnan had married Nuala in the summer when Cormac was born. Oddly, thought Mara, marriage had made his love grow while Nuala's seemed to cool. Partly, she guessed, it was due to the intensity that Nuala invested in her profession. Partly, also, perhaps, Fachtnan felt that he was unsuccessful while his wife was immensely successful. Mara sighed. If only she felt that Fachtnan, with the learning-by-rote problems which had plagued his boyhood, and had not got better with age, could take a step forward and at least qualify as a teacher of law and if only she could persuade King Turlough to replace the usual ten-year sentence of banishment of Boetius MacClancy with a permanent one, then Fachtnan might be able to take over the MacClancy law school and Brehon Mara could manage the legal affairs of north-west Corcomroe in addition to Burren. But Fachtnan had grown from a sweet-natured boy to a very reserved man in his thirties, and ultimately only he could solve his problems.

In the meantime, she had to see to her drenched and probably hungry scholars.

She had temporarily shunned Ballinalacken Castle as the king's wife, but it made sense as a place for a busy official of the law to snatch a meal. Breakfast was a few hours past and when Mara saw how wet and cold her scholars were after their ride, she decided to take the small narrow road which led up to the hilltop where the castle, a wedding gift from King Turlough Donn to Mara, his second wife, reared up against the sky.

When they arrived, she turned a preoccupied eye and a deaf ear towards the various appeals made to her for decisions, noting that several seemingly important matters had already been determined in her absence and that the urgent questions about how many wall chambers to prepare for use had been solved by the simple solution of crowding into every space as much bedding as it could hold. Already the long table in the Great Hall had been spread with several large linen cloths, the joins neatly hidden by silver bowls and platters borrowed, probably, from Bunratty Castle. The burning question of how to seat everyone had been neatly solved by lining each side of the table with cushioned-adorned short planks, supported by trestles, and reserving the ornate chairs for the top and bottom of the table.

'Let's go down to the kitchen,' said Cormac, eyeing the festive room with an air of boredom. Like Turlough, he was immediately at home with the kitchen staff, teasing the girls, joking with the men and contriving to have a taste of everything that was going while the embarrassed steward tried to get them all back upstairs again. However, Cormac had his way and they sat cosily around the kitchen fire and made a hearty meal, sampling all of the dishes being cooked in preparation for the great day.

The kitchen house at Ballinalacken faced north so when they came out they were astonished for a moment to see how the day had brightened. The strong wind was still gusting in from the Atlantic, but now it was driving the clouds across the sky. Large patches of blue and the bright sunshine of late March had turned raindrops into tiny balls of liquid crystal and the gorse bushes on the hillside blazed bright gold. As they rode down to Oughtdara the catkins from some early flowering hazel branches quivered softly yellow in the sheltered laneway and the wintry blackthorn showed tiny buds of snow-white blossom on the tips of its black branches.

All three brothers were waiting for them when they reached the church at Oughtdara. Deirdre emerged from her house full of smiles and as pleased as though she had personally cooked the sunny afternoon to serve up to them. Her presence took Mara slightly aback. She had hoped to talk to Pat without his wife's anxious surveillance. She would prefer to hear his full account of the finding of the body and of Clodagh's behaviour.

'I wonder could we leave little Orla with you, Deirdre,' she said, seizing the opportunity to affect the absence of both. She wanted Fachtnan's whole attention to be on the words that fell from those brothers, all of whom had substantial lands to gain from the death of their cousin. Orla would chatter continuously and distract him.

'I want to see the moon milk,' whined Orla.

'Another day, perhaps next Saturday afternoon, if you're good,' promised Fachtnan hastily. Mara felt a bit sorry to have disappointed her, but Orla was a sweet-natured child and was soon placated by Deirdre's loud whispers about secretly baking a cake for her father to eat when he came home.

'What would you like to see, Brehon?' asked Pat. He did not seem in any way worried by her presence, just gravely polite. Gobnait was his usual placid self and Dinan's eyes were sparkling with pleasure at the prospect of having a new audience for his stories, while Ug the sheepdog herded them all into a tight pack in a professional fashion which excited Cormac's envy.

'I'd like to see the lands that each of you own; those that you inherited from your father and those that originally belonged to your uncle Danu,' said Mara, avoiding the mention of Clodagh's name. There would be time enough for close questioning at the end of the expedition. 'Shall we leave our horses tied up here?'

'Turn them loose inside the enclosure,' said Pat. 'They'll be quite safe in there. The grass is good and the walls are high, still. We'll tie up the gate so that anyone who comes will make sure to shut it again.'

He and his brothers, with averted heads, passed the *Fár Breige* standing sentinel by the entrance to Dunaunmore and Mara followed with her scholars while Fachtnan hovered by the gate for a moment, staring curiously at the stone pillar and glancing all around at the surrounding hills.

'So this is Dunaunmore,' said Mara as she watched her fastidious Arab steed tear the lush green grass in greedy mouthfuls.

It had been a cold wet February, followed by a wet and blustery March. The grass on most of the fields at Cahermacnaghten and around Ballinalacken had a yellowish tint, but the grass within the high sheltering walls of Dunaunmore appeared as it would appear after a month of summer sun and mist: a deep, fresh shade of green and as thick as the best velvet. Mara bent down and plucked a few rooted pieces. The soil on the roots was dark and rich and held a faint heat from the stone below.

'Just three inches of soil above the limestone, but it's enough with the rain that we get.' Gobnait watched her action with a smile. 'There's probably been tons of seaweed put on it long before any of us were born, but in my lifetime, I've never known it to need anything. It's always the same, winter and summer. Your horses will enjoy it, Brehon.'

'Do you know, I don't think that I've ever been in here before,' said Mara. She remembered Clodagh's words about her fine house. It had been important for the woman to get back this place and she had plans for it, and, of course, with an army of workers, a carpenter, a thatcher, a blacksmith to make a new gate, with all of these, the place, built on a small hill, with its view of the restless Atlantic, could be very beautiful. But where was Clodagh planning to get the money or the goods with which to pay these people? Land by itself would give nothing. Aengus had no stock and Clodagh, herself, had just a couple of sheep and a pair of goats. By law, she would be forbidden to sell the land; it was hers only to care for and to use for the duration of her life, after that it went back to her kin, to her nearest blood relatives, those who had descended from the same grandfather. The house itself would need work and materials.

It was a fine place, a very large enclosure, built in the old style with massive squared-off stones, each the size of a wooden chest and within the wall there were many buildings: the house, the kitchen house, the place for visitors and a couple of other houses, storage places, perhaps, or a dairy for milk and cheese. Each one of these was built in the same fashion with large, carefully hewn stones, narrow slits for windows; there was no glass anywhere and the shutters were broken and hanging loose.

Worst of all, the thatched roofs were ragged and decaying, covered in green moss and several large holes had appeared here and there. Danu, Clodagh's father, had been a carpenter and the wooden doors were massive and well shaped. But the red lead paint had blistered and fallen to the ground, leaving great stretches of rotting timber and there were marks of rodents' runs beneath at the thresholds of most entrances. It had been just as well that Deirdre or Pat had salvaged some of the furniture and placed it within their own well-cared-for and well-heated house.

'So this is where it all started, Brehon; this is the place where the first blows were struck in the wars,' said Dinan.

Mara controlled the start that she gave. Of course he was going back thousands of years ago, back to the *Fír Bolg*, back to the arrival of the *Tuatha Dé*, to the time when gods clashed with men and terrible cruelties and savage punishments were the norm.

'Show me the Cave of the One Cow where you were yesterday morning while the nanny goat gave birth to the twins,' she said to Pat and as they walked up the steep hill to the north of the enclosure, Mara tried to turn a deaf ear to the tale that Dinan was chanting to the scholars which seemed to involve a man's intestines being wound around an oak tree. The sea was visible by the time that they got to the top of it and Mara paused for a moment to look down over the shining blue-black slabs heaped one on top of the other, fringed by the blue sea with the white-capped waves and beyond it the misty azure outline of the Aran Islands, and then she turned back to look down at Oughtdara.

'You can see the stone pillar and the enclosure of Dunaunmore very well from here,' she observed to Pat and he looked uncomfortable. He had understood her implication.

'On a clear day, Brehon, you can, but yesterday, even the gods themselves would have been hard put to see anything through the mist. It was only when it cleared a bit that I thought there might be something wrong. I didn't take any notice for a while, to be honest with you. I thought that it was Clodagh up to tricks again.'

So Pat also witnessed the tormenting of the priest by

Clodagh. Mara raised an eyebrow at him and he nodded mysteriously.

'It's a terrible thing to say, Brehon, of my own flesh and blood,' said Dinan breaking off his story and turning from the scholars to her, 'but I do believe that old queen came back again in her. No mortal could torment the way that she could.'

'The old queen,' breathed Art. 'Morrigan, the blood-drenched one.'

'What! Clodagh! *Dhera!*' Cormac was thrilled.

Normally Mara would have been amused by the two of them, but somehow Dinan's intensity had got under her skin. She felt herself give a slight shiver.

'Let's walk on,' she said.

The cave was large once you were through the ivy-screen door and there appeared to be plenty of air. Once her eyes adjusted, Mara found that she could see everything. It was difficult to see how far back into the hillside it stretched, but she guessed that it might go a considerable distance.

The two baby goats were curled up beside their mother in the cave. They were sleeping peacefully while she chewed on the dark green leaves of the ivy that hung like a curtain over the entrance to the cave. Mara admired them, while in the background Dinan chanted the lay of the Morrigan. 'This is the way the story goes,' he said. '"The cry of the Morrigan is terrible and fearful to the ears . . ."'

'You have a great view from here,' said Mara to Pat, trying to ignore some gory details about the horse of the Morrigan which had one leg, one eye, and one ear and the pole of the chariot passing right through his body so that the peg in front met the halter passing through its forehead.

'We have, indeed, Brehon,' said Pat.

'So when you came out to the entrance of the cave, you could see that there was something wrong back in Oughtdara?'

'It was the crows,' said Pat in a slightly defensive fashion. 'I could see them all hovering around. And one big black crow came and perched on the . . . on the head . . .'

'On top of the stone pillar, is that what you mean?' said Mara.

'That's right, Brehon.' He sounded uncomfortable and his eyes slid across to Dinan.

'She's a shape-changer, so they say,' observed Dinan. 'In lots of the old tales, the Morrigan disappears, leaving only a crow in her place. Many have tried to kill her, so they say, but her soul will go into a passing crow and then she'll be reborn again. It is told that this world will never be free of her, not until the time of the second coming.'

'When did she first come; when was she first seen in this world, Dinan?' asked Cian eagerly.

'Well, you know all about the *Fír Bolgs*, the little dark men that came from across the sea, don't you? They were here first of all and she was their chief god, the most important of them all and then the *Tuatha Dé* arrived from across the sea. In the old stories, the Morrigan appeared first in the great battle between the *Tuatha Dé* and the *Fír Bolgs*.'

'And she's been around ever since,' stated Art.

'She finds plenty of forms to hold her spirit,' responded Dinan. His voice sounded dreamy, slightly dazed and Mara wasn't surprised that the four younger scholars were hanging on his words. Slevin, however, had a twinkle of amusement in his eyes and Domhnall looked bored, until Dinan turned and pointed dramatically towards the small church in the distance.

'And they say that when she is killed, a crow takes her spirit and flies with it to the cave of Sionnach MacDara and keeps it there until a new form has been woven and then it is released upon the world again.'

'Have you ever been in that cave, Dinan, the cave of Sionnach MacDara?' Domhnall's eyes were suddenly sharp with interest. Fachtnan, who had been standing in the doorway looked back and Slevin moved a little closer towards his friend.

'That's something that I can never understand. How can a fox be a son of a priest and a saint?' asked Cormac lightly and Domhnall gave him an exasperated look.

'Ah, these were the old days; some very strange things went on in the old days; things that no mind could fathom or under-standing could grasp.' Dinan, Mara noticed, had answered Cormac's question, but not Domhnall's.

'So how do you get into the cave of Sionnach MacDara, Dinan?' she asked. 'Or do you know, Pat?'

The two brothers looked at each other and then at Gobnait, and Gobnait was the one who replied, saying hastily, 'You don't want to be going down there, Brehon. That's a terrible dangerous place. And you'd be torn to shreds before you got near to it. The blackthorn's been let grow something shocking all around it. It's only the foxes that get in and out of that place. They've got their own little tunnels, cute, they are, these fellas.'

'You'll have to get your goats on to it, Pat, if it's that bad; they eat blackthorn, don't they?' The advantage of being a Brehon, thought Mara, was that one could offer advice on all kinds of subjects and no one was rude enough to advise you to mind your own business.

'Well, you see, it's by way of being church property, Brehon,' said Pat apologetically.

'So the entrance is quite near to the church, then, is it?' Mara could see the purpose of Domhnall's question. However, she thought that she might approach the subject slightly more obliquely.

'I remember Brigid, my housekeeper, telling me that the whole land under here is like a honeycomb with caves and passageways going everywhere,' she observed. She touched the fronds of luxuriantly cascading mass of maidenhair fern and murmured lightly, 'How on earth does this grow so well with so little light.' It was, she thought, significant that her observation about underground tunnels and passageways went unmarked whereas all three brothers hastened to tell her about different varieties of ferns that grew in the caves.

'I suppose the Morrigan would have gone down this tunnel, wouldn't she, Dinan?' Slevin had cleverly brought the two halves of the conversation together and for a moment, even Dinan looked disconcerted.

'That's right, lad, she would have,' he said and then the temptation was too much for him and he said in a whisper, 'You know about the Morrigan, don't you? When she made water it flowed down and through the earth, carving out passageways wherever it went.'

'Oh, blessed Jesus!' muttered Cormac, rather inappropriately, thought Mara.

'Are there any underground tunnels, leading from this cave?' she asked.

'Not from this one, that I could swear,' said Pat so quickly that she was inclined to take his word for it. She looked around the cave and he added, 'This is a good cave, Brehon. I wouldn't put my nanny goats' little kids in here if it had any passageways for them to get lost in.'

'No, of course not; I'm sure you are very careful with them.' It did not mean, though, that one of the other caves could not have afforded a means to get secretly back to Oughtdara without anyone seeing you. Pat was, she thought, the most uneasy of the three brothers, but then he was the eldest and perhaps used to taking responsibility.

'I'm just trying to imagine yesterday morning, the morning when Clodagh was murdered and wondering whether it was possible for you to see anything of what happened, and, more importantly, whether you saw anyone near to the place where the crime was committed. It would be quite possible,' she said, improvising fluently, 'for you, for any of you, to have seen someone and then in the terrible shock of discovering the murdered body of your cousin, for that picture to have gone completely out of your head.'

Mara let the sound of her words die away. She had purposely spoken slowly, with pauses after key words. There was a slight echo in the cave, but she was a practised orator and echoes could be made to play their part in adding a weight to the words. She swept a glance around her scholars, her eyes warning them to say nothing. She didn't want any more silly talk about the Morrigan or any facetious interruptions.

'I'd like you to think back to that time yesterday morning, Pat. It would have been earlier than now, of course, it would have been about an hour about noon. You had been seeing to the nanny goat, had helped her to deliver her twins and then, the crisis was over, the mother was suckling the babies, you walk to the entrance of the cave, you were probably cramped and stiff, so you walk out and you see that the mist had begun to lift, that's right, isn't it, Pat?'

'That's right, Brehon.' Without being asked he moved slowly

to the cave outlet. Mara followed him, concentrating so hard that she was unaware of the others.

'Yes, you're right, Brehon, that's what I did. I'd been kneeling down on the ground beside her and my knees were sore, and I'm a bit tall for that sort of work, so I straightened up, went outside, right outside . . .' Pat moved forward so that he was on the edge of the cliff and Mara saw the slow sweep of his head, moving from the sight of the Atlantic breakers where he would have sniffed the salt wind, backwards and then she saw his head stop. 'And I could see that there was a sort of glow there behind the clouds to the back of Ballinalacken Castle.' He was staring up at the hill and the stately stone building and she saw him give a small nod. 'And I said to myself, the mist is going. And it was just then, Brehon,' he said turning around to face her, 'it was just then, that I saw the crows. I'd been hearing them, you see, I'm sure I'd heard them when I came out of the cave, because I'd been saying to myself: Thank God, they're under shelter, the two little ones, because things are hard for them for the first few days – crows trying to peck their eyes out, foxes waiting for the mother's eye to be off them for a few minutes, waiting to nip in and tear the throat of them. And then I saw them circling around and around the *Fár Breige* so I thought that I would go down and see what was happening.'

And risked leaving the newborn kids; the thought crossed Mara's mind, but she said nothing. Pat, she thought, was telling his story well and it did seem, she thought, as though he were reliving the experience of standing up there on the cliff edge on that fateful Monday morning and gazing out, seeing the sun behind the clouds, and the mist rising from the valley floor and then becoming aware of the predatory crows.

'And then when you were about halfway down, you hollered for me,' put in Gobnait. 'So me and Ug came across to join you.'

'And what could you see?' Mara turned swiftly to the younger brother.

'I could see Pat.'

'But not the crows; did you notice them?'

Gobnait turned that over in his mind, half-nodded, but then shook his head.

'I couldn't tell for sure, Brehon. I think the sight of her . . . the way she . . . I think all that put everything out of my head. I just don't remember the crows, but Pat saw them so . . .'

'I see,' said Mara. 'And where was Pat when he shouted for you.'

'I was quite near the *Fár Breige* by then, Brehon,' said Pat. Gobnait had looked at her helplessly and then at his dog so it was not surprising that his older brother had intervened. Nevertheless, she was slightly sorry that she hadn't sent Gobnait off with Fachtnan while she was talking to Pat.

'And then when we got down and we could see her there and we got nearer – yes, I remember the crows now!' said Gobnait. 'Ug went flying at them and scattered them and then he came back to us, and, you wouldn't believe this, Brehon, but all the hair, all around his neck, all down his spine, every single hair, well, it was all standing on end. He knew she was dead, you see. He's a clever fellow.'

'So he is,' said Mara. She looked down at the astute Ug who was staring at her with a look of sharp intelligence on his narrow face. What a shame that he couldn't talk! Had Pat actually come down from the cave, climbed down from the cliffside, only realizing that Clodagh was dead when he came quite near to the stone pillar, or was there another explanation.

'And Dinan,' she said. 'How did he come on the scene?'

'Well, when we saw that—' began Pat, but he was interrupted.

'Not a bit of it, not a bit of it,' said Dinan's deep, melodious voice and every head turned to him with interest.

'That dog wouldn't turn a hair because of a dead body. He's seen plenty of them in his time, plenty of his own killing, too. No, the dog knows the truth about what killed the woman, and what's more, the crows knew it also.'

'What did you think, Fachtnan?' asked Mara as they went to collect their horses from Dunaunmore enclosure. She placed a hand on his arm to detain him for a moment. The three younger boys were arguing vociferously about whether the

Morrigan had anything to do with the crows or not – Cormac and Art inclining towards the belief that the goddess was involved somehow or other, and Cian pouring ridicule on the whole matter. Cael was listening quietly to a low-voiced conversation between Slevin and Domhnall. It was a good moment for the Brehon and his assistant to confer in privacy, but Fachtnan looked taken aback, his eyes, going towards the gate.

'What did you think?' she repeated, suppressing a feeling of impatience. After all, it was good that a man loved his daughter. She just wished that he could detach his mind from her during working hours. He looked guilty and ill at ease, she thought and felt rather sorry for him.

'I thought that Pat seemed like an honest man,' he said with an effort. And then, with a note of sincerity in his voice, 'I just felt all of the time that he was telling his story that it was the truth.'

Mara nodded. This was what she valued in Fachtnan. His judgement, even when he was just a boy, was always excellent. He had a mature understanding of people. She said nothing, though, and waited. There was a slight frown between his bushy eyebrows.

'I thought that Dinan was uneasy and overanxious to keep turning the talk towards the Morrigan,' he said and then continued rapidly, 'that could mean something, or it could mean nothing. They are all uneasy, and it may be, that as yet, none of them have opened up to the others. They may still be all wondering whether a brother has done this deed.'

'I agree with you,' said Mara. She stood back and let him go. No point in detaining a man who has something else on his mind. In any case, she thought, I have nothing else to say at the moment. There are three men, three brothers, all of whom had something to gain from the death of this woman.

And all of whom, she realized as she walked her horse through the gate, might have been able to get to Sionnach MacDara's cave, unseen. Without mounting, she crossed the roadway and joined Domhnall, Slevin and Cael as they stood in deep conversation in front of a seemingly impenetrable thicket of blackthorn.

'Fox runs,' Slevin was saying in a low voice as she came up.

'Isn't there some sort of proverb, or wise saying: "Where a fox may run, a wise man may pass"?' enquired Domhnall.

'Would want to be a very small, thin one,' said six-foot-high Slevin, looking with disfavour at the thorny passageways.

'Look,' said Cael softly. While the boys had been bending down and peering at ground level, she had moved around the side of the thicket and was standing beside a twenty-foot-high rock face. The black thorny branches were flat against its pale grey surface, but Cael had reached across, leaning slightly down, and plucked something from a needle sharp blackthorn. She passed it to Mara.

'I thought it was a piece of wool, first,' she said, 'but it's not, is it?'

'No,' said Mara thoughtfully. 'It's a linen thread, come from someone's *léine*.'

It pointed to the fact that someone had squeezed their way between the bushes and the rock face, but there would be no means of telling who.

Children and men wore them knee-length and women wore them full-length, but everyone in the kingdom possessed these garments woven from the linen threads harvested from the flax that grew high in a sheltered valley in the Aillwee Mountain.

Eight

Cis Foðhla Tíre?
(How Many Kinds of Land are there?)

Land is valued in cumals.

*The value of a cumal of land ranges from twenty-four milch cows
for best arable land, down to eight dry cows for bog land.*

The area of a cumal is approximately thirty-four square acres.

That evening after Mara had finished her supper, she spent
a long time thinking about the three brothers. How much
did Dinan believe of those tales that he told with such admiration, she wondered. And would he allow his admiration to
influence his deeds? The heroes of the legends became heroes
because they rid their kingdom of an evil spirit such as the
Morrigan, that demon woman who could urinate powerfully
enough to carve passages and caves through the landscape.
Would Dinan allow their heroic behaviour to influence him?
There had been something odd, something childlike in his
insistence on dwelling on the horrors and the suffering
inflicted. Mara, though very fond of children, had few illusions
about them. Children, she believed strongly, had to be trained
in the way of the righteous, as Brigid would say. Left to themselves, they would undoubtedly always seek what profited
them, would sweep aside whatsoever frustrated them in their
desires, had to be encouraged on a daily basis to put themselves
in the place of others, not to give way to fury, to share with
others, to work, to gain the esteem of others, ultimately self-
esteem and above all to learn to live at peace in a community.

Brehon law, she thought with a half-smile, was an ideal
training ground for the young: keep the rules, or pay the
penalty. And then she thought back to Fachtnan and sighed.
He wanted a school for Orla and there were two schools on
the Burren, one for law, and one for medicine, but they were

only for highly intelligent, highly motivated young people. Perhaps there should be a third, one that taught less exacting knowledge and skills. She had been reading a book that she had bought from a bookseller in Galway by an English lawyer called Thomas More about an ideal land called Utopia – the book itself was named *Utopia* and it had a few pages about an ideal school. Thomas More, like herself, would have been brought up with the relentlessly hard study of Latin – his book was written in Latin – and then of the law, but he wrote about a gentler school, a school where, not only did the children learn to read and write, but where the whole community took part in teaching the children, each one instructing in a particular skill, such as growing food, caring for animals, building houses and walls, fashioning articles from wood, weaving and sewing. Every neighbourhood of the Burren had its expert in these matters and could impart their knowledge to a schoolroom of children. Mara's mind ranged over other possibilities: music, dance, making of pots, binding of books, even perhaps an understanding of the law that would govern their lives as adults. That would be her contribution.

Mara gave a sigh and a shrug of her shoulders and turned her mind back to the murder. Were those tales about the Morrigan just an effort to distract her from the fact that these three brothers had, by the death of their cousin, Clodagh, more than doubled the amount of land that they had previously held? She thought about that for a while, half wondering whether to have a word with her farm manager, Brigid's husband, Cumhal, but there was another matter that had been nagging at her subconsciously and she decided to pay a visit to Ardal O'Lochlainn, instead.

As usual he was working, and as usual he made a polite pretence of being just about to finish as soon as he saw her. She salved her conscience about interrupting him with the thought that he worked too hard, anyway, and allowed him to escort her up to the room on the top of the tower house, making light conversation about the preparations at Ballinalacken for her fiftieth birthday party. It was only when the wine had been poured into the cups and they were alone that she turned the conversation back to the murder case.

'I've been walking around the lands of Pat and his brothers this afternoon,' she said, 'and I've come to you for information. You inspected those lands closely so you should be able to give me an answer on judgement day about the case that Clodagh brought about laying claim to her land. Now I'd like to ask you a slightly different question. How well did the brothers profit from the death of Clodagh?'

He looked slightly taken aback at her plain speaking. She knew that she could trust him, though, and she knew that he would give an accurate and a well-considered answer. She knew, also, that he would be turning over in his mind the opinion that he had given at Poulnabrone that the whole of the portion owned by Clodagh's father, Danu of Dunaunmore, was merely 'land fit to graze seven cows'. And in fact, when he spoke, it was to that verdict that he referred, though he approached the matter obliquely.

'Land is a strange thing,' he said, taking a thoughtful sip from the wine in his cup. 'You, Brehon, could come here to my lands and you could look at one of my best fields and to you it would only be useful as a place where your scholars could play at hurling. You would consider, perhaps, how well it would drain in the winter so that they did not get too muddy, you would look to see how level a surface it had so that none of your scholars could trip and break a leg; now I could look at the same field and I would look to see the quality of the grass; I would estimate how well it could feed many of my horses throughout the winter and whether it would still produce new grass for the foals in the spring and then go on to have a crop of hay in the summer, I would be concerned with the depth of the soil, with its fertility and whether it drains well; and so, Brehon,' he concluded lightly, 'this field in my mind's eye is more valuable to me than it would be to you.'

'So, what you're saying is that land which you valued as only sufficient to graze seven cows, would in fact, be infinitely more valuable for someone who wanted to graze goats and sheep on it. Is that right?'

Ardal gave her an approving nod and swallowed some of his wine before answering. 'As always, Brehon, you put the matter in a nutshell. Goats don't take any notice of rocks and stones;

boulders that might break the legs of my racing horses, would be as nothing to goats, just an amusement and source of food, they don't require rich grass as they will nibble the herbs that grow under and beside the clumps of stone through the winter in the warmth of the limestone, and the growing shoots of the hazel will nourish them in spring and the ivy on the walls of the rocks and the caves will keep them healthy all the year around. And the young kids will just strengthen their legs leaping from rock to rock, and, of course, our mountain sheep are like goats.'

'So the brothers got land of value to them?' It was interesting, thought Mara, how Brehon law always used a cow, a milch cow, as a unit of value, equating it with a piece of silver. And yet pigs, sheep and goats were also of value to a farming community. Perhaps some changes should be made in this law.

'Three of them; three of the brothers,' corrected Ardal. 'Finnegas's share was probably of little value to him, but there is a strong bond between the brothers and he would do what he could for them.'

'And what about Dinan's share, the bawns?'

'Not worth at all as much as his two elder brothers' shares,' said Ardal and added, 'though it seemed to me that, on the day when I was valuing it, that he was the one that seemed the most worried about the prospect of losing it, the most upset of all the brothers. It appeared that he was much attached to that piece of land because it was a battle site between the *Tuatha Dé* and *Fír Bolg*s. He was almost hysterical, crying out to Clodagh that the old people would be revenged upon her, rather as he did on judgement day at Poulnabrone. In fact, Dinan was so set on owning the bawns that when it came to the division of the land – as you know, Finnegas, the youngest divided it, and then before the brothers picked in order of age, apparently, according to my steward, Dinan had asked for that piece of land. It's possible,' said Ardal in the tone of a man who is inured to the eccentricities of his fellow creatures, 'that he may have set particular value on these lands because of the tales connected to them.'

'Do you think that he truly believes all of these old stories?' Mara thought back to the legends that Dinan had told them. Though intensely sceptical herself, she could see how her scholars, even Fachtnan, had been disturbed by the horrors of the tales. Dinan had seemed, she thought, frowning slightly, almost to confuse his cousin, Clodagh, with the goddess Morrigan. Did Morrigan really have ten bright red tresses, or was that a memory of Clodagh's hair before it turned grey?

'I feel that it would be dangerous to assume that he does not,' was Ardal's reply and she nodded her agreement. Instinctively she felt that there was something rather odd about Dinan's intensity and she had learned over the years never to dismiss any such feelings but to subject them to a rigorous analysis. If the man truly believed that Clodagh was a reincarnation of the goddess Morrigan, who was so known for her shape-changing abilities, then he would have felt justified, felt a hero, if he had killed her. During her short walk back to her house, Mara thought back to the stories that Dinan had told, visualizing the ominous figure of the *Fár Breige*.

'There is one other matter that I wanted to talk to you about, Ardal,' she said. She would have to be careful, here, she knew. Ardal was an extremely religious man and the older he grew, the more important church matters and churchmen seemed to be to him. 'Brigid was talking to me about Clodagh as a girl and said that she worked as the priest's housekeeper.' She waited, but his face was blank and so she was forced to continue. 'She mentioned the bishop to me,' she continued, wondering how to approach the matter obliquely. She saw him stiffen, wince slightly and she guessed that he would not be willing to betray anything that the bishop may have said to him. 'She mentioned she had heard that the bishop and you got together and made up a marriage between your shepherd, Aengus, and Clodagh so as to remove her from the young priest's household.'

'*Sin sceal é*,' said Ardal lightly, quoting the old country proverb. He smiled, but his smile was forced and Mara guessed that Brigid, as usual, had the true story. It had been a poor match for that pretty girl, the daughter of a craftsman and a landowner. It wrecked three lives, and to no purpose, but the bishop would have had great influence over Ardal.

'Funny how these old stories linger in the minds of some; now I myself don't have much of a memory for the past,' he said and there was a stern note in his voice. She would get no more out of him, she thought, as she rose to her feet to take her leave. He had not denied it, and that was enough for her.

But it was not of Father O'Lochlainn, but of Dinan that she thought as she walked down the moonlit road towards her house. She had asked whether the man took these legends seriously and he had replied instantly to her question. 'It would be dangerous to assume that he did not', had said Ardal and his words reverberated in her mind during her short walk back to her own house. She got to her gate, put her hand down to open it and then changed her mind.

There was a candle lantern burning in the schoolhouse a hundred and fifty yards down the road. Someone was working late. She wondered whether Fachtnan had stayed behind to make notes. It would have been something that he would have done in the past, but these days he seemed to be lacking interest and to be preoccupied with his younger daughter. Orla was a problem, or at least Fachtnan was making her to be a problem, she thought with a sigh of exasperation that this matter kept intruding upon more important affairs of the kingdom. Left to herself, the child would play happily under the care of her nursemaid. However, Fachtnan seemed to feel that Orla should be studying for a profession, if not medicine, then the law. Perhaps she should talk it over with him, give him her honest opinion of the little girl's ability. It would be a cruel thing to impose rigorous study on a child whose intellect or temperament was not able for that burden.

But when Mara pushed open the door of the schoolhouse there was no sign of her assistant, but all of the scholars were there from twelve-year-old Cormac to eighteen-year-old Domhnall. They were, once again, spending their free time working on the case.

Domhnall was standing at the whitewashed board on the wall with a stick of charcoal in his hand. Down one side were written five names: of the four brothers and of Deirdre and across the top Domhnall was writing the headings: MEANS. OPPORTUNITY. MOTIVE.

'I don't know why there has to be means *and* opportunity. They mean the same thing, don't they?' Cian was a good person to have in the law school; he challenged everything, argued with everyone.

'No, they're not, birdbrain,' said his sister. 'You could say that little Orla had the opportunity to murder Clodagh, but she wouldn't have the means as Clodagh was killed by a pair of hands squeezing the life out of her and Orla would not have the strength to do that.'

'What about Deirdre; would she have been strong enough?' asked Domhnall. He had already put a tick under opportunity opposite her name.

'I'd say yes,' said Mara decisively. 'She does a lot of churning and that must strengthen the hands and arms.'

They all nodded. All had tried their hand at this from time to time, more for the tastiness of a piece of new butter than from a desire to be helpful. Domhnall put a neat tick under 'means'.

'Yes, she'd have to have strong wrists,' agreed Cormac, 'and she did have the opportunity, didn't she? She was in the house quite near to *Fár Breige*. I agree with your ticks, Domhnall,' he finished condescendingly.

'Hm,' said Cael, 'I wouldn't be too keen on her motive, myself. Why would she do it?'

'To get more land for her husband like any good wife,' said Cian.

'She probably didn't want it; if they have more land, they have to have more goats, and that would make more work for Deirdre, churning all that milk and making all those cheeses,' said Cael vigorously.

'Cael's right, in a way,' said Slevin, 'but I was thinking when we were up there this afternoon that all of those caves are on the land that Clodagh had before she was killed; the only one that Pat has on his own land was the Cave of the One Cow. Now they have about four or five, don't they; the Thieves' Cave, the Bones Cave, the Daghda's Cave, Moonmilk Cave and the Through and Through Cave, so that means that they'll have plenty of nice dry, warm places for the kids when they're young, and they're probably safer from foxes, too, as the mother goat can easily guard the entrance.'

'You're probably right, so her motive will be the same as the men – greed.' Cael nodded at Domhnall as he added ticks to the names.

'It's a bit of a boring list, isn't it,' complained Cormac. 'They've all got opportunity, except for Finnegas; they've all got motives and they're the same motives; and they've all got means; they would all be able to strangle someone. And that mist made everything so easy for the murderer. We might as well stick a pin in and choose by that.'

'Let's agree on the least likely one out of Pat, Deirdre, Gobnait and Dinan,' suggested Domhnall.

'Deirdre,' said Cael. 'She looks too sensible to commit murder just because she wants to have more cheese to make.'

'Dinan,' said Cormac. 'He's not the type.'

'Yes, he is,' said Slevin. 'Dinan gets himself very worked up. People like that are more inclined to lose their temper and there's many a death caused by a loss of temper.'

'He might have killed her because he thought that she was the Morrigan come to life again,' said Art in a low voice. 'I know that sounds stupid,' he added quickly.

'Not to me,' said Mara. 'It was interesting listening to him this afternoon, wasn't it?'

'He did sound quite creepy, didn't he?' said Cormac to Art. If Cian had said such a thing, Cormac would have poured scorn on him, but Art was Cormac's best friend; they were reared in the same bed, were fed by the same woman and the relationship was very strong. Cormac would never ridicule his rather sensitive and shy foster brother.

'I'm debating whether we were right to rule out Finnegas completely,' put in Slevin. 'After all, with a fast horse, he could perhaps take the coast road and then cut across the fields, down into the valley.'

'There's a lot against it,' said Cael. 'You heard him say that he was in sight of his workers almost all of the time, he's not too likely to say that unless it were true. He'd know that the Brehon could check on that.'

'A horse wouldn't help too much, anyway. That's a birdbrain idea. It's the rocks and the cliffs that make it slow. Art and me were climbing around there last summer, during the holidays, and it takes for ever.'

'Well, we'll go over there tomorrow, but I must say that I think it is unlikely that Finnegas would come over. He'd have to be sure of finding Clodagh and then there is the point that he hasn't got much of a motive as, according to Ardal O'Lochlainn, Finnegas had the very worst piece of land. It's not limestone land; just waterlogged clay.'

'Perhaps, though, Brehon, he might have hoped to find another lead mine on that land since it's near to his own land. In fact, he might have found signs. My father says that lead sells for almost the price of gold in Galway as there is so much demand for it with everyone putting in new windows and building new houses with slate roofs,' said Domhnall.

'It's a possibility,' said Mara. 'Well, we'll see it tomorrow and we can make up our mind then. I think, though, that I would have heard if there was any talk of the seam of lead running out. King Turlough sent his steward to purchase some for bullet making not long ago and I think that he would have reported if there were any problems. In fact, I seem to remember him remarking on what excellent lead it was.'

She was about to suggest that they left the problems for a moment and had a game of chess or read a book before going to bed, but Domhnall said hesitantly, 'What about Father O'Lochlainn, Brehon? What did you make of him? Or would you prefer not to say?'

I would, thought Mara, but she could not justify excluding her scholars from part of the investigation. She had her long-accustomed and most successful methods of training young people to become lawyers, law professors or even Brehons and these included making them part of the legal work of the kingdom, making the dry laws of the texts come to life by witnessing their practical application. At the beginning of each Michaelmas term in September they all swore an oath to be discreet and never to reveal confidential matters talked about in the course of their work and she reminded them of that oath from time to time. There were grave reasons to suspect Father

O'Lochlainn in this murder case and she would have to confide them to her scholars. None of them had been sheltered from knowledge of ordinary sexual relationships among men and women, but there was something so odd, so perverted and so very ugly about that strange link between the priest and Clodagh that, for a moment, she wished that she could say nothing.

However, she had to tell them so she did as well as she could, adopting a dry, matter-of-fact manner and emphasizing that she thought there might be a streak of madness in both of them.

'God, so she used to go out and pretend that she was, you know, *doing it* with the *Fár Breige*! No wonder that Dinan thought that she was the goddess Morrigan brought back to life again. Do you remember that bit about Morrigan *doing it* with one of the other gods across a river, one foot on either bank – must have had legs the length of a *forrach*.' Cormac, perhaps because he was the youngest, or perhaps because of his temperament, seemed to be the least embarrassed.

'Well, you've got your wish, Cormac,' said Cael dryly. 'We've certainly now got a different motive, a very different motive. I would say, Brehon, that the motive would be anger, in the case of Father O'Lochlainn, would you? Rage would, perhaps, be a better word.'

'Yes, I agree, Cael, rage would be a good word and rage can be the cause of a killing.' Mara kept her face very serious but she was amused at the elderly tone that fifteen-year-old Cael adopted. 'What would you think, the rest of you?' She was anxious to keep the conversation going for a few minutes. Art was crimson with embarrassment and she wanted to give him time to recover.

'I'd like to borrow your copy of the *Táin Bó Cuilinge* to read tonight, if I may, Brehon,' said Domhnall. 'I think that these old tales might hold some of the answers to this mystery.'

'I haven't read any of those legends for such a long time,' confessed Mara. 'They sit and gather dust, but I do think that you're right, Domhnall. We may be meeting something more complex here than we usually encounter. It just crossed my mind, as you spoke, that many of those early legends have four brothers in them, brothers who have such strong bonds between them that make a brother's welfare come above all other things. And then there is the introduction of the Morrigan, the goddess of battle and, of course, of sexuality.'

'And she has certainly got this case looking very much more interesting; Morrigan and his reverence the priest, both of them,' said Cormac, his eyes sparkling with a touch of mischief.

'It could have been the priest, but I've got another idea,' said Cian, his half-broken voice rising uncontrollably. 'What if it is the whole family, the whole kin group, who decided that she had disgraced her kin by going on like that in public and that she was doomed to die, to redeem their honour. They could have all had something to do with it. One brother to strangle her, one to move the body out from the house and another, no, you might need two for this – two to tie her up against the *Fár Breige* so that she looked like she was doing what she did when she was alive. What do you think of that for an idea, Brehon?'

'What about Aengus, could he have been in on it, too?' queried Slevin. 'After all, she had disgraced him even more than her cousins.'

'Yes, but she was not of his blood,' said Cael wisely. 'Clodagh was a disgrace to the whole kin group. If he had minded so much, then Aengus could have come to the court for a divorce. The family could not get rid of her; once a member of the kin group, always a member of the kin group, but Aengus need not have anything to do with a divorced wife.'

'In any case, Aengus had gone up the mountain, everyone saw him. And if he came back,' added Cormac, 'he would have had to pass Pat and he would have had to pass that place where Gobnait was dumping his seaweed and Dinan was around there also. And one of the other shepherds would have noticed that he had been gone for a long time.'

'Where do we think that she was killed?' asked Slevin suddenly. 'I've been sort of imagining that she was killed in the house, weren't you, Domhnall. We'd assumed that, didn't we, when we were talking it over, but it occurs to me that there's no reason why she shouldn't have been killed just where we found her, standing up against the *Fár Breige*, pretending to, to . . . well, you know . . .'

'And the murderer came behind and put his, or her hands around Clodagh's neck and squeezed hard.'

'And had a length of rope handy? Is that likely?'

'People do, Cael,' said Slevin. 'Especially people with goats – it's the easiest way to catch them, throw a noose over the horns. The noose might have been already tied so he or she just slipped it over Clodagh's head.'

'Took a terrible chance, didn't he? I know it was very misty, but these valley mists can clear suddenly, or someone could have come over towards Dunaunmore and seen him tying the body. And what was the point, anyway, of tying the body, why not just leave it lying on the ground?' Cian looked around at the others.

'That's a very good question,' said Mara. 'I've been wondering about that, myself.'

'I don't think that we need to speculate too much about that,' said Cael. 'The fact is that the body was bound to the *Fár Breige*. We should just deal with facts.'

'I don't agree,' said Domhnall. 'I think that at this stage in an enquiry we should speculate as much as possible. It's important for us to enter into the mind of the murderer as far as we are able to go. Without knowing *why*, we can't find *who*.'

No one spoke for a short while after that. Domhnall had great influence over his fellow scholars. Cael, in particular, was not going to argue with him. But after a few moments, Art broke the silence, his voice low and embarrassed.

'Do you remember that place in the Bible where it says: "God is not mocked",' he said hesitantly and then stopped.

The bishop, thought Mara, would not be too pleased with the implied comparison, but she knew what Art meant. There was an odd sensation about this case, a feeling of evil forces at work.

'So, why was Clodagh O'Lochlainn killed?' she asked aloud, though speaking to herself.

And Art answered quite simply, quite earnestly, almost as though she had asked him a routine question during the repetition drill at the law school.

'She was killed, Brehon, because she was evil.'

Nine

Bretha Étgid

(Judgements of Inadvertence)

A man may open a mine if he has ownership of all the land around it. He may only dig one shaft and may not dig side shafts leading towards the lands of other men, but only beneath his own property. He must cause no harm to other property.

If harm is caused, then a fine must be paid. This will be decided by the court and will take into account the damage caused.

Mara woke early. Though normally someone who slept as soon as her head touched the pillow, she had lain awake for hours the night before, thinking about Clodagh. Was she truly evil as young Art, under the spell of Dinan's mesmerizing storytelling, had said? Mara suspected not. Clodagh, she had thought, remembering Brigid's picture of her as a young girl in a cloak of many colours, had been ambitious; clever and ambitious. She had wanted to stand out from the crowd, had wanted to make something of herself; had, perhaps rightly, felt that she had qualities which raised her above those around her. The liaison with the priest had been another step up and out of the position into which she had been born. However, being a woman meant that she had borne the consequences of the sexual act; while Father Eoin could walk away once the relationship became known to the bishop and his minions, Clodagh was left pregnant and facing the wrath of the males who were in command of her. The marriage with one of Ardal's shepherds was hastily fixed up with the assistance of the clan *taoiseach* and that should have been the end of the matter, in the eyes of all.

But it wasn't. Clodagh was still Clodagh. That burning ambition might have appeared subdued into a sullen fury which erupted into abusing her unfortunate husband and tormenting her faithless lover, but, Mara suspected, the ambition was still there. The long-expected death of her father found her prepared to make a new life for herself. There was the puzzle of the derelict house that she proposed to renovate. And even more intriguing, the quest for men skilled in the use of pickaxe and crowbar. Had Clodagh proposed to open a stone quarry? Unlikely. Most people in the kingdom of the Burren mined their own stone, built their own houses with the help of relatives and neighbours, erected the miles of stone walls from rocks and boulders taken from their fields.

And then suddenly Mara swung her legs over the side of the bed and lit the candle that stood on a small table beside her bed. She poured out a cupful of fresh spring water from the pitcher and drank it slowly, sitting very still and visualizing the landscape of the valley of Oughtdara in her mind's eye. The morning spent scrambling around the lands belonging to Pat and his brothers had paid dividends. Today's expedition would confirm her suspicions. The rain pattered against the glass in her window, but come what may she had to go to Ballyryan next morning. She replaced her mug, blew out her candle, resolutely shut her eyes and began to count the sheep, white blobs of wool, on the hillsides above the valley.

When she woke in the morning everything seemed very quiet and when she opened the window shutters she could see why. The rain had stopped and the temperature had risen, but the land was drenched and a mist steamed upwards, obliterating all the familiar landscape, blotting out thatched roofs, chimneys, the wide spreading ash tree, even deadening the lowing of cows. She went to the kitchen to eat her usual frugal breakfast of milk and a slice of Brigid's nutty bread, thickly spread with unsalted butter, but her mind was so busy that, minutes later, she was surprised to see an empty plate and pitcher in front of her. She exchanged her light shoes for a pair of substantial boots and took her woollen cloak from the back of the door. It had been made in the traditional way, in two layers, its outer surface felted and then treated with honey to render it waterproof.

When Mara came out of her own gate, she could hardly see the hedge opposite and she almost had to feel her way along a road that she had walked several times a day for almost fifty years. For a moment she wondered whether to postpone her visit to the lead mine but she had sent a message to Finnegas yesterday and she was averse to wasting the time of a very busy man. She could send an excuse by one of Cumhal's farmhands, but there was no reason why it should be easier for anyone else, rather than for her who knew the way so very well. In any case, she was driven by urgency to settle this case. The countryside was alive with rumours. Brigid had been full of lurid tales of terrible happenings in the past when the gods had been stirred and she was anxious to put a stop to these circulating, causing unrest and suspicion. A belief in the supernatural, she had found in the past, can be a cloak for man's misdeeds. This murder of Clodagh O'Lochlainn had to be solved swiftly and the murderer brought to justice at Poulnabrone as soon as possible.

There was a clanging of pots from the kitchen house as she groped her way through the tall iron gates that were set into the massive wall that enclosed the buildings of the law school, but no sound of young voices.

'You're never going out in that fog.' There was nothing wrong with Brigid's ears, though she was nearly seventy years old. 'And going all the way over to Ballyryan,' she added, demonstrating that, as usual, she knew what was going on.

'It'll lift once the sun strengthens,' said Mara with more optimism than she really felt. Still this had been a month of strong winds and perhaps one would blow in from the Atlantic as they made their journey towards the western coast. 'Where are they all? Not still in bed, I hope.'

Brigid snorted, implying ironically that they would have a chance while she was around.

'All ready for you, Brehon,' she said. 'They're over in the schoolhouse. Domhnall was saying something about looking at that map you made, long ago. Do you remember when Fachtnan was a boy, and Enda and Moylan and Aidan, and you had them out measuring and drawing on that big skin from the dun cow?'

'I remember,' said Mara. 'That was clever of Domhnall to think of that.'

She repeated her words to Domhnall himself when she went into the schoolhouse. He was calling out bends in the road and heads were nodded and words repeated. She sat and listened while scholar after scholar chanted the route from Cahermacnaghten to Ballyryan, but when Domhnall began to roll up the map again she stopped him.

'It would be interesting to look on the map at the portions of land that the four brothers have inherited. Let's look at Finnegas's land first, since we are going to see him this morning.'

'It's almost in north-west Corcomroe, isn't it, just on the border, just like Ballinalacken Castle,' said Cian.

'That's right,' said Mara. 'In fact, the old part of Ballinalacken Castle, the old tower house, was deliberately built there by the O'Lochlainn clan to guard against the O'Connor clan of Corcomroe crossing the border into the Burren and stealing their cattle. Of course, as you know,' she added, 'the kingdom of the Burren was owned by the O'Lochlainn clan from time immemorial. The O'Brien clan only completely conquered it less than a hundred years ago.' Unobtrusively, she looked at Cormac from under her eyelashes and was glad to see that he looked uninterested. There were already too many looking to be Turlough's heir when his delicate eldest son, Conor, died, or perhaps even before. The clan had a right to choose a new *tánaiste* if they thought that the present man would not be equal to the task. Some sought favour with powerful members of the clan, while Turlough's second son, Murrough, was openly in rebellion against his father and all that his father stood for. She did not want Cormac to take either of those paths.

'I'd say that Finnegas's portion from his father probably ends just there,' said Domhnall calling back her attention by pointing at a spot on the map. 'I remember Brigid talking about him building a road of a hundred paces, when he was only a boy, so as to connect on to the road leading down to Doolin Harbour.'

'And isn't it good that the three kingdoms are now united under one ruler; in the old days the O'Lochlainns of Burren and the O'Connors of Corcomroe were at daggers drawn and no one from the Burren would have dared to go to Doolin Harbour.' Mara spoke absent-mindedly. Staring at the very detailed map, her suspicions of the night before seemed feasible. But how to prove it, she wondered.

'And that King Turlough has ordered that there should be free movement between all three kingdoms: Thomond, Burren and Corcomroe,' said King Turlough's twelve-year-old son. Cormac sounded proud. As he grew older he was beginning to identify more with his father. Up to a couple of years ago, his birth parents had taken very much second place to his foster parents, Art's mother and father.

'Let me just look at that map again,' said Mara, dismissing with an effort the thorny question of Cormac and his future. She studied it carefully. She would be able to tell better when she was in the actual place, she thought and gave a sigh. It would be so much quicker and easier to go by the road, but she thought it might be more fruitful of results if they walked across from Oughtdara. She wondered which of the brothers she would ask to accompany her and decided upon Gobnait. Pat was too anxious and Dinan, when he emerged from the cloud of legends, was sharp and quick-witted and might guess what she was doing.

'I think on balance that we might just ride to Oughtdara and then walk across from there,' she said and then, seeing their astonished and disappointed faces, she added hastily, 'I know that you would all be able to find your way through the mist, after all the memorizing of the map, but I want to have a good look at the land which Finnegas has inherited from Clodagh and I don't want Finnegas to realize what I am up to.'

'Have you got an idea, Brehon?' asked Cael.

'But she doesn't want to talk about it until she tests it out,' said Cormac with a grin and Mara laughed.

'I've a hard task in keeping my secrets from you people,' she said and then added quickly, 'Art, could you ask Cumhal if he could give you some of his measuring rods, the three-stride ones. Perhaps one for each of you if he can spare them.'

'I'll ask him to put them in a tarpaulin bag for us, shall I?' suggested Art. 'I can just take them myself, then. They're very light.'

'In-ter-es-ting,' drawled Cormac, but Mara refused the invitation to divulge her plans. Fachtnan had not yet arrived from the home that he and Nuala shared at Rathborney, but she sent Slevin over to Brigid to leave instructions to tell him that they had gone to Oughtdara and he could follow. She was anxious not to delay and risk finding that Gobnait had already gone to the beach for seaweed, or to the mountains to tend his sheep. Then she folded up the large piece of skin and put it into her satchel.

Oddly enough, although the mist had been thick on their journey, once they turned to go down to Oughtdara it began to clear and only the bottom of this hollowed-out dip in the hills was obscured. As they turned down into the road, they could see below them the slopes of the green valley with its soaked grass and then the cloud of mist that enveloped the valley floor, its few bent and twisted stark blackthorn trees looking as though they had sprung from a pale lake. Though there still hung a great silence and the thick soft clouds still capped the valley basin, there was now a slight freshness in the air, a coolness on the left cheek which showed that the wind from the sea was beginning to blow in, although the headlands and the cliffs between them and the Atlantic were still shrouded in mist.

They were just in time to catch Gobnait who, booted and cloaked, was peering out of his front door. In the usual polite fashion of the neighbourhood, he declared himself delighted to escort the Brehon and her scholars over to Ballyryan and denied that he had any particular plans for the morning, and only regretted that he had left Ug guarding a lambing sheep, as otherwise the sagacious animal could have been sent over to warn Finnegas of his impending visitors. Anu came to the door to invite them in and Mara took the opportunity of showing the map to both of them.

'Can't make head nor tail of it,' he said staring at the large piece of ox hide in a puzzled way.

'It's drawn as if you were looking down from the heavens on the fields and the roads,' said Mara, using the explanations that she normally employed with young children. 'Look—' she seized a half-burned stick that poked from the bottom of the fire and drew on the hearthstone from memory a sketch of

Dunaunmore enclosure with its buildings represented by circles and drawing a thick circular line around it to outline the wall and then a narrow oblong for the path leading away. After a moment's thought, she added a small circle to show where the *Fár Breige* stood and then called on Cormac to interpret the whole, and to explain about scale.

'It's a pity Dinan isn't here,' said Gobnait. 'He's the boy who'd like to see a thing like that done in front of his own two eyes.' He stared at the drawing in a respectful, but bemused manner.

'I've made a mess of your lovely clean floor, Anu,' said Mara apologetically. 'If you'd give one of my scholars a damp rag, they'd clean it up.'

'Not at all, not at all,' said Gobnait in alarm. 'No, leave it there, Brehon. I was just thinking to myself that we'd have the neighbours around this evening and have a bit of a ceilidh. Everyone would love to see that.'

'We'd make sure that no one would dance on it,' Anu assured her earnestly.

'Well, if you're sure . . .' Mara yielded gracefully. Gobnait would tell the story to Finnegas and then Finnegas would not question why the scholars were going around with measuring rods. Map-making would form an excuse and cover for her real purpose. She had the power to do what she wanted to do, to inspect any land in the kingdom, but she preferred to keep her thoughts to herself for the moment. At this stage in the enquiry, matters could change very rapidly and she had no intention of enlightening or alarming any one of her suspects.

'Perhaps, Anu, you would tell Fachtnan where we are gone if you see him. Tell him that we are walking across to Finnegas's place. May we leave the horses in the enclosure again, Gobnait?' she asked.

'Of course, you can and be very welcome.' He had the grave courtesy of all the brothers. It was strange how well-mannered and almost courtly they were and how wild and uncouth their cousin Clodagh had been. Who was her mother, wondered Mara and decided that she must ask Ardal. He was an excellent *taoiseach* and knew all that was to be known about the members of his clan. The affairs and the honour of the clan were the whole life of that solitary, reserved man.

In the meantime, she continued to talk to Gobnait about map-making and as they walked along together she explained to him that she hoped to mark in the boundaries on her map, and obligingly he pointed out boundary walls and boundary stones to her.

'This is where Pat's new land, the land from our uncle, ends and Finnegas's land from our uncle begins.' He pointed at a boundary stone, engraved with the name of Danu in the ancient ogham script, the lines cut so deeply that even the yellow lichen had not managed to obliterate them after the centuries. Some ancestor, also called Danu, had caused that stone to be erected and his name to be engraved upon it.

'So Finnegas's new portion is not the old family land,' she commented.

'No, our uncle Danu was a very clever man, a very clever man. He was a carpenter as well as a farmer. He could make chairs and chests and anything you wanted. He used to take things to Galway and sell them for silver and then he bought this extra land – it was one of the last things that he did before he dropped into second childhood. I think myself that he hoped to find lead on it, just as Finnegas had found on his land from our father, but Danu never had a chance. He turned forgetful and got old very fast, poor man. Look, over to the right there, just over that wall, is the land that Finnegas had as his share of our father's land and over there is his lead mine.'

'What am I thinking about?' Mara shook her head at her forgetfulness. 'I meant to have marked in the boundaries. Well, let's at least do this one. Art, get the measuring rods out and we'll make a start beside this wall. Where does Finnegas's land, the land he got from your father, where does that end, Gobnait? Show me the boundary line between that and the land owned by Clodagh's father.'

'Over there, just at the end of the rough road, and the wall marks it out on both sides, it's quite a small piece of land, just one big meadow, reaching as far as the sea cliff. I'll go and get Finnegas and tell him that you're here, Brehon. I'll tell him about the maps too. That'll interest him. He's a clever fellow, Finnegas. The brains in our families, they say, sank down to the bottom pair of brothers.' And with a cheerful wave, he went off.

It was very different land here to the land in the Burren. Mara looked at it with interest as Art handed out the measuring rods and Domhnall marshalled the scholars into a line, each three paces away from the other. The field was dotted with pools of standing water. On the Burren the porous limestone absorbed even the heaviest rain and stored it in vast underground lakes and caves until saturation point was reached and then the water welled up. The vegetation here was different, also. The grass was interspersed with large patches of winter-brown rushes and brass-yellow king cups, marsh irises and dark purple marsh orchids flowered instead of the cowslips of the dryer pasture on the Burren.

'We measure from this boundary to the next boundary, to a point nearest to the entrance to the mine, Brehon, is that what you want?' said Domhnall in a low voice and with an eye on the departing figure of Gobnait.

Mara would not be surprised if he had followed her thoughts and had understood the real reason for her interest in mapping the land here, close to the boundary with north-west Corcomroe. Domhnall always had his wits about him. She gave him a quick nod, and Domhnall made an almost imperceptible signal to the scholars to stay with him as she went forward to join Gobnait and Finnegas, map in hand.

Finnegas listened with interest to Gobnait's garbled explanation of the meaning of those straight and curved lines that represented the familiar landscape of stone walls and winding roads and Mara put in a word here and there while observing from the corner of her eyes how Domhnall set the scholars to work with low-voiced instructions. Domhnall seemed to be working quickly and efficiently, the scholars forming a straight line, each ensuring, by means of the pole, that they were an accurate three paces distant from the next and then rapidly the last in the line became the first and so on until the entire meadow, from the boundary to the lead mine entrance, had been measured. She allowed him plenty of time and did not intervene until she saw that Art was replacing the measuring poles in the tarpaulin bag. Then she beckoned them to join her and to see the wonders of the lead mine.

'I'm so very grateful to you, Gobnait, for bringing us across. I'm afraid that I will have wasted about an hour of your morning by the time that you get back,' said Mara. It had, she reckoned, taken them about half an hour to get across and she noticed that Gobnait had not disagreed with her estimate, just protesting how much he had enjoyed himself and what a privilege it had been to be associated with the drawing of maps. It would, she thought, have been just about possible for Finnegas to murder Clodagh and return to the mine – and, of course, Ug, the sheepdog, intelligent though he was, could not relate whether he met Finnegas at the mine, or just halfway across.

On the other hand, there was no doubt that he would probably have been missing for at least an hour, more probably an hour and a half, from the lead mine and if that were true, his workers would know of the fact.

'So the lead comes from these ordinary-looking rocks, does it?' she asked, looking around her with interest and noting that the mine ran from north to south, certainly in the direction of the land Finnegas had received from Clodagh's father, Danu.

'That's right, Brehon. Years ago, when I started first, I just took the stuff from the rock beneath the soil. I could see that there was lead there by the way nothing would grow, the land was poisoned, but by the time I was at it for a couple of years, that seam was used up, so I moved down the hill and hacked my way through that passageway that you can see there. I had a few men working for me by then, but I had a terrible disappointment in the beginning because there was no lead in the rocks. I nearly gave up. I thought there might just have been a little bit of lead there and now it was all gone, but I took a chance at it. We just kept hacking away, day after day, week after week, using the broken rock to build up props at the sides of the passageway, come and see.' He broke off and led the way, showing the supporting pillars, one on each side and one in the centre, and pointing up to the boards that spanned the gaps, above their heads. He made a good story of it; Mara was reminded of Dinan's tales of the gods in this dramatic recital of one man's battle with the sullen, dark hued, heavy grained rocks, so unlike the lighter, more friable limestone.

'Perhaps, one of your young lads would like to have a go at splitting one,' suggested Finnegas. He was very at ease, no trace of guilt or of anxiety that he might be suspected of his cousin's murder showed in him, and yet the fine would be a big thing to a man without cows, as it would have to be paid in hard-earned silver. An easy conscience, or a firm belief in his own cleverness; Mara could not decide.

'Cael,' suggested Cormac mischievously.

'Not me, thanks.' A year ago Cael would have accepted the challenge, but she had grown up a lot in those last twelve months and now she smiled kindly on Cormac and said, 'Don't strain yourself,' in a motherly fashion as he grasped the pickaxe.

'No, no.' Finnegas was calmly determined that the king's son should not run any risk. 'Another few years and you'll be better than any of them but you still have your growing to do. We'll try the big lad here.'

Domhnall made a few perfunctory efforts to chip out the dark seam from within the reddish-coloured rock, but soon put down the pickaxe.

'Not my sort of thing, I'm afraid,' he said without a hint of embarrassment. 'You have a go, Slevin.'

Slevin, with his farm-trained muscles, made a better job of it than Domhnall, the son of a prosperous merchant in the city of Galway. During the noise from his thunderous blows Domhnall said, very quietly, right into Mara's ear, 'Just over forty strides from the entrance to the boundary.'

Mara made no answer, but intervened to stop Cian seizing the pickaxe, promising that he and Cormac could come back, if Finnegas permitted it, when they had finished their growth spurt and diverting them by asking whether they could explore the mines.

'We'll divide you up,' decided Finnegas. 'Oscar, here, will take you four to see the place where the lead is melted and the two big boys can come with me and the Brehon.'

Finnegas was well used to showing the mines and he made an interesting story of it. Domhnall had been discussing the subject with his father and knew a lot about the use of lead piping to convey water to the fish market in Galway and he kept Finnegas busy with well-formulated questions, while Slevin, to Mara's amusement, was keeping slightly to the rear of the others, stepping the distance out in long-legged strides.

'And here's how far we've gone to this day,' said Finnegas genially when they reached a forbidding rock face straight in their pathway. He lifted a lantern and showed them the dark seams. 'But you come back in a couple of weeks, and you'll see we'll have gone another few feet through here. Step by step it has to be done, the supports have to be built, the ceiling put into place before we have too much hacking at the walls. Now come and see the *bole* and I'll take the others along to see what you have just seen.'

While Domhnall was cross-questioning Finnegas about the *bole*, Mara fell back until she was beside Slevin who was thoughtfully tracing a lead seam with one well-kept finger and then ruefully examining the welts on his palm.

'Interesting, isn't it? Very hard work, though. My hands have gone soft with wielding the pen, not the axe. I'll have blisters tomorrow,' he said aloud, and then in a low voice, he added, 'Sixty strides into the cliff face.'

Sixty strides. Even if Slevin's strides were slightly smaller than Cumhal's measuring rods, it seemed without doubt that Finnegas had been mining under the land belonging to his uncle Danu and then to his cousin Clodagh, long before the woman's death had made that land his own.

This seemed to solve the puzzle of why Clodagh had declared at Poulnabrone that she was going to be rich and why she was looking for men with stone-working skills. Clodagh had worked out that the lead that was being mined now was being taken from her own property. She had envisaged her successful cousin's mine would be handed over to her. The law was quite clear on the subject, thought Mara. It said that minerals in the ground belonged to the person who owned the land above it.

If Clodagh had suspected that her cousin's mine had encroached upon the land that she now owned, then she would have checked the position with poor old Fergus, who would, no doubt, have immediately trotted out the words from *Bretha*

Étgid that he had committed to memory over sixty years ago. Clodagh, according to Brigid had been a clever girl, and no doubt had kept that sharpness of intellect.

Deep in thought, Mara followed Domhnall and Slevin up to the *bole* where an immense fire burned within a beehive-like structure that cleverly used an existing circular gap in a cluster of rocks, filling some of the gaps with a mixture of clay and small stones to provide shelter, while the filtered strength of the Atlantic wind fanned the flames to a high temperature. There was a little runlet hacked out from a limestone slab ending beside a pool of spring water and the liquid lead poured down this and into the pool, where it cooled and turned into solid lumps. One man tended the fire and another picked out the lumps of lead and placed them in baskets.

'It melts easily again,' said the man called Oscar. 'It's great stuff; can take any shape. Easy to use and never rusts. More use than gold.'

Mara watched with her eyes, but her brain was busy. Finnegas now had a strong motive, but she still was not sure that he had an opportunity. It was possible, she thought, that Clodagh had some sort of showdown with him, had perhaps offered him a share in the profits if he would continue to run the business for her. She may have given him time to think about it and appointed a time to meet him, two mornings ago – at perhaps an hour or so before noon, when Aengus would be well out of the way, up the mountain caring for Ardal O'Lochlainn's sheep.

'I suppose you are very busy all day long,' she said to the man who was taking the lumps from the pool. 'Do you always do that job?'

He straightened his back, glad, she thought, of an excuse to pause in his labour.

'We all do a bit of everything, Brehon, just as Finnegas orders us,' he said politely.

'So what would you have been doing at around this time the day before yesterday morning?'

'The day before yesterday, Brehon, oh, yes, I remember. Myself and Oscar were helping the master in the tunnel, bringing in some of the waste stone and piling it up ready for building the new supports. We got a couple of feet built by the end of the day.'

'Hard work,' commented Mara. 'Did you keep at it all day without a rest?'

'Except for just an hour or so in the middle of the day when we went in the cart with the load to Doolin Harbour; the master wanted us all to go so that it could be got loaded up quickly. He had promised the boat owner to give some extra help this time.'

'How long would it take for the cart to go to Doolin Harbour from here?' asked Domhnall in a nonchalant fashion.

'How long would you think, Oscar?'

'Best part of an hour, I'd say,' said Oscar.

This would give Finnegas barely enough time to keep an appointment with Clodagh, to kill her, and then to return to his mine, but these men would have very little notion of what exactly was an hour's length of time. They would use the word 'hour' as an approximation; it might easily have been an hour and a half, or even two.

'And I suppose that he was jumping up and down waiting for you when you arrived back eventually,' said Slevin with a chuckle that sounded very natural.

'Not a bit of it; he'd gone for a stroll himself and we were already at work when he came back. But there you are, no pleasing him. A face on him that would cut you in two. Driving us as though the sky was going to fall in.'

Mara strolled off to meet the party coming back from the tour of the caves. She turned the matter over in her mind as she went. On the one hand, it did appear that Finnegas might just have had time to rush across to Oughtdara, murder his cousin and then rush back. However, on the other hand, she had to admit that it was an unlikely crime for him to undertake. How did he know that the law position was as Clodagh had stated it to be? Quoting the elderly and senile Fergus MacClancy would not impress this practical man of business who lived so close to Corcomroe and would undoubtedly have heard of the mental state of its Brehon. He, unlike Mara, was not to know that Fergus's memory, for some odd reason, held tightly the sum and substance of the laws that he had learned in his youth though all else fell away from him like water from a leaking bucket.

No, she thought, Finnegas would not have been hasty. She would have thought it would be more likely that he would stroll over to see the Brehon of the Burren and ask her some pertinent questions about rights of landowners. After all, the entrance to the mine was definitely on his own land and so was at least half of the tunnel. He wouldn't see the justice of Clodagh being able to seize the fruits of his hard labour. Yes, from what she had seen of Finnegas, she would expect that he would come to see her at the law school, would ask her advice. And if she confirmed Clodagh's words, he probably would want to compromise with his cousin, rather than murder her.

Unless, of course, he had already made an offer and had been rejected.

She would take no further steps today, she decided, but turn the matters over in her mind. Finnegas, though, would now go onto the list of suspects. He had means, opportunity and motive.

Ten

Cóic Conara Fugill
(The Five Paths of Judgement)

There are five paths along which a case must be pursued by a Brehon:
1. fír *(truth)*
2. dliged *(entitlement)*
3. cert *(justice)*
4. téchtae *(propriety)*
5. coir n–athchomairc *(proper enquiry)*

'Did you see Fachtnan, Anu?' asked Mara when they returned. She had forgotten about him while at the lead mine and only remembered him when they were almost back at Oughtdara. There was no sign of him when they arrived so she addressed her question to Gobnait's wife, while still looking around for a sign of Fachtnan. She was conscious of some annoyance and tried to suppress it, but she could hear a crisp note in her question.

'I did, indeed, Brehon,' said Anu. 'He came in here not too long after you left. He came into the house and had some buttermilk, he and his little girl. I gave him your message and he said that it was too far for the child to walk and he couldn't take his horse across that rocky land so that he would meet you when you came back. He hasn't gone, though. His horse is still over there with the rest of your horses, grazing in the enclosure. I saw it a while ago when I went to pick some cress.'

'Perhaps he went to join Pat,' suggested Gobnait.

'Or Dinan,' was Anu's suggestion.

'We'll find him,' said Mara firmly. She already felt guilty that she had taken up a couple of hours of Gobnait's time and didn't wish to delay the couple any longer. They would want to be checking on the lambing sheep and all the hundred and one tasks of busy farmers.

'Perhaps he went into the church,' suggested Cael. 'If I know Orla she would start to whine if Fachtnan made her walk more than a hundred paces. She'd have something to sit on in there and he could keep her occupied by lighting candles or else telling stories.'

I wish he'd leave that child at home, thought Mara, though she was conscious that her exasperation was a little unfair. There was a time when the Cahermacnaghten Law School did admit five-year-old children, but it wasn't always a success. For the first few years they were only capable of learning by rote while they solidified their skills of reading and writing. When her son Cormac and his foster brother, Art, had been successfully taught to read and to write by Art's mother she had allowed them to attend for just two hours in the morning and together they had memorized large numbers of law triads and mastered the early stages of Latin nouns and verbs, reciting verses from the *Latin Grammar*, written by William Lilly, High Master of St Paul's School in London and presented to Cahermacnaghten Law School by St Nicholas's Grammar School in Galway City. If there had been a second child of similar age to keep Orla company, she might possibly have considered it, but Orla, as the only five-year-old in the school, would inevitably demand much of her father's attention, and had, in any case, little desire to learn.

And, of course, seven years ago, Brigid had been very much younger and could take over the care of these small children when the law school was busy with serious legal matters. Mara would never have dreamt of involving a child of the age of little Orla in gathering evidence during a murder investigation in the way that Fachtnan seemed to be doing by bringing his small daughter with him. She would have to talk with him and settle this matter before the day ended.

But Fachtnan was not in the church; it was empty except for the figure of the priest praying earnestly in front of the altar. Mara gave a swift backwards movement of her hand to warn her scholars to keep at a distance and went up the church and sank to her knees beside him. She had been about to ask him a question about Fachtnan until she saw his face.

'How are you?' she asked with concern. The day was dark and murky, the narrow window slits emitted virtually no light, but the candle on the altar faintly illuminated his features. From what she could see of him, his eyes were heavily shadowed and lips bloodless. His shoulders sagged and he looked as though he would collapse. His hands were clasped together, fingers firmly interlaced, but even still a strong tremor ran through them and she could hear his breath come short and quick through a half-opened mouth.

'How are you, Father?' she asked again, moved by his utter misery and this time he seemed to hear her. He turned his face towards her and she now could see a horror in his eyes.

'Is something wrong?' she asked quickly.

'It was the bishop,' he said, his voice barely audible. 'I've only just realized that it was the bishop.' And then he turned away from her again, burying his face in his hands. 'I had thought that it was the god. It should have been the god. She had disgraced the god and the god should have been the one who had vengeance on her. Holy Mother Church should not have contaminated anyone by putting its hands on her unclean flesh.'

The man was unhinged, thought Mara.

'Come now, you must not give way like this,' she said in firm, authoritative tones. She beckoned to Domhnall and Slevin.

'Father O'Lochlainn is not feeling well,' she said, endeavouring to keep her voice soothing and unthreatening. 'Take him over to Deirdre. She's in her house, I know. I heard her pumping water. Tell her that Father O'Lochlainn has become weak and faint with too long hours of praying and fasting. She'll look after him. Go with my scholars, Father. You will be quite safe with them; they will look after you.'

They were two strong, well-grown boys and in a moment they had raised the man from his knees, each with a firm hand grasping his upper arm. He hung between them, shivering like a man who has received a terrible shock. Mara hoped that he was not going to have some sort of an epileptic fit. Perhaps she should despatch him to Nuala, but she had a feeling that Deirdre's mothering might do more for him than Nuala's practical, common sense. Nuala had little time for illnesses caused by the emotions, saying that the body was complicated enough without having to understand humours and such-like nonsense. No, Nuala would be the wrong person to deal with a man who did not have a fever, nor a stomach ache, but was nevertheless sick to his soul. A cup of buttermilk and a slice of freshly-baked bread might work better than medicine for this strangely childlike man.

'Oh, and ask her whether she saw anything of Fachtnan,' she called after them as they set off down the small church, walking at a smart pace, half-dragging, half-carrying the priest.

'What on earth had he meant by the bishop?' asked Cael when they had disappeared through the door.

'I have no idea,' said Mara. The church was freezing cold and reeked of damp. Spots of bright green mould bespeckled the white cloth on the altar table and a faint miasma hovered over the burial slabs beside the wall. What a dismal substitute for a wife and a family. And Father O'Lochlainn had about thirty years of this, after perhaps a couple of years of the company of a pretty and intelligent young girl.

'Is the bishop going to be a suspect?' enquired Cormac with a mischievous spark in his eyes belying the innocent air he had assumed.

'Don't be ridiculous?' snapped Mara. She could not imagine the stately and very elderly Bishop Mauritius O'Brien coming down to this obscure valley, strangling a woman, tying her to a pagan god and then going back to his princely home in Kilfenora.

Father O'Lochlainn, now, that was a different matter. Guilt, shame, repentance could have wrought upon a mind that had never been very stable and madness could have been the natural outcome. If the murder were proved against him, then the bishop would, according to the law, have to take charge of him, treat him humanely, but ensure that he was never unsupervised and that he posed no threat to any other person. Father O'Lochlainn would confess; he might have done it there if she had pressed him, but she would have been reluctant to cross-question a man as distraught as that. No, let him rest and be comforted and perhaps tomorrow morning she would come to him, accompanied by two witnesses: Fachtnan and Domhnall, she thought. She would make the accusation and hear what he had to say. If he admitted his guilt or if he was incapable of rational thought, then she would send for the bishop and inform him what she was going to do. The case, she thought, might be finished, but it was not going to be wrapped up in clean linen and stored out of sight. The people of the kingdom had to know what had happened; had to be told the truth. No violent death should ever be left without public acknowledgement if she could possibly help it. Peace and order in the kingdom depended upon open government.

'Where can Fachtnan have got to?' she said aloud, hearing her voice sound both irritable and uneasy. Cormac looked at her rather anxiously and she forced herself to apologize for her rebuff. Her scholars had to feel confident to put forward their opinions without fear of ridicule.

'I'm sorry, Cormac,' she said, 'you were quite right to query that; and, as always, we should keep an open mind. And of course, no one, not even a king, is exempt from the law. I do feel, however, that the bishop would be a most unlikely murderer. I think that he would have taken a very different course, don't you? Sent a message to me, probably, and asked me to deal with the matter.' As she spoke she began to walk quickly down towards the small north-facing door. *Where was Fachtnan?*

Domhnall and Slevin were returning as she emerged. Domhnall shook his head when he saw her looking at him.

'No, no sign of Fachtnan,' he said. 'Deirdre didn't see him at all. She was busy all through the morning. She was churning. She told me to tell you not to worry about the priest. He would be welcome to stay with them until he is more himself. That,' said Domhnall in his precise manner, 'was the way that she put it: *more himself.*'

'But what is *himself*?' Cael picked up on the note of query in Domhnall's voice.

'That's a good question,' said Mara responding to the glances that passed between her two cleverest pupils. 'I suppose that in a case like this, it is our task to peel back the layers and to discover what lies beneath. People are seldom exactly as they appear to be on the outside.'

'And, of course, sometimes, extreme fear and guilt can do the peeling, like Brigid when she pours boiling water over the onions.' Cael proffered this thought, not to Mara, but to Domhnall who responded with an approving nod. Cael's freckled face turned slightly pink.

'The priest said something interesting, Brehon, when we were walking back with him. He was rambling on about the bishop killing Clodagh and I thought that I'd better try to distract his mind from that in case he upset and annoyed a lot of religious people, so I said—'

'You should have heard him, Brehon,' interrupted Slevin. 'He sounded like you or even the bishop himself. He was so definite.'

Domhnall blushed a little, but then recovered when she did not smile, just looked at him inquiringly. 'I just said to him, "Oh, no, no, no. The bishop doesn't have a rope, Father." But it was what he said in answer that was interesting. He stopped dead in the middle of the path and looked at me as if I were the mad one and he said, "Oh, he didn't need to bring a rope; he just used her own rope." And do you know, Brehon, Slevin and I were talking it over afterwards and we both can remember seeing her at a fair with her rope coiled over one shoulder, underneath that terrible old cloak of hers.'

'So she used,' said Cian. 'Yes, I remember it now. Slanting across her chest. I remember it. Loose enough to be pulled off in a hurry. She could have just slipped it over her head without even taking the cloak off, or, I suppose someone else could have done that, too. After all she was strangled by someone's hands. It was only afterwards, only after she was dead, that the rope was wound around her.'

'Do you think that it was really the . . .' Art stopped and then said nervously. 'You don't think that she did it herself, tied herself to . . . do you think it might have been something like that? Something to do with the Morrigan?'

'It's the rope that we're concerned with now, Art,' said Mara firmly. 'Let's not get involved with any of those old stories. Where is that rope, by the way?'

'Cormac took it. Cormac, what have you done with the

rope? You did take it; don't deny it; I saw you myself.' Cael faced Cormac like an angry mother, ignoring Art's mutterings.

'Calm down! I've got it. I knew it was important evidence.' Cormac swung the cloak from his shoulders, opened the loops on the short leather jacket that he wore beneath it and revealed the rope coiled around his waist and chest, over his white *léine*.

'Yuck!' exclaimed Cael. 'Imagine wearing a rope that strangled a woman.'

'It didn't strangle her, birdbrain, don't you listen? Nuala told us, don't you remember. She was strangled by a pair of hands, just the way that someone will do to you some day if you don't mind your tongue.' Cian, these days, was at odds with his twin sister who seemed to be growing up a lot more quickly than he was doing himself, but still that reaction was unwarranted. Mara wondered whether, though tougher and less open than Art, he also was worried by the possible supernatural element in this law case. Even Cormac had looked a bit taken aback at the venom of his intervention.

Nevertheless, she gave Cian a long, cold look that caused him to flush uncomfortably and after a minute, he muttered, 'Sorry.' Mara decided to leave the matter. She took the rope from Cormac as soon as he had uncoiled it and examined it carefully. Of course, Clodagh had a pair of nanny goats of her own, presumably given as some sort of dowry by her father, so she would have as much use for a rope as would her cousins.

Forgetting about the puzzle of Fachtnan's whereabouts, Mara sank down on a convenient flat-topped boulder and looked at her scholars.

'This is very interesting,' she said, her eyes going from one to the other. 'To my mind, this changes matters. What do you think, Cian? Speak quietly, won't you?'

'Makes it possible that the murder was committed by someone who would not be expected to own a rope,' he said pointing with his head in the direction of the church. The allusion to the priest was obvious and the others nodded agreement. 'Now we know,' Cian continued, 'that the rope was there, to his hand, probably slipped off her shoulder when he was strangling her, the murderer, I mean,' he added, looking defiantly at Cael in case she suspected him of believing in the *Fár Breige*.

'Exactly,' said Mara, nodding approval at him.

'And makes it possible that the murder could have been unplanned and possibly unintended,' said Cael, her blue-grey eyes focussed and intent.

'Two very interesting points,' said Mara. To her mind both points seemed to indicate the priest. He could have been driven past bearing point by Clodagh's obscene mockery and rushed out and strangled her, perhaps hardly knowing what he had done. And then the mind shutting down the conscious-ness of wrongdoing, he told himself that it was the work of the god of evil; and then came the effort today, to cast blame on Bishop Mauritius who had probably told him to get that woman out of his life, but who had given no assistance to do so.

And yet, somehow she was not sure. It couldn't be the bishop, of course. That was nonsense, but the priest had said, 'he used her own rope'. Somehow, that sounded as though he had witnessed the murder rather than perpetrated it. She remem-bered thinking that there was a very good chance that he had looked out of his window and seen something on that morning. Although the mist was thick, he could have seen a figure, heard the obscene cackling suddenly cut off, and then had seen the rope being wound around the body.

And, as for the bishop, in the mist, Bishop Mauritius was just like any other man.

'So anger seems to be the more likely motive than greed,' mused Domhnall, looking thoughtfully around at the rocky landscape.

'I wouldn't go quite as far as that myself,' observed Mara. 'If Clodagh's own rope were used, then I would say that the big difference that this new discovery has made is that it might turn the crime into something which was not planned, some-thing which perhaps happened on the spur of the moment.'

'Finnegas, for instance,' said Slevin and Mara nodded.

'Exactly,' she said. 'It's quite feasible that he came across to reason with her, found her there, shaming his family, embar-rassing the priest and that he strangled her. In the struggle the rope could have slid from her shoulder, as Cian suggests, and he got the idea of blaming the stone god.'

'And the same could go for the other brothers,' pointed out Domhnall. 'I agree with you, Brehon. If that really was Clodagh's rope, then this murderer could have been someone who just seized an opportunity.'

'I think that we should endeavour to get a second opinion on this rope. We won't bother Deirdre; she'll have enough to do with the priest, but Cael, would you just slip along to Anu's house and ask her whether she recognizes it, and if she can't exactly identify it, just ask her whether she remembers Clodagh carrying a rope under her cloak.' There was no harm in getting confirmation, though Mara knew that her scholars were keen-eyed and observant.

As she expected, Cael was back in a very short time with the information that, according to Anu, Clodagh definitely carried a rope, over her shoulder as Cian had remembered. 'She said to tell you, too, that the *taoiseach* came over early this morning to say that they didn't need to worry about Aengus, because he was going to stay in one of the workers' cabins at Lissylisheen until the weather got better,' she added.

'That's good,' said Mara. 'And did she think that the rope looked like the one that Clodagh carried?'

'She said that she couldn't be exactly positive, Brehon, but that she thought it looked like it. She said that Clodagh made her own ropes, she had seen her out twisting them and she knew that she used ivy because about a year ago she had asked Gobnait to bring her some and then did nothing but complain about it when he brought back a huge load to her, according to Anu!'

'So it looks as though it was Clodagh's, then,' said Cormac enthusiastically. 'There's lots of ivy in that rope, it's good stuff, Cumhal always says, as long as you have enough of it, and you soak it well beforehand, that's what he says.'

The crime, thought Mara, was a simpler and more haphazard one than she had envisaged. Someone had suddenly seized an opportunity on that morning when the mist was almost impenetrable and had murdered Clodagh, either because of the property, or because of hatred for the woman, herself.

'Tomorrow, we must try to pin these six people down to exact times,' she said aloud. 'We'll have to do it properly, perhaps interviewing all of the people who live around here, and the herdsmen on the hills. It will be a matter of careful examining of detail,' she said to her scholars. 'I'll get Fachtnan to make out . . .' And then Mara stopped. 'I was forgetting about Fachtnan. Where on earth is he? Cormac, run over to Dunaunmore and check that his horse is really there.'

Cormac was back in a moment. 'His horse is still there,' he said cheerfully. 'But, I've been thinking and I've got a sudden inspiration. I know where they might be, Fachtnan and little Orla. Do you remember yesterday that she was moaning about not being allowed to come with us, you know, when she was left with Deirdre, do you remember she was saying something about moon milk? Perhaps she persuaded Fachtnan to take her there, to the Moonmilk Cave.'

'But they can't be still there. Anu said that they arrived not long after we left for Ballyryan. That must have been about three hours ago.' Mara gave a hasty glance upwards. There was no sun to be seen among the lowering clouds, but a slightly brighter patch towards Ballinalacken showed that midday was approaching.

'Where is this Moonmilk Cave, anyway?' She looked at Art who knew more about the locality than the others did. His mother ran her sheep on the common land of the foothills of Slieve Elva, close to the O'Lochlainn commons on Knockauns Mountain.

'I'm not sure which one of them it is, there's such a lot of caves there, all lined up along the cliff,' he said hesitantly, looking at Cormac.

'I'm not sure either, I know we went there with Dinan, but I got in a bit of a muddle with them all. Dinan would know. Hey, Ug! Go and find Dinan, like a good boy.'

The sheepdog was trotting in the direction of his home, soaked wet, but with the air of a dog who has done a good morning's work. He turned his one pricked ear towards Cormac, and then stopped and waited, looking back, checking with his master to see whether this was an official command. A moment later Gobnait came into view.

'How's the lambing sheep, Gobnait?' shouted Cormac.

'Well, well, thanks be to God. A lovely little girl-lamb, she's had. Me and Ug got the two of them into the shelter of a cave and we hung a dead fox up on a sally bush next to it, just to warn off the other fellows. You should have seen Ug smile when I did that. He killed it himself, this morning. Smile, Ug!'

Obligingly Ug stripped his teeth in the ghastly semblance of a smile and then basked in the admiration of the scholars.

'We were wondering whether Dinan was around, or whether Ug could fetch him for us; I'm a bit worried about my assistant, Fachtnan. Anu said that he left her hours ago; his horse is still in the enclosure and one of the scholars thinks that he might have taken his little girl to see the Moonmilk Cave,' said Mara, apologetically looking at the soaked and dripping sheepdog.

'Ug will take you there himself and be more use to you, too, than young Dinan. He won't be pestering you with all those old stories. Doesn't say a word; just gets on with his orders. If there's anything wrong, Brehon, just send the dog back to me for help. That cave is a nasty, slippery old place, though there's plenty that swear by the stuff.' And with those cryptic words, Gobnait pointed at Mara, turned to the dog, and said, 'Go to the Brehon, Ug.'

The intelligent Ug gave one sharp, crisp bark, the canine equivalent of 'Yes, my lord,' guessed Mara and he came over and sat at her feet.

'Moonmilk Cave, Ug,' ordered Mara, wondering whether this miracle dog knew the name of every nook and cranny in the area.

Ug gave another bark and ran twice around the little group of Mara and her scholars, and then raced ahead.

'We'll never keep up with him,' said Mara in dismay, watching the dog sprint across the rocky ground.

'Don't you worry about that, Brehon; he'll be backwards and forwards, keeping one of his eyes on all of you. He won't let anyone fall behind. I must go in now and have a bit of dinner, but send the dog for me if there's anything wrong. Don't go in too far. Stay near the entrance. Myself

and Pat will come with lamps and a stretcher once we see
himself come back to fetch us.' With a casual wave, Gobnait
went off to his meal and Mara looked anxiously after Ug
and hoped that he would live up to his reputation. It had
been an inspiration of Cormac's to think about the Moonmilk
Cave. It was very likely that they had gone there since
Fachtnan had promised Orla a trip. What had possessed him
to give in to the child and take her to one of those uncomfortable and fairly dangerous caves? Of course, to a little girl
it probably sounded like a magical place. The moon is made
of cheese; Brigid used to chant to her when she was about
Orla's age, but milk seemed to be a more likely idea and
suited the whiteness better than yellow cheese. Orla probably
had some fanciful notion that the moon was kept in this
cave during daylight hours.

'Don't run, you'll fall over the stones; Ug will wait for
you,' she called ahead to her younger scholars who were trying
to keep pace with the sheepdog. Sure enough, Ug did turn
frequently to make sure that they were all with him, and
from time to time, he came back and swept in a wide circle
behind and around them, herding them skilfully. They were
going in the direction of Ballynahown, and it appeared that
Moonmilk Cave was probably in the same cliff formation as
the Cave of the One Cow, but quite a bit further east. She
remembered thinking when she was young that the stark
stone facade was like a row of stone buildings in ancient
Rome, and now she thought, as they came nearer, that the
numerous caves were like the doors to the buildings. I don't
think that I've ever come up as far as this before, she thought
and wished she had done it a few years previously when she
was younger and had more of a spring to her step. It was
hard going, with levels constantly changing, rocks blocking
the path and deep crevices disguised by lumps of winter grass.
It didn't help to be burdened with her satchel, but there was
no help for that. She would have been uneasy without it and
unwilling to hand it over to anyone.

'That's Moonmilk Cave over there, Brehon,' shouted Art.
'Look at the ivy hanging down. When we were inside, I

remember thinking that it was like a dark green curtain over the doorway, just like they have at the king's place at Bunratty.'

'And Ug is sitting outside the doorway, looking pleased with himself,' said Cael. 'Clever dog.'

Eleven

Brecha Crólige

(Judgements on Blood-Lettings)

Every physician should cultivate a herb garden in order to have the means to make medicines for the sick. Other materials should be diligently sought for on mountains, in caves and by the sea.

There must be something wrong, Mara thought. Surely if Fachtnan were in the cave he would have heard the voices of the scholars shouting to each other and calling playfully to the dog.

Ug, unlike Cormac's dog, Dullahán, had his mind strictly on business. He bustled around them as though they were a group of unusually stupid sheep, herding them into the cave, going straight for his goal and refusing to acknowledge any blandishments or commands from his charges, but forced them to go ahead through the thick curtain of ivy until he had them all inside the cave, looking back out at the daylight through the lace-like fronds of the dark green triangular leaves. There was a cluster of boulders that seemed to block the entrance, but Ug squeezed past these and they all followed. And then they were in a high cave about five or six metres long.

'This is the place that Dinan brought us to; I remember this place.'

'Look, Brehon, that's the moonmilk, look, that white crumbling stuff on the rocks.'

Mara's eyes were becoming accustomed to the gloom. The moonmilk substance encrusted the rock face on their left-hand side, looking like clumps of dirty snow. Here and there water dripped from above and its colour was a blue-white, like watered milk. It was an extraordinary sight.

'I've never seen anything like this,' she said. 'In fact, I've never heard of this. I wonder whether Brigid knows about this place. I've never heard of moonmilk, before.'

'You can eat it,' said Cormac. 'We all tasted it when we were here with Dinan. He told us that the great god of medicine, Dian Cécht, made this cave for mortals with bad stomachs.'

'Really,' said Mara, almost forgetting Fachtnan in the interest of the mention of such a familiar name. 'I wonder does Nuala know about this stuff. I suppose that she must since little Orla had heard of Moonmilk Cave.

'I told Dinan that Dian Cécht was in our law books and he said that was good that we were learning these things and that we must make sure that we hand it down to our children and to our children's children and to the people of the kingdom,' said Cael with a giggle and a quick glance at Domhnall.

'Taste it, Brehon; it's quite safe. We all tasted it and we're still alive,' said Cian.

Mara tasted. It had a powdery taste, neither pleasant nor unpleasant.

'It's supposed to cure you if your food burns in your stomach, according to Dinan, and Dian Cécht, apparently,' said Domhnall. 'He said that Gobnait used to have a bad stomach when he got married first – he wasn't used to all the fancy cooking that Anu did for him. Anyway, this stuff made a new man of him, or so Gobnait said.'

At this second mention of his master's name, Ug gave a quick sharp bark that recalled Mara to the purpose of her presence. 'Fachtnan,' she called, cupping her hands around her mouth and then called again, and heard the echoes return her voice to her.

'Hold back the ivy for me, Cormac, so that we get some more light.' It would have been easier to pull it down, but she didn't want to interfere with the goats' feeding of it. She was beginning to understand the value of this seemingly barren land to the brothers with their flocks of sheep and goats. The caves were as useful as barns and cow houses would be to more prosperous farmers; places of shelter – warm in the winter, and cool in the summer. And better than barns and cow houses, they were providing food and water as well as safety for the animals.

'The clouds are moving off the sun, now, Brehon,' shouted Cormac. 'You'll soon be able to see.' The cave was facing south and the sun had eventually come through the clouds and, just as Cormac spoke, it shone down the cave, revealing the length and the height of the whole chamber.

'It goes back further than this,' said Slevin, 'I remember we went quite a way. See, just about five or six paces down, it turns into a very narrow passageway, with that moonmilk on a sort of shelf. We went along that, one behind the other; it goes quite steeply up a hill and then you come to where the moonmilk shelf actually turns into your floor. Dinan wouldn't let us go any further. He said that it was too slippery and that you could break a leg on that surface. Do you think that is what happened to Fachtnan?'

'Odd he didn't hear me call, though,' said Mara. 'Let's all shout together. I'll count. One, two, three.'

To her alarm, the resulting yell and the dog's barking seemed to cause some sort of vibration within the cave. Great clumps of solidified moonmilk and bright green hart's tongue ferns fell from the ceiling and, what was worse, some small rocks tumbled down, also; one of them narrowly missing Art's head.

'We mustn't do that any more,' said Mara urgently. 'Are you all right, Art?' She guessed that this moonmilk was something to do with rainwater taking the lime from the rocks and weakening them, just as the rainwater on the stone pavements of the fields seemed to wear the rock away and cause small hollows. There was no sign or sound of Fachtnan and if he were anywhere near he could not fail to have heard the shouting and have responded. She had no intention of taking her young scholars through the labyrinth of the cave. With the strong March sunshine they could see to the back of the first part and there was no sign of anyone there.

'I'm not sure whether we should send the dog for Gobnait and Pat, or not,' she said, feeling worried and hesitant. 'I can't imagine that Fachtnan would have taken Orla any further into the cave.'

'Orla was going on about moonmilk,' said Cael. 'She went on and on and on about it.'

'It might have been something for her mother to make stomach medicine from,' said Mara. She remembered Gobnait's remark: 'there's plenty that swear by the stuff.' She had a memory of Brigid talking about limewater for babies and this stuff certainly had a taste of lime from it. So that was the explanation for Orla's insistence and Fachtnan's acquiescence. It was apparent, even to her, that Orla was jealous of the strong link between her mother and Saoirse so the gift of the moon-milk substance would have been an attempt to gain Nuala's attention. Fachtnan, a very sensitive man, would have been aware of Orla's jealousy, would have been sorry for his younger daughter and anxious to help her to bring a present to her mother.

'But they wouldn't have needed to go any further in,' pointed out Domhnall. 'They could have gathered bags of the stuff here.'

'Well, you know Orla,' said Cael with a shrug. 'She always wants her own way and Fachtnan usually gives into her. I could imagine her saying that she wanted to see if there was something better in the next cave, something whiter, some drier stuff, or wetter stuff.'

'You could be right,' said Domhnall and then they all looked at Mara.

'I know I am probably fussing but I feel uneasy about you all going any deeper into that cave,' she said. 'What I'd like to do is just to go forward myself and try calling out fairly softly, just projecting my voice but keeping the pitch low. So if you'll just wait outside the cave, all of you. I'll be calling from time to time so that you'll know that I'm all right. Oh, and Cian, will you keep Ug? He has a very ear-splitting, high-pitched bark and I think that might have been what caused the problems the last time.'

'Come on, Ug, good boy, let's find a fox,' said Cian.

'Dinan thinks that foxes are the souls of the dead gods of evil,' said Art as Mara nerved herself to step forward into the cave.

'Keep as much of the ivy back as possible,' she said softly without replying to this interesting thought. What with Father O'Lochlainn and the *Fár Breige*, Dinan and his ghost-inhabited foxes, she felt that she was thoroughly sick of the supernatural. She switched her mind from the murder case and focused it upon finding Fachtnan.

Step by step she moved forward and when she reckoned that she had gone about sixteen paces, she came across a narrow passageway leading to the left. She peered into it, but it looked uninviting and far too narrow. In any case, there did not appear to be any of the powdery white moonmilk there so she continued going up the slope along the main passageway. The floor of hard rock beneath her feet became slippery, just with mud, she reckoned. Her night vision had begun to improve and she could see a rock shelf covered with moonmilk by her side. She kept going steadily. There was little danger, she reckoned; it had only been the unfortunate combination of the six voices and of the dog's high-pitched, ear-splitting bark that had caused the fall from the roof. Otherwise, this seemed a good cave with plenty of headroom.

'Fachtnan!' she called in a low voice, but there was no response so she went on. The cave started to slope more steeply uphill and to become decidedly narrower. Now the shelf of moonmilk had become the floor and she had to walk very carefully with her arms outstretched to keep her balance on that slippery surface. The air was good though; in fact, she was aware of a slight breeze blowing in her face.

'Fachtnan,' she called again, but she had begun to despair of receiving an answer. This is where a sensible person would return, she told herself. Oddly she had a feeling that there was something malevolent in the air. Perhaps it was just the effect of all the stories that Dinan had been reciting. She even caught herself wondering whether the malicious Morrigan had any connection with that particular cave. Odd, she thought, how Dinan seemed to be intent upon drawing comparisons between the goddess of evil and his cousin. He had laid great emphasis on the ten tresses, or perhaps it was braids, of rich red hair that the Morrigan wore. Clodagh, perhaps, encouraged these ideas. She must have been a woman filled to the brim with hate. She had been a lovely girl with rich red hair and she had turned into a sour malevolent old woman who continually strove to embarrass and disgrace her husband, her kin group

and even her clan, not just in her home or her village, but in
the market places and fair grounds, at the great festivals of
Imbolc, Bealtaine, Lughnasa and *Samhain*, spring, summer, autumn,
and the start of winter when the four clans of the kingdom
came together. She had shamed them all on those occasions.

And then suddenly a memory came back to her from her
own childhood. She had gone to the *Samhain* festival with
Brigid. It had been very dark, no moon, no stars that night,
but the huge bonfire blazed up at the entrance to the cave
where the spirits of the dead would emerge for their few hours
of freedom and would mingle with the living and try to entice
foolhardy young men and girls to accompany them back into
the cave. And then suddenly a great shriek went up, 'The
Morrigan, The Morrigan,' and a girl with red hair came out
from the dark cave and had stood there, with the light from
the bonfire no brighter than her hair. Mara remembered as
though it was yesterday, the intensity of her own shriek and
how Brigid, always a mother to her, had swept her into her
arms and taken her home immediately.

I wonder whether that could have been Clodagh, thought
Mara, it would be just the sort of thing that she would have
done, slipped into the cave in a moment when the fire was
dimmed and then emerged into the full glare when the flames
leaped up again. She caught herself shivering slightly and tried
to summon up a laugh. How stupid she was being. She had
not the slightest belief in the supernatural, but she did fear the
effect that such practices could have on people, and she feared
the way that some unscrupulous persons would use these
superstitions to cloak evil.

She would go back and send the dog Ug, with his four
agile legs, across the rocks, back to Oughtdara and summon
men with lamps. By now she really could not see anything
other than a faint gleam of moonmilk underneath her cautiously
moving boots. The air on her face, though, increased and that
kept her going for another few paces in the hopes that there
might be an exit from the cave. She turned a corner, feeling
the rock face carefully with her hands. The light now became
stronger and it appeared to be coming from some spot ahead
and above her.

And then she almost fell. Something lay across her path. She bent down and touched wool, harsh woven wool. A cloak. And then flesh. A face. She moved her hands up and down. It was definitely a body, not dead; breath came loudly and with an almost snoring sound from it. Her hand moved over the face and then felt a clump of springing wiry curls. It was Fachtnan, she knew that hair, had known it since he was an untidy-looking eight-year-old with an unruly crop of curls. She sank to her knees beside him, thankful that she had found him, but where was his little daughter?

'Orla,' she called softly, but there was no reply.

Mara straightened up. Her vision was beginning to improve. There was another corner ahead of her, but around that corner a faint and very dim light seemed to be coming. Keeping one hand on the wall, carefully she stepped over Fachtnan and rounded the rock face. Now she could see everything and she could see where the light had come from. There was a small opening in the ceiling, an opening just about big enough for a man. At some stage there had been a rock fall, rather like the minor one that they had caused, but this was not minor. There was a large hole – about six feet long, or even longer, and almost as wide, and the floor of this part of the cave was littered with jagged-edged rocks.

The roof was very far up, about thirty feet, she reckoned, but the light was good enough for her to see that a long rope hung down through this hole reaching the floor inside the cave. She stared at it for a moment and then remembered that she still had to find Orla.

But there was no sign of Orla anywhere. She had a sick feeling in the bottom of her stomach. A small child, a nervous little girl, lost in the labyrinth, terrified; there was danger in this situation. She had to get help as soon as was possible, but first she had to check on Fachtnan, to see what had happened to him so that she could send a sensible message to Nuala.

Mara went back and knelt beside Fachtnan, moving her hand tentatively over his head and then finding a clot of something sticky at the back. He had fallen and struck his head. She hoped that the thick springing curls of hair might have cushioned his head to a certain degree. His right leg seemed bent at a strange angle and she guessed that he might have broken it. However, he was a strong and healthy young man and she was sure that Nuala would be able to deal with his injuries. She was more worried about Orla. Where, on earth, had the six-year-old gone?

'Orla!' she shouted as loudly as she could and repeated the name over and over until the caves rang with the name. She shook her head with exasperation at herself. There was something ghostly about the echoes and Orla, not a very clever little girl, but a child who loved stories, would no doubt have heard the tales about the 'old people' and stories of haunted caves from her nursemaid and from the scholars at the law school. There was a possibility that the child was not far from her, cowering into the shelter of a rock, with her hands over her ears. Mara waited until the sounds died down, and then tried saying the name quietly but still it seemed to come back with the wail of the *banshee*.

Mara gave one more look at the unconscious Fachtnan and decided that she would have to go back to her scholars. They would have heard her cries of Orla and would be very tempted to come and join her. By now she was fairly convinced that the cave was safe if you were cautious, but she knew how meticulous Domhnall was about obeying orders so she did not want to put him in the difficult position of being forced into restraining the impatience of the other scholars. She took a last look at the rope hanging down, tied to a blackthorn or something, upon the field at Ballynahown, she guessed. She wondered what its purpose was. Some of these caves flooded, but Moonmilk Cave was remarkably dry, especially considering all the rain that had fallen in March.

There was no chance that Orla could have climbed that rope. It must stretch for about thirty feet upwards, she thought. No six-year-old child would be able to do that and Orla was not a particularly athletic or courageous child. She thought back to Cormac and Art at that age. Setanta, Cormac's foster father, used to tie a rope to a tree branch for them, but that would have been only about six or seven feet long and they were both very tough, very adventurous boys. In any case, this rope reached only to a few feet above her head. Possible for an adult to leap and catch it, but impossible for Orla.

She had to get help.

The scholars were grouped around the entrance to the cave and she was touched to see the look of relief on all their faces when she arrived.

'I've found Fachtnan,' she said immediately. 'He is unconscious and I think that he has probably broken his leg. But there is absolutely no sign of Orla and that is what is worrying me the most. Cormac and Art, I want you to go back and collect your ponies and ride, safely and sensibly, to Rathborney and get Nuala to come to Oughtdara with the cart; don't tell her that Orla is missing, because we might well have found her by then. She's probably hiding somewhere, feeling terrified. Let's send Ug for help first of all so that Gobnait is prepared.'

What a pity, she thought, that these people could not read, otherwise she could have given the useful Ug a note tied to the broad leather collar that he wore – a defence against a fox bite on the neck, according to Gobnait – and the situation about the missing Orla could have been explained. Still, her scholars would go as quickly as possible and would doubtless meet the brothers on their rescue mission.

'Go on, Ug, good boy, find Gobnait,' said Cormac encouragingly and the dog shot off, as though he were an arrow that had been released from a bow.

'You others follow him, and safely – be very careful, won't you?' said Mara. 'I'll go back and wait with Fachtnan in case he comes back to consciousness.'

'Would it be all right if I stayed with you, Brehon?' asked Domhnall diffidently. 'There's plenty to go back and I think that one of us should stay. You always say that there is safety in numbers.'

'Well, I can't argue with my own wise words,' said Mara. She spoke lightly, but she was touched by her grandson's concern for her. And, she admitted to herself, glad of his support. One could keep an eye on Fachtnan while the other searched for his daughter. She was much more worried about Orla than about Fachtnan. A broken leg on a healthy young man was a nuisance, but not a tragedy; a missing six-year-old in a possibly dangerous cave was a more serious matter.

'I wonder if Orla would have had the sense to run for help when Fachtnan fell over and hit his head?' she said to him.

'I doubt it,' he said laconically. There was an ironic twinkle in his eyes that made her feel a lot better. She had been like that at his age, she thought, looking back over the thirty-two years that had elapsed. She was more outgoing than Domhnall, but she had been calm and confident and able to deal with whatsoever arose. Domhnall had inherited her abilities and her confidence. He was a very fine young man and she was proud of him.

'Oh, come on now,' she said bracingly, 'after all, this is a child who has grown up seeing injured people come to her mother. Surely the sensible thing would be to run back out of the cave and try to get back to where Deirdre lives. She would remember spending the time with her making a cake for Fachtnan.'

'Sounds sensible,' said Domhnall politely. 'The only trouble is that Orla is not very sensible. I'd expect her to panic. I'd say that she's still in the cave.'

'You may be right,' said Mara with a grimace. 'We'd surely have seen her, I suppose, as we were coming across.'

'And she'd have heard us. Cael and Cian were shouting at each other, and Cormac was making jokes about the goddess, Morrigan, at the top of his voice.'

'That's true,' said Mara with a sigh. 'Still we'd better look for her out here before we go back inside again. I can remember once a case, long, long ago, when a small child went missing up on the bog on Slieve Elva. Everyone was busying cutting the turf and *footing* the wet sods and a little girl went missing. There must have been forty people there, all searching for her, shouting her name, all the dogs running around. They went further and further afield – you can imagine what the family were feeling like, thinking that she had drowned in a bog hole – and then in the end she was found curled up fast asleep, only a couple of hundred yards away from the family's plot. Small children do that, just fall asleep if they are lost and frightened. Mind you, this child was only about two years old. Still, Orla is young for her age and quite timid. I think that we should try searching for her. Where would she go, I wonder, if she ran out of the cave?'

Mara stared across the rock-littered landscape, trying to see it with the eyes of a six year old. She moved her hand trying to recollect Orla's height. About to her waist? She really could not remember. Even so, she crouched down and looked across. The cliff that was tunnelled by all those caves with their splendid names was higher than the rest of the valley and here they were standing on a ledge. No matter how small Orla was, she must still have been able, quite clearly, to see across to the small settlement at Oughtdara. The church roof was plainly visible and even more so, the huge walls of Dunaunmore, the ancient fortified place of the *Tuatha Dé*. Even Orla must have known the way to go back to where her father had left his horse and to where a kind person like Deirdre lived in a cosy house filled with the smells of baking.

'Look, Brehon,' said Domhnall urgently. Mara straightened and turned to the side. For a moment the south-western sun shone straight into her eyes and then her vision cleared. She was looking along the line of the inland cliff face towards the sea and there seemed to be a figure in the distance. She blinked rapidly and then shaded her eyes. Yes, there was a man approaching, carrying something. Her heart seemed almost to stop for a moment and then begin its slow steady beat.

Only a lamb, perhaps . . .

But instantly Domhnall was gone from her side, moving fast, climbing over rocks, going around groups of boulders and then climbing a flat cube-shaped stone, stopping, standing quite still. And then he turned towards her, his fist raised in a gesture of triumph and his words rang out against the cliff face.

'He's got her. Aengus has got Orla. She's all right. She waved to me. Aengus waved and then she waved.'

Twelve

Gúbrecha Caracniað
(The Judgements of Caratniad)

Heptad 47
A man may divorce his wife for the following reasons:
1. *Unfaithfulness.*
2. *Persistent thieving.*
3. *Inducing an abortion on herself.*
4. *Smothering her child.*
5. *Being without milk and refusing to engage a nurse.*
6. *Being a cause of war.*
7. *Bringing shame upon his honour.*

'Good old Aengus,' said Domhnall, when he arrived back at her side. 'I wonder how he managed to spot her, wandering around down here; that man must have eyes like a hen harrier's to be able to see such a tiny little girl from such a distance. It's lucky for her that he was up there. Gobnait says that Aengus is up on Knockauns or Ballynahown all day with flocks until the light goes. And he stays up there until the light fades, or all night sometimes. In fact, he's moved back up there, Brehon, did you know; back into one of the shepherds' huts; Deirdre told me that.'

'I didn't know,' said Mara. She was conscious that she spoke in a slightly absent-minded way. A lot of things had begun to come together for her: the hole in the cave roof; the rope; the misty morning; the powdery-white moonmilk, so good for the stomach. And Cian's remark. She awaited the arrival of Aengus with a slight feeling of dread in her heart.

'No, I don't suppose that Orla was wandering,' she said aloud. 'She probably did what Orla would do. You know what she is like. She probably just sat down beside Fachtnan and wept and shouted to him to wake up, until someone came. It's all come together really.'

Domhnall, of course, had not seen the inner cave where Fachtnan had fallen. He had not seen the rope which went up so high and through the rock, through the broken ceiling of the cave; a rope that would allow someone to descend from Ballynahown's lower slopes to drop straight down twenty feet below and to emerge on the ground above Oughtdara. And, of course, the morning of the murder was a morning of thick mist. He gave her a puzzled look, but she ignored it. She had to think. She sat down on the flat stone and pondered her next move. Orla had to be taken back, Fachtnan had to be lifted safely and without injury across the stony ground. And she had to talk to Aengus.

By the time Aengus came up to her, she had made up her mind and she went forward, smiling at him.

'Aengus, how good you are! How on earth did you manage to climb down that rope? Tell me what happened?'

'Rope!' exclaimed Domhnall. 'What rope?'

'I got very frightened,' said Orla, determined to be the centre of attention. 'I thought that he was a bad god coming down from heaven and I runned away.'

'That was silly,' remarked Mara. Orla, she thought with amusement, was confusing two sets of religions. The gods from the *Fír Bolg* or *Tuatha Dé* did not, as far as she knew, indulge themselves with lounging around on clouds playing harps in a heaven above the blue sky. 'So where did you run to, you silly girl,' she asked lightly.

Orla looked at her sulkily. 'Not telling you,' she said.

'Sure, God help us, she got a bad fright when she saw me coming down,' said Aengus. 'I tried to shout down to her, to tell her that I was coming to help her, but she went mad, she was screaming and then she ran away. Lord bless us and save us, Brehon, I had my heart in my mouth, I thought that she would kill herself, or be lost for ever. They're dangerous places, them caves.'

'I'm sure,' said Mara. 'It's a good thing that you were there, Aengus. How did you manage to find her? You can put her down now, Aengus. Stand up on your own two feet, Orla. You're a big girl now. Aengus has carried you for long enough.'

'If you don't mind, Brehon, I'd like to keep a hold of her now that I've got her. I wouldn't want to be squeezing through any more of those little passageways if she took a notion to run off. Desperate dangerous they are. Lucky I knew those caves like the back of my hand. You'd never believe it, but she had nearly ended up in Sionnach MacDara's Cave by the time that I managed to catch her.'

'Well, we're very grateful to you, Aengus.' There was no doubt that without him Orla might have been lost forever in the endless labyrinths of those caves. Mara felt her legs a little unsteady and concealed a shake in her voice by speaking briskly. A problem had now been solved. But had the last link to the previous problem been put into place?

'Domhnall, would you take Orla and bring her back to Oughtdara. Orla, you can walk now, but you must hold Domhnall's hand and don't you dare run away again or I shall be very angry indeed. Do you understand what you must do?' She looked sternly at the child and waited until Orla gave a reluctant nod.

'I'll go back to stay with Fachtnan, Domhnall,' she continued. 'I'm worried that he might regain consciousness and look for the child and then do something stupid like trying to stand up, or crawl. Perhaps you'll come back into the cave with me, Aengus, will you? I'm sure that you know more about broken legs than I do.' These shepherds of the hills were often excellent physicians according to Nuala. Up there, isolated from all assistance or advice, they learned from experience what to do when animals were ailing or had broken a limb or were wounded in some way.

'Take my cloak with you to cover him, Brehon,' said Domhnall. 'I'll be warm enough scrambling across those rocks. I'll probably end up having to carry her. Come on, Orla, your mother is coming down here with the cart and you can go back with her.'

Orla went off without a backward glance. She had not enquired after her father; perhaps she had managed to blot his accident out of her mind. Mara shrugged her shoulders and turned to Aengus.

'Orla's mother and father will be so very grateful to you, Aengus. You were up on Ballynahown and you heard Orla crying, is that right?'

'That's right, Brehon.' He was waiting politely for her to go ahead of him but she waved him on and then followed. He did not seem to mind the sudden darkness that came as they stepped into the cave from the bright March sunlight and he went steadily and rapidly ahead. They passed the shelf covered with moonmilk and Mara reflected how, when she saw Aengus on the day of his wife's death, she had noticed that his mouth and lips were coated with a white powdery substance. Aengus probably knew this cave very well. Poor man; marriage to a wife like Clodagh would give anyone a bad stomach!

'You know where he is lying, don't you, Aengus; you came down the rope. You tied your rope to a tree, didn't you and started to come down. Was that what frightened Orla?'

'That's right, Brehon. I called down to her that it was all right; that I was coming. But she gave a God Almighty scream. I heard her running and she was screaming and screaming. I couldn't see where she went because I had to keep my eyes on the rope and let myself down hand over hand and keep looking for footholds on the rock, so that I wouldn't slip down too fast and fall myself. I could hear her feet running. I knew that she was going down that passageway – lucky, she kept on screaming, "Don't come near me; don't come near me!" that's what she kept on about. Poor little thing! I frightened the life out of her. Here, Brehon, this is the place that she went down.'

By now they had come to the end of the first main cave. Aengus indicated an almost impossibly narrow passageway. Mara marvelled at how he had managed to follow the child. It was a piece of luck for Orla that the man was so small and bone-thin.

'I thought that I should go after her; though I didn't like leaving the poor fellow lying there, but by the sound of him, I didn't think he'd come back to consciousness too quickly and the little girl could lose herself for ever in these caves.' He sounded apologetic and Mara hastened to make up for her silence.

'You did absolutely the right thing, Aengus,' she said. 'Everyone will be so grateful to you. You saved the child's life and Fachtnan will come to no harm. You would have had to leave him, in any case, to get help for him. But Orla could have been killed. I can't bear to think of what might have happened to her if she lost her way. I remember someone telling me that the whole of this district has a network of underground passageways and caves beneath the surface and that only a fox or a badger would be able to find its way through them. I hope that Orla was grateful to you,' she added, thinking that the terrified little girl had probably kicked and screamed when he had eventually caught up with her.

'I didn't need any thanks, Brehon. I'm very fond of children.' He said the words in a low voice and there was a note of sadness in it that touched her. Cormac, she thought, was very fond of Aengus and Cormac was a good judge of a person, seeming instinctively, from a very early age, to be able to distinguish between those who liked him for himself and those who were trying to ingratiate themselves with his distinguished parents. Dogs and children liked Aengus. Even little Orla, after her fright, and her terrifying ordeal, had been calm and happy when carried by him.

'I hope that Fachtnan is all right.' A new worry had come to her mind. They must be quite near where they had left him, but she could hear nothing.

'There he is, the poor fellow.' Aengus was quicker than she to hear Fachtnan. The horrible snoring sound had finished, and now there were a few groans and then silence.

'He's coming back to himself,' said Aengus as they rounded the protruding rock. 'Ah, here he is. Now, my lord, don't be upsetting yourself, we'll soon have you better.'

Only silence greeted that. Fachtnan had lapsed into unconsciousness again. Mara reached out, feeling around tentatively until she touched the woollen cloak. One hand had been flung out and it felt very cold. Mara decided not to move it. The leg, she reckoned, was definitely broken, but that did not mean that there might not also be an injury to the arm, or collarbone. Carefully she spread Domhnall's cloak over the outstretched body. That was about all that she could do for Fachtnan – other than keep him from injuring himself any more, or from endeavouring to look for Orla. In the meantime they would just have to sit and wait – it would take perhaps an hour before Nuala and the stretcher-bearers would arrive, and at least half an hour before Gobnait and Pat arrived, escorted by Ug, and hopefully carrying lamps and also a stretcher.

And while they were waiting, she could be carrying on with the affairs of the kingdom.

By now her eyes had, once again, become accustomed to the dim light. She could see Fachtnan lying there under Domhnall's cloak, breathing a little easier now, with the occasional groan, but not tossing or turning. She could examine the rope that dangled down from the broken top of the cave. The little section where they sat was a high point, she reckoned. On both sides the ground sloped steeply downhill. It would probably be flooded down there, but here it was relatively dry. She and the unconscious Fachtnan could wait here in comparative comfort until the rescue party arrived.

But opposite her sat the small thin figure of the herdsman, Aengus, and she could not shirk her duty.

He could, she thought; leave whenever he felt like it. She would not put him into an intolerable position; weigh him down too much with guilt for something that perhaps had been almost involuntary. In the past she had put herself into danger by questioning a suspect who had thought that all suspicion would end with the death of the Brehon. Now she realized that had been foolhardy. Without vanity, she weighed the consequence for the kingdom of her death in counterbalance with the conviction of a murderer who probably had not meant to kill, and who, in any case, had been pushed beyond all reasonable bounds. The ancient laws of Ireland could, and would, she thought, take into account the mental state of the accused, would weigh in the balance of his crime the crimes that had been committed towards him, would estimate the provocation, take evidence of words and deeds. The reputation of the dead woman would not, could not, be spared when it came to a trial. *De mortuis nil nisi bonum* had said one of her scholars, but the living had rights, also. She would be gentle and careful with this man who must have suffered greatly, behind the screen of blank incomprehension that he had presented to the people of the kingdom.

No direct questions, she thought. Nothing that would provoke him to violence. She would not be misled by his apparent fragility. This was a man who climbed mountains almost every day of his life, who lifted waterlogged sheep and carried them to safety, a man who had sixty years of hard work to tone every muscle in his body. There was a business-like knife at his belt, also.

'You've had a bad time, Aengus,' she said gently. 'I wish that you had come to me and I wish that I had approached you. There were measures that I could have taken, ways to make things more bearable for you.' She thought through all of the contents of Heptad 33 that listed verbal assaults such as mocking a person's appearance, publicizing a physical blemish, coining a nickname that sticks – all of these could be punished by a heavy fine. And, of course, there was worse. She remembered Cian and how he had aroused the wrath of this poor man before her.

'You were angry with one of my scholars when he repeated Clodagh's words,' she said softly. She could guess the taunt that his wife had flung on him and was only sorry that any scholar of hers could repeat them. There were times when Cian seemed to betray a hidden anger that just seemed to have to erupt. She wondered whether he had heard somewhere of his father's ignoble death, though she had planned to keep it secret until the twins were sixteen years old. I shall have to keep an eye on Cian, she thought and then switched her mind back to her present problem.

Aengus was staring at her blankly. His face bore a look of total incomprehension. It was as though she were speaking some foreign language to him.

'I wish you had come to me,' she said. She spoke, she knew, with the greatest sincerity; she could have done something for this man. The hell that he lived within might have been a joke to young and old, but it was no less real for that. It should not have been allowed to continue. The law, she thought, was right to punish satire, even taunting, with the greatest severity, exacting a full payment of the victim's honour price. Words could sometimes hurt more than blows. They could destroy the spirit.

Fachtnan stirred and groaned and she leaned down and touched his face. He was quite warm. She took his wrist in her hand and tried to count the beat of his blood as Nuala had taught her and it seemed to be quite strong and regular. He, she thought, was not her worst problem at the moment.

'You had grounds for divorce, Aengus.' The words were out of her mouth before she could recall them, but she knew that they were worse than useless. It was too late now for him to have redress to the law. He had taken the law into his own hands, had silenced the woman who had tormented him. And yet he must have heard of cases of divorce in the community, must have known that the possibility existed for him. The word 'divorce' had taken his attention. He had turned to look at her. Her sight had adjusted to the light so well by now that she could see tears flood into his faded old eyes.

'I wouldn't have done that to her, Brehon,' he said piteously. 'I wouldn't have shamed her. I wanted her to be happy. I thought that we might be happy together, but I wasn't right for her. She was the one who was going to divorce me. She was going to shame me in front of the people of the kingdom. She had learned about a law from Brehon MacClancy. She had gone to see him to find out if she could get rid of me. She wanted a fine new husband, she told me. I was no good to her. She was going to be rich and she was going to have a fine house and a fine husband, not a useless old fellow like me.' Mara heard him sob, heard the few broken words, words that were almost lost in the hands that he had placed over his face. She understood, though. Clodagh had learned the law well from poor old addle-witted Brehon Fergus MacClancy. She was going to sue for divorce on the grounds of impotence and attribute her childless state to her husband's lack of ability to perform his marital duty. An unpleasant woman, she wished to enjoy her newfound land without having to share it – perhaps hoping that it might give her back her youth and the love that she had evoked back in the days when her red tresses and cloak of many colours had lit up the stony valley.

'I wish that you had spoken to me, Aengus; I might have been able to settle matters quietly, persuade her. I'm here for everyone in the kingdom that has a legal problem. You shouldn't have kept all of this to yourself . . .' Mara felt so distressed that even a groan from Fachtnan went almost unnoticed by her.

'I spoke to the *taoiseach* a few days ago. I thought that I should tell him of my shame before it was known throughout the kingdom. He said that he would speak to you,' said Aengus with a simple dignity that she found almost unbearable.

'I wish that he had told me.' But as she spoke she reflected that it was probably just the day before the murder that Aengus had told his pitiable tale to his *taoiseach*. Ardal had said nothing about it during their meeting that evening, but Clodagh was by then dead. Ardal would have reasoned that he could not betray what was said to him in confidence. His clan was his life; their concerns were his.

Mara thought hard for a moment. She had all the information that she needed. Motive; yes, of course: Clodagh had made the man's life a misery and was planning to shame him in front of the kingdom. Means: he could certainly have strangled her; she would have had a great contempt for him and would have not feared any danger from him. Opportunity: she had thought that was lacking, but she had not known of the possible descent from Ballynahown into the Moonmilk Cave and then the hidden way through caves and underground passageways until he reached the cave of Sionnach MacDara beside the church. From the cave it was only a few yards to the pillar of stone, the figure of the *Fár Breige*, the god of evil. Not knowing about all of that, she had dismissed him from her mind, and thought that he had lacked opportunity, since he had been seen to leave the area as dawn broke. But now with that knowledge, she could see that it had been easy for him. He could have made his way carefully, possibly waiting behind the thick barrier of blackthorn until the mist was at its thickest. She looked across at him, conscious that the silence had gone on for a long time. He was no longer looking at her, but glancing over at the unconscious figure of Fachtnan.

And then he had taken his knife from his belt.

It was a long knife, long in the handle, long in the blade. To her it looked wickedly sharp, but he held it out and scraped it against the rock edge, turning and twisting it, making sure that both sides were whetted to a keen edge. It had a long point on it, and she could imagine how he might plunge it between the ribs of an unwary fox.

Or, perhaps, into the heart of anyone who threatened him.

Mara felt her mouth grow dry, though there was no threat uttered, no angry glances, just the relentless scrape of the knife. She held her breath until eventually, with a quick puff of air along the blade, he held it out to the light that filtered down from the broken rock face above them and examined it carefully.

And then he got to his feet. Mara stayed very still. The moment for doing anything had passed. He stood above her, holding the sharpened knife in his hand.

'You'll excuse me if I leave you for a moment, Brehon,' he said.

She nodded. She could not trust her voice to be under her control. There was nothing to do, she thought, and wished that she believed in prayer.

For a moment after he had left her she eyed the rope above her head, but she knew that she was incapable of leaving the unconscious Fachtnan behind her. She would have to rely on her wits and on her tongue; she would have to control her fear and preserve a friendly and unconcerned attitude. How long had it been since Ug the dog had gone flying across the rocks to fetch his master?

And then she heard the footsteps. Aengus was coming back very quickly. What had he gone to do? Perhaps to check that the rescue party were nowhere in sight; that would be sensible. He appeared around the rock face, not looking at her, his eyes on the man on the ground. He was carrying a short, stout stick of a willow bush and as she watched, her mouth dry, he knelt down beside Fachtnan, measuring the stick against the broken leg and trimming it to size with his sharp knife. When he was satisfied with the length, he took a hank of twine from his pouch and bound the stick against the leg, winding it around and around, knotting the loops from time to time and then finishing off with a double knot.

'Just as well to keep it steady while they are lifting him onto the stretcher,' he remarked.

Mara did not trust her voice to say anything, but she nodded weakly. She was conscious of a great feeling of shame and surreptitiously unclenched her fingers.

'They'll be here soon,' he told her in a reassuring way. 'I saw the dog running ahead of them. Very clever dog, that fellow, Ug.'

'He is, indeed,' said Mara weakly. She bent over Fachtnan, busying herself with feeling the pulse of blood that beat in his wrist, tentatively touching the clotted blood on his hair.

'He hit his head when he fell,' she said to fill the silence and waiting anxiously for the bark of the dog.

'He'll come around soon, don't you worry, Brehon. He's better off as he is until they get across the rocks.' And then when she didn't reply, he said, 'I broke my leg once up on the hill. I had to crawl back down to the hut, but there was a sally bush outside and I had my knife and I tore a strip from the bottom of my *léine* and I bound up the leg and waited until someone found me. The *taoiseach*, God bless him, was very good to me; he sent someone up twice a day with food and drink for me. I mended well, not even a limp. He's a great man, the *taoiseach*; he'd do anything for his people. He was very kind to me when I told him about the divorce. He said that he'd take care of it and that I wasn't to worry any more about it. I felt better about it all once I told him. Be easy now, poor man, be easy now, we'll soon have you right.'

Fachtnan had groaned loudly and Aengus stroked his forehead. 'I hate to see things suffer,' he said simply. 'Even an old sheep with a broken leg; I'd stay up all night to give her company, not let her to herself in her pain; I'd talk to her, sing to her sometimes, just to be with her.'

Jesus, himself, thought Mara, had asked for no more. 'Could you not watch one hour with me?' was what he said to his disciples. This man was willing to sacrifice his night hours of sleep in order that a sheep would be comforted.

'Listen, did you hear that?' In a moment he was on his feet and left the cave. He must have great hearing, she thought, telling herself that she would stay with Fachtnan, but glad of the excuse to sit quietly for a few minutes. Her mind was very busy, weighing up motive, means and opportunity, reviewing the evidence. The motive; well, that was obvious. The means – Aengus was a man that had worked with animals all of his life. Despite his size he would be strong with well-trained muscles. And the rope above her head, and the knowledge that the network of passages beneath the ground would lead him to the cave that stood so near to the *Far Bréige*, all of these things told her that she could have come to the end of her quest to find the murderer of Clodagh O'Lochlainn.

Facts, logic, reasoning; all those things she valued, but she had been Brehon of the Burren for nearly thirty years and during that time she had investigated many crimes, judged many motives, talked with the innocent and the guilty. Her long years of experience had taught her not to devalue facts, not to skip one single step in the gathering of information, but at the same time to trust to that accumulated wisdom, an instinctive certainty; this man, she said to herself, is not a killer.

Aengus, as her son had told her, was a gentle, kind man. Aengus was fond of children, fond of dogs, even fond of elderly sheep. His were not the hands that had choked the life out of Clodagh O'Lochlainn after forty years of marriage, forty years of forbearance.

And then suddenly, everything slotted into place like the threads on a weaver's loom. The bishop! Why had she not seen the significance of that? She had been looking in the wrong direction, had been misled completely. But now her thoughts were moving so rapidly that by the time the light from a lantern shone on the wall opposite to the entrance, she had come to her conclusion and stood up to welcome the rescue party.

'Aengus bound his leg to that stick,' she said as Nuala knelt on the stony floor beside her husband, touched his cheek for a moment and then signalled to Dinan to shine the light on the leg. Strangely unemotional for a wife witnessing her unconscious husband, but perhaps just now Fachtnan was a patient to her. When she spoke her voice was business-like as usual.

'Made a very good job of it, too. Well done, Aengus. We brought a stick, but this is fine, I'll just move that bone a little, tighten this here.' As she spoke, Nuala removed Domhnall's cloak, and then opened Fachtnan's own cloak, spreading it widely, like a blanket, on the rock face. 'Put down the stretcher, Pat, just here beside the cloak. Now, Brehon, could you take the lamp and the four of us will lift him, each take a corner; get comfortable everybody. We can do this quickly and easily, there's plenty of room, thank goodness. I'll give the signal.'

Mara held her breath for a moment, but it was quick and competent. All knew what they were doing. Broken legs were well known in this stony part of the world. In a moment, Fachtnan was placed on the stretcher; a minute later he had been bound to it by long strips of linen; and then Domhnall's cloak was spread over him. Mara held the lantern high, shining the light so that it lit up walls and ceilings. Illuminate, she thought. *Lumen luminis*, that was one of the names of God Almighty in the doxology and it was, indeed, a divine gift to be able to illuminate matters, to see the truth. She was glad that she had had that long quiet time with Aengus. It had saved her from making an error, from accusing him directly, had allowed the light of truth to shine into his childlike soul. Let him stay with the feeling that the gods had killed his wife, for the moment. The truth would have to be known to everyone quite soon.

As soon as she got back to Oughtdara she would get that priest into a room by himself. She would take no denial, listen to no nonsense about supernatural forces and, above all, any mention of the *Fár Breige* would bring forth from her a storm of rage which should shock him out of his self-indulgence and bring his wits back to him. She had no patience with that sort of nonsense.

By one means or another, she would force Father Eoin O'Lochlainn to shed the light of truth upon this matter of the murder of Clodagh O'Lochlainn.

The priest was basking in front of the fire when Deirdre, rubbing some life into her hands red with the cold, ushered Mara into the cosy room. He had been sitting on the cushioned settle and had slipped sideways, his grey hair falling over his forehead with his cheek resting against the soft lambswool covering, his eyes shut and one hand dangling downwards towards the floor. For all of his sixty-odd years, he had the appearance of an exhausted child.

And sitting opposite him, on the other settle, was Dinan who rose to his feet as soon as Mara entered.

'Sit here, Brehon,' he said hastily. 'I was just waiting for his reverence to wake up.'

Mara took his seat with a nod and a smile, but did not speak. Was there any polite way of getting rid of him? It was difficult to send a man out from his own brother's house without some good excuse.

Unfortunately Dinan seemed pleased to see her. 'I promised Deirdre that I wouldn't wake him,' he said in a penetrating whisper, 'but I just wanted to talk to him about the *Fár Breige*. Deirdre says that he keeps muttering about the god, but she can't make head or tail of it. She says that it's just some old *rameish*.'

Mara muttered something, but Dinan wasn't to be deterred.

'You see I'm finding out that we know very little about the *Fár Breige* – even a scholar like yourself, Brehon, you don't know much, do you? And think of all the stories about the Morrigan – I could write a book about her, that's if I could write.' He gave a short laugh and ran his hand through his hair, gazing down at the sleeping priest with an air of exasperation. Mara nodded sympathetically, moved by his frustration at his illiteracy. Why should Dinan not write a book as good as Sir Thomas More's *Utopia*, she thought. It would be much more thrilling, much more vivid, more tightly constructed. Dinan was a born storyteller; a man who knew how to hold an audience spellbound.

'And yet, *he* knows all about how the woman was killed, how the *Fár Breige* managed to do it. He was there.' Dinan, encouraged by her interest, jerked his thumb at the sleeping figure so that she would know he meant the man, not the god. 'He was there, peeping from his window, like he always does. Deirdre says that he saw it all. I'd love to hear what he has to say, wouldn't you, Brehon.'

'You know, Dinan,' said Mara, 'it's not being able to write or to read that is the important thing. Any fool can do that if they are taught it early enough. It's having the brains and the imagination to tell the tales; having the words that hold attention; a man who can do that is a man who will live in the memory of the people. Why don't you get one of my young scholars, Cormac or Art, to write them down for you and they'll make a book for you.' She could see that he was taken by the idea so she hastened to use the opportunity to get rid of him.

'Go and talk to them,' she said authoritatively. 'They're waiting for me in the Dunaunmore enclosure, with the horses. Leave Father O'Lochlainn to me. He'd just be worried about the bishop if you ask him anything.' It worked like a miracle. He was on his feet instantly, his face blazing with excitement.

'You're right, of course, Brehon. I should have known that for myself. Deirdre did say that he was going on about the bishop. He won't mind about telling you. You're more important than any bishop in the land.'

And with that extravagant compliment, Dinan withdrew to go and confer with her scholars about his book. It would be rather a nice thing to do, she thought, as she heard his boots clatter on the paved road outside. One of her father's most treasured possessions was the *Book of Lismore*, full of the tales of the past; perhaps the *Book of the Burren* might rival it. It would be good for Cormac and Art to have this as their special project. Art drew and painted pictures very well and Cormac had a fluent pen. They might make something quite beautiful out of it.

And then she dismissed the Morrigan and the *Fár Breige* from her mind and deliberately shook the sleeping priest from his slumbers. It took her a while; she had a strong impression that he was resisting her, that he did not want to wake up, but wanted to continue to take refuge in sleep from the nightmare of guilt that filled his waking hours.

'Tell me why you thought the bishop was responsible for the woman's death,' she said sternly.

Thirteen

Gúbrecha Caracniað
(The Judgements of Caratniad)

A lord must care for his kin and his clan because they are of the same blood. He may lose his honour-price for a wide range of offences and failings such as sheltering a fugitive from the law, tolerating satire, eating food known to be stolen and betraying his honour.

Likewise he loses his honour-price if he fails to fulfil his obligations to his tenants.

Ardal was in the steward's room when she arrived at Lissylisheen Castle. She was shown straight into the room, but then paused for a second, feeling slightly embarrassed. The table had a green cloth spread over one end of it and this was strewn with piles of small pieces of silver, with silver coins and even a few gold ones.

'You're busy,' she said.

'Not at all.' Ardal, as always, was the soul of courtesy, rising to his feet immediately. 'We've just finished counting everything. Come and look at our coins. We have quite a collection here. Look, there's a gold angel from England. No king's head on it. It's surprising that the young king, King Henry VIII, still uses his father's coinage. He must have become king about fifteen years ago, but there, you can see still the old coins: still St Michael slaying the dragon on one side and a ship on the other, the coinage of the old king, King Henry VII.'

'Odd, that,' said Mara, bending over the board and picking up various coins. 'He's supposed to be a very handsome young man. You would think it would have been one of the first things that he would have done: sat for an artist and then put the king's head onto the coins of the realm. There's Francis I of France and Charles V, Our Holy Roman Emperor, beloved of the Pope. They've all got their picture engraved upon their coins.'

'I suppose he's been too busy with all of his wars: the Italian war, the French war and now Scotland. I hope he decides to leave us alone. King Turlough thinks that while the Earl of Kildare remains, in Turlough's words, the lackey of the king of England, then we'll never get our country back, but for myself, I'm happy if he leaves my kingdom of the Burren alone.' He spoke, she thought, as though he, like his ancestors, was the king of the Burren. And she wondered, not for the first time, how well she knew this complicated man.

'What's that angel coin worth?' She had changed the conversation rather abruptly, she knew, but she did not want to talk about any invasion or about the Earl of Kildare, who was the sworn enemy of Turlough. Her husband was war-like and adventurous, but he was getting a little old for warfare now and she wished that she could induce him to stay at home and not to be always in the forefront of any opposition to the Earl of Kildare and the troops from England.

'Just about half a sovereign.' Ardal did not elaborate. He was a sensitive man and knew that she had visited him for a purpose.

'Lock the coins into the small chest, Danann,' he said. 'We'll take them to Spain when we go there next month. I've a mind to purchase a stallion with Arab breeding and I think that I know just the horse. It won't be cheap, but the foals will pay for the sire, over and over again. Now, Brehon, I'm at your service. Will you have a cup of wine with me? I've just got a small half barrel of wine from Bordeaux and you shall be the first to taste it.'

'That sounds tempting, Ardal, but no; thank you. I feel like a little fresh air. I sat in a cave out in Oughtdara for what seemed like hours.' And then she told them both the story of Fachtnan's accident and of how Aengus had saved little Orla. Ardal smiled with satisfaction, merely remarking, 'He's a good fellow. I must remember to have a word with him. Perhaps get him something, a good warm rug for his room, Danann, or something like that. What do you think? Whatever you think he'll appreciate – I'll leave it to you, Danann.'

'Aengus will be pleased about that. He has a very high opinion of you. As do all of your clan,' she added lightly. She waited until the young steward had locked away the coins and handed the key of the strong box to his master. 'Let's walk down the road, Ardal,' she said and saw him look enquiringly at her. She said nothing, however, until they were out on the road. There was a strong wind blowing, but the sky was a clear blue and there was a perceptible deepening of the green on the roadside grass.

'First of April,' said Ardal. 'March has done its worst.' He surveyed his fields on either side of the road with a professional air. 'Soon see an improvement. I can almost hear the grass when it begins to grow in those valley fields. I've been looking at them long enough, I suppose. I've been looking at them now for well over fifty years, winter, spring, summer and autumn.' He ended with a slight laugh, but Mara could see how affectionately he regarded his land.

'I was thinking the other day about the year when Domhnall's mother, Sorcha, was born,' said Mara meditatively and saw him smile with a look of amusement.

'That's an odd way to refer to my own daughter, I know,' she said, 'but somehow that's the way I think of her, as the mother of my grandchildren. She was married to Oisín more than twenty years ago and the years when she was a child were short years, such busy years for me. Brigid did a lot of the mothering of Sorcha. I'm not much of a mother, I suppose, always too busy with the law.'

'You were a very young mother when you had Sorcha,' he said. 'What were you, fourteen, no, fifteen years old – that's right, isn't it?'

'That's right,' she said with a sigh for her stubbornness. Her early and disastrous marriage was her fault; her father had done his best to persuade her against it. 'And you became *taoiseach* a month after I became a mother. I think you were more able for your responsibilities than I was.' It had been a difficult time for him, she thought. His father had persuaded the clan to pass over the eldest son and, according to the law, to pick the fittest of all the descendants of the great-grandfather for the position of *tánaiste*, not realizing how soon the eighteen-year-old would be called upon to shoulder the whole burden.

'You were just eighteen,' she said.

'Too young,' said Ardal.

'You were equal to it,' she replied.

'If my wife had lived,' he said and then stopped. She was surprised. It had been over ten years at least since he had alluded to that early and tragically short marriage.

'If your wife had lived then I think that the balance would have been more even between your life as a private person and your life as a *taoiseach*. Your clan would have always been important to you, but there would have been other interests, other matters to keep everything in balance. But so far as your land and your position of *taoiseach* was concerned, I don't suppose that you could have done better. You brought wealth to yourself, but also prosperity to your clan.'

He looked at her enquiringly, but continued to walk, matching his step to hers. They strolled in silence; following the narrow road as it went climbing steeply upwards. They had left the valley now and were going up onto the High Burren. The well-kept fields on either side of the road had gone and now there was the true Burren, 'the stony place', in the old language. To their right the field sloped steeply towards the sky, lines of pale grey rock, looking like miniature buildings, protruded from the ground and small, sturdy winter bullocks nosed out tufts of grass from among the cowslips.

'Not like my valley fields, are they?' Ardal broke the silence.

'No,' said Mara. She looked around at the rocky fields, at the orange tip butterflies hovering amongst the pale purple lady's smock flowers. 'But I like the hills myself,' she said. 'The air is so good on the hills. The valleys get the mist. I don't like mist; I suppose there is something slightly supernatural about it. Something evil.' She paused, leaning on a gate and from the corner of her eyes, saw him hesitate and then come to join her.

'Dinan has some great stories about the mist,' she said and then without a pause, she continued, 'Were it not for the mist, I suppose Clodagh would not have been murdered. What do you think?'

He made no reply to that, but he was standing so close to her that she felt rather than saw him stiffen.

'The impulse of a moment might have evaporated if it were not for the way that the mist cloaked all.' She let the sentence hang in the air for a few minutes, but he did not reply. He was a man who had great control over his tongue.

'You see,' she went on, 'I was misled for some time about this murder. The fact that it had followed on from my judgement at Poulnabrone when Clodagh had been granted all of her father's lands, well, that misled me. I had been looking into the four brothers. All of them had a motive. The land, as you pointed out, was not valuable in terms of cattle, but in terms of sheep and goats, well, it was valuable to them. And then when it comes to land, it's not just the grass that grows on it, but what lies beneath it, and here on the Burren we have silver, a little gold and, of course, lead, which may in these days turn out to be almost as valuable. So Finnegas, as well as the other brothers had a motive.' She looked sideways at him, but his well-cut profile was impassive, his lips firmly closed, his blue eyes fixed on the small black cattle on the hilltop.

'So I was led along the road to investigate the four brothers, but in the end, I did not think that there was any evidence that any one of the four had done the deed, so I was forced to look elsewhere.'

He turned to her then, a keen look and she nodded. 'Yes,' she said, 'I moved on from considering the, well, I suppose, the cold motive of greed, to the hot motives of lust, anger, rage . . .'

'Hardly a likely candidate for lust,' remarked Ardal dryly.

'Do you remember her at all?' asked Mara with sudden curiosity. 'Do you remember her when she was a young girl, about your own age, I suppose; at the time when the bishop came to see you, to tell you that there was a bit of scandalous gossip about the young priest at St MacDara's church in Oughtdara.'

There was a slight flash of irritation from his eyes. 'I haven't any recollection of her,' he said brusquely and without reference to her he released his hold of the gate and began to continue their walk down the road.

'But you remember the bishop,' she said, joining him, but deliberately not trying to catch up with him.

He glanced over his shoulder, slowed down and then grinned reluctantly. 'I suppose,' he said, 'that I was young enough to be flattered that he was the one who came to me.'

'And you were able to do his business for him?'

He would have been, too, she thought. Looking back at herself at a similar age, she was amazed at how much she achieved through sheer self-belief and youthful self-confidence. How sure I was, she thought. How certain that I understood all. Now, I am not certain of too many things. Everything, now, is more nebulous, more uncertain; more open to too many points of view.

'It wasn't too difficult,' Ardal was saying. 'Liam, you remember Liam? He arranged it all. He just went through our records; he was a great man to have everything written down. He picked out Aengus. Just about the right age. Not married. No female friends. Everything was right.'

'Except that it wasn't,' said Mara. She could imagine nothing more disastrous. If Liam had looked to match up two men to go on a journey together in a state of amicable friendship and co-operation, he would not have chosen two people with such diametrically opposite tastes.

'Well,' he said with a shrug, 'perhaps it did not turn out too well.'

'So, the bishop paid you another visit; no, he summoned you this time, didn't he?'

He gave her a sidelong look, but decided that she had her sources and agreed with a slight nod.

'He's a lot older now, than he was then,' he said lightly. 'His days of journeying are over. He holds court now, and does not go on progress around his domains.'

'This meeting, I imagine, would not have been quite so amicable. He would have pricked your pride, wouldn't he? He would have either said or hinted that Clodagh's behaviour in public was a disgrace, a disgrace to the O'Lochlainn clan.' Mara thought back to Cian's words: *What if it is the whole family, the whole kin group, who decided that she had disgraced her kin by going on like that in public and that she was doomed to die, to redeem their honour.* Mara had considered this, but had decided that the brothers were perhaps too down-to-earth, too humble, or too commonsensical to feel that anything Clodagh did would impugn their honour in any way. The honour of the clan, was, perhaps, a different matter: the O'Lochlainn clan who had ruled over the Burren from time immemorial, up to only a hundred years ago, the honour of that clan belonged to its *taoiseach*, and it was the whole life, the whole reason for living of that solitary, reserved man, she remembered thinking. The bishop, in his arrogant way, would not have spared him.

'So he ordered you to do something to put a stop to this scandalous behaviour.'

One of the tenant farmers on this high stony ground was moving his young heifers from one field to another, so Mara and Ardal stood in the middle of the road, in the time-honoured fashion, blocking access to the way that descended into the rich valley.

'Lovely day, Conn, isn't it; I think we'll get the good weather now for a week or two,' shouted Ardal once the gate was slammed closed on the lively young animals.

'It is, indeed, *taoiseach*, and that will be very welcome after the bad March that we've had. God bless you, and the Brehon, too.'

'You are so well liked by them all, every one of your clan knows you and every one of them feels honoured by your notice,' said Mara in a low voice. 'As soon as Conn gets back to his house, even before he takes off his cloak, he will tell his wife about meeting you and what you said about the weather, and what you looked like and they will both bless you and feel grateful for your prediction. And you, of course, have made sure over the years that you will never disappoint, never visit a place without saying the right thing, without making contact, without giving an item of good news, even if it's only the weather.'

He looked amused at that, and then slightly embarrassed. 'I don't suppose that I think about these things at all,' he said. 'No more than you do, I suppose.'

'I'm not sure that I have the instinct to spread good news in the way that you do,' said Mara, thinking about her often preoccupied murmur in answer to greetings. She added, 'So when you were in the Ballynahown region today, you made a point of dropping down to Oughtdara and reassuring Deirdre that Aengus was well cared-for and happy and that you were

looking after him. That was kind of you. But, of course, there
was no mist today.'

And then when he said nothing in reply to that, she added,
'It is a great responsibility to place upon a man, giving him
the status of God in the Old Testament.' The God of the
Old Testament, she thought, was a god of wrath, who did
not hesitate to bring death and destruction down up those
who angered Him. She thought about that for a moment and
then continued, 'Because there was no mist today, because
you could be plainly seen, because there could be no confu-
sion between a human figure and that of the grey stone pillar,
the *Fár Breige*, then Father Eoin, the half-insane priest, peering
fearfully through his window, could see the truth. He, in his
own words, had thought that it was the god who had strangled
Clodagh, had felt that it should have been the god, but now
he realized that by talking to the bishop he had shifted the
burden over on to your shoulders and that you had carried
out the bidding of His Lordship. He saw it all, you know;
that is the problem with mist, it comes and goes, thickens
and clears in a matter of moments. He even saw how you
had used the dead woman's own rope to tie her dead body
to the pillar, but the mist distorted his vision. When he saw
you there today, a day with no mist, he realized that it had
been you who had strangled Clodagh.'

She wondered for a moment whether he would deny it.
It all made sense to her but the evidence so far was flimsy
with only Father O'Lochlainn's word for it. If he did deny it,
then she would have to seek more corroboration; it should be
easy enough. The *taoiseach* was not a man who could move
unseen and unnoticed.

'It was not intended, you know,' he said eventually.

'I could guess that,' she said quickly, conscious of a great
feeling of relief that he was prepared to confess and of thank-
fulness that she did not have to ask among his tenants and his
workers, did not have to go through the wearisome procedure
of asking for sightings of their *taoiseach* on that morning, and
tempting loyal followers to lie and prevaricate.

'Tell me what happened.' They had reached the brow of the
hill. Ahead of them lay the Carron Valley, territory of the O'Brien

of Leamaneh Castle. Not as green and well-tended as the valley that they had left behind; lots of hazel scrub occupying valuable grazing land and most of the walls were ill-tended and had large gaps where cattle had knocked stones onto the ground.

'I went across to see her at the request of the bishop – it was a bad morning with the heavy rain, but I had already wasted quite some time as I wished to allow Aengus time to be out of the way.'

That had been kind, thought Mara. Other men might have interviewed man and wife together, implying that it was the husband's duty to keep his wife under control.

'By the time that I got to Oughtdara the rain had eased but a dreadful mist had risen up in the valley.' Ardal's face took on a remote look, as though gazing back into some nightmare. He stayed silent for a moment and then turned to her as though to explain. 'I was worried about my horse as I could hardly see my hand in front of my face, so I dismounted when I came to the trackway leading down and I tied the horse to a tree. And then I went on foot down the rest of the way as far as the church. I was going to go to the house inside the Dunaunmore enclosure; I thought that she would be indoors on a morning like that, but then I heard a sharp crack. And then a voice, shouting at the top of her voice.'

'Clodagh?' Ardal had half-turned his face away from her, his eyes were no longer on the Carron Valley, but were turned towards Mullaghmore Mountain, its swirling layers of white limestone burnished to silver by the setting sun in the west. At the end of the month, on the eve of Bealtaine, after judgement day at Poulnabrone, all the people in the kingdom, except the very young and the very old, would climb that mountain and build a great bonfire on the peak. It was a very special place for him, she reckoned; she had never known him to be missing on those occasions. The O'Lochlainn, king of the Burren, hundreds of years ago, would have regarded that mountain as the most sacred place in his kingdom.

'What was the crack?' she asked, bringing him back to his story. A tap with a stick on the window of the priest's house, she thought. Clodagh up to mischief; no doubt tormenting

her long-lost lover. It was a pity that Ardal had not identified
the sound. It might have saved him from committing the crime
if he had realized that there was a witness.

Ardal shook his head. 'I don't know,' he said. 'I didn't think
anything of it. I just followed the direction of her voice. She
had once been an intelligent girl; I remembered talking to
her all those years ago, persuading her into a respectable
marriage, and I thought that I could talk to her again, perhaps
influence her to bridle her tongue for the sake of decency;
I was even prepared to bribe her to be silent in public, or
to consider a sensible separation. After all, she had just inherited
the land belonging to her father – I had found her keen-
witted and well-informed on that occasion when I valued
the land and checked on whether a will existed.'

'But on that morning . . .'

'The woman acted as though she were insane. I never heard
such filth as issued from her mouth.' There was a harsh note
in Ardal's voice. 'She acted as though she were possessed by
the devil. I wouldn't offend your ears, Brehon, by repeating
what she said. That unfortunate man!'

'Her husband?'

'He also; I was thinking of Father Eoin, such a pious man.
She tormented him, would not leave him alone.'

Had Clodagh confined her foul-mouthed obscenities to the
subject of the priest and her husband, or had she made sexual
advances to Ardal himself, as well? Judging by the look of
distaste she guessed that the latter was true. It accounted for
the fury with which he attacked her.

'I just felt that I had to stop her, to stop those words
coming out of her mouth; I just felt that I could not listen
to any more of that stuff,' he said, almost as though he read
her mind.

'So you put your hands around her neck.'

'I shook her first, just trying to stop her. And then she
turned her head and spat at me, right in my face. I was mad
with fury. I just didn't know what I was doing. I just had to
stop her; I had to silence her.' Ardal picked up an angular
pebble and flung it with all his strength. It hit a standing stone
about a hundred yards away and a startled hare bounded out

from the grass nearby and went leaping down the hill propelled to great speed by his powerful back legs.

'I can understand that you were angry, that you lost control, but I find it hard to understand why you did not come and tell me what had happened, make open confession, offer to pay the penalty . . .'

He threw up his hand in an odd gesture, almost an appeal for mercy, she thought, but she waited. She had to be impartial. No one was above the law.

'I couldn't bear it,' he said eventually.

'And yet others had to bear the burden of suspicion.'

'I would not have allowed any injustice.' His colour had flared up and his blue eyes were angry.

'You must have known how the weight of suspicion would fall upon her husband, poor Aengus, and upon her cousins.'

'I tell you that I would not have allowed any harm to come to them. I would have compensated them.'

'That was not good enough, though, was it? Murder is a terrible deed and no amount of benevolent paying of a fine would compensate for the lifelong burden of a false accusation, of the mark of Cain in the eyes of kin, of clansmen and of neighbours.'

He said nothing, did not even look at her, just stared intently at the mountain. She waited for a moment, but knew that he would say no more. And she had no more questions. He had killed the woman. Out of sheer rage and disgust, he had put his hands, the strong hands of a horseman, around her neck and throttled her. And then in an effort to hide his crime he had bound the body to the stone pillar and had disappeared back into the mist. Pride, of course, had prevented him from acknowledging his crime. And perhaps there was a certain thread of arrogance woven into the decision to remain silent.

'I shall want to hear this case as soon as possible,' she said abruptly. There had been too much talk, too many superstitious fears aroused. All needed to be explained to the people of the Burren and the wild rumours laid to rest. 'I would like to hold the hearing on the day after tomorrow.' This would get the matter over before Turlough arrived back, and before those celebrations of her fiftieth birthday.

'You will be there?' A half nod in response.

'If you wish to plead innocent, you may desire to have a lawyer to represent you, an *aigne*. I can give you a list of suggestions if you wish.'

He shook his head. He would not plead innocent, she thought. That terrible, overweening pride that had prevented him from acknowledging his crime would now prevent him from denying it.

'I will be there,' he said, his voice so low, so broken that it was almost impossible to identify it as his.

The stone-paved field of Poulnabrone was almost empty for judgement day. The notices had been read at all the churches, at the inns, at the blacksmith's shop and at the mill – all as the law directed, but when the Angelus bell sounded, the only member of the O'Lochlainn clan who was present, as well as the *taoiseach*, was Aengus, and he was only there because Mara had sent Fachtnan, leading the law school cob, to make sure of his presence. There were a few members of the O'Connor clan, one of two MacNamara men from Carron and otherwise only the O'Brien farmers and tenants from the nearby townlands. The O'Lochlainn clan remained faithful to their highly esteemed *taoiseach* and did not want to witness his humiliation.

The English had derided Brehon laws, castigating them as a free licence to kill, for those who had the silver to pay the fine. But no one seeing the face of Ardal O'Lochlainn and noting the sunken eyes, the mottled pallor of his cheek, the stooped shoulders, would have felt that this man was getting off too lightly as, step by step, the Brehon took him through the morning of his crime and got him to describe the actions that led to the death of Clodagh O'Lochlainn. He acknowledged his guilt with bowed head and husky voice.

'According to *The Great Ancient Tradition*,' said Mara, 'the fine for killing a person is fixed at forty-two séts, twenty-one ounces of silver or twenty-one milch cows. This was an unacknowledged killing and so is classified as *duinethaoide* and therefore this doubles the fine to be paid, so the fine is forty-two ounces of silver or forty-two milch cows.' Normally, at this stage of the proceedings, she allocated a time limit within which the fine had to be paid. In most cases the culprit would have to call upon kin members or perhaps the whole clan to enable him to pay, but in the case of Ardal, an honourable man, she merely finished by hoping that sum would be paid as soon as possible. Aengus, she noted, looked stunned and acutely miserable. He sank down on a stone and put his head within his hands.

Aengus, as a man with no land, had no honour price of his own and so Clodagh, as his wife, had none, either. Nevertheless, this was a huge sum of money. Aengus could now become a well-off farmer. He would need, she noted, guidance and assistance in order to manage this fortune. Most of the people who had attended were now leaving, sidling past Aengus as though he were the culprit, not the victim. Fachtnan finished stowing away her papers and law scrolls in the battered leather satchel that accompanied her everywhere and Mara directed her steps towards the miserable figure of the shepherd, but Ardal forestalled her, walking over, putting out a hand and then pulling Aengus to his feet. The man swayed as though he were ill, but Ardal kept his hand firmly gripping the upper arm and walked with him to where the horses were tethered. He held the cob while Aengus mounted and then together they rode down the road towards the Carron valley.

Watching them go, Mara felt comforted. The law had done its duty, now was a time for healing. The Bible, of course, said that: 'whoever sheds man's blood, then his blood will be shed by man: for God made man in his image.' Brehon law, on the contrary, was concerned that there should be no unnecessary bloodshed, so substituted a financial penalty, much to the disgust of England and of Rome.

However, even the bishop himself, she thought, would probably not allude to the matter again. He would, with secret relief, consider that God's wrath had descended upon a woman who had mocked the man of God. And most of the people in the mountain valleys would probably secretly continue to feel that the *Fár Breige* and the Morrigan had something to do with it. And Ardal, she was sure, would make sure that Aengus knew how to handle his newfound wealth.

Fourteen

Brecha Nemeð Coisech
(Laws Concerning Nobility)

The status of a briugu (hospitaller) depends on three things:
1. *A never-dry cauldron.*
2. *A dwelling on a public road.*
3. *A welcome before every face.*

On a day of bright sunshine, when the lambs raced in the fields and when primroses, violets and early orchids flowered in the roadside verges, Mara celebrated her fiftieth birthday. She woke early, conscious of having slept heavily after the exhausting evening of greeting her guests and half-expecting to see her husband by her side, but there was no sign of him. Surely he had not forgotten the elaborate birthday party that he had been so insistent on staging. Unlikely, she thought. He was surprisingly good at turning up when expected, even despite all of the trials and difficulties of journeys during these unsettled times. She stretched out luxuriously for a minute before getting up. The room was beautifully warm from the heat of the many charcoal-burning braziers, with an ewer of water simmering in a basin above one of them, and already the early morning sun penetrated the curtains. She went to the window, admired the lambs and the spring flowers, and then turned back to the task of looking like the king's wife in front of all his invited visitors. Brigid, her housekeeper, had probably been in the room already as a lace-trimmed gown of soft dark green wool had been laid out ready to be worn for the morning. Quickly she washed, plaited her hair, enclosing the braids in a fine silver net at the back of her neck and then dressed, buttoning the long sleeves with care and pulling on soft leather shoes over her woven stockings.

'Let me see you.' Brigid was in the room, inspecting her

with care, looking her up and down severely, checking that she was going to do honour to the Davoren family, whom Brigid had served for over fifty years.

'And now you're going to tell me that I looked better than this fifty years ago,' said Mara resignedly.

A smile crept across Brigid's stern face. 'You were a lovely baby, the first baby that I ever looked at properly, I suppose.'

'I wonder what I would have done without you?' said Mara. She owed a lot to her father who had cared for his motherless daughter, had allowed her to join in the lessons in the schoolhouse, had nurtured her talents and encouraged her on the ambitious pathway to become a lawyer and the only woman Brehon in Ireland, but Brigid had given her love and security, and confidence in herself, had supported her through that disastrous early marriage to the idle drunken law scholar Dualta, and then after her divorce, had cared for her daughter Sorcha while Mara, bereft of her father, struggled to keep the law school going and to manage the legal affairs of the kingdom.

'I owe you so much, Brigid,' she said softly. 'Fifty years of looking after me!'

'Would you listen to that!' said Brigid, hastily. 'What's got into Cormac? He is like a seagull in a storm this morning. He's been running up and down those stairs, screeching at the top of his voice, since dawn broke. And in his best clothes, too. Very fussy, he was this morning, his lordship. Nothing would do him, but his saffron *léine* and his new fur-lined jacket.'

'It's the king,' said Mara, her sharp ear distinguished the word from the boys' shouts. Despite her annoyance at his late arrival, she felt her lips part in an irresistible smile. She went quickly across to her window and the empty road was now full of sound and colour and movement. First came the standard bearer, the long triangular banner of blue and saffron linen rippling in the wind and then the men-at-arms. The mail-coated galloglass, battleaxes slung over their shoulders, formed the vanguard, as though they were going into battle, then came the lightly-armed kern with their bows, their throwing knives, wooden shield and short swords, and then behind them the mounted bodyguard and behind them came Turlough himself, and a group of his friends, a very large group, she noted, hoping they had room for them. But all would probably turn out well. It usually did with Turlough. Mara had contemplated receiving them in the Great Hall, but one look at Turlough's face, eagerly scanning the tower house walls, made her change her mind. She snatched up her fur-lined cloak and went clattering down the stairs on the heels of Cormac and his friends.

The courtyard was thronged but the crowd opened a passageway for her and she made her way to the gates, pausing there for a moment and allowing her son and his friends to race up the road.

'These boys get so excited,' said Cael with an elderly sigh and Mara did her best to hide a smile. Cael was growing up fast, she thought, and almost felt a pang of nostalgia for the shorthaired little girl in the knee-length *léine* who had been so resolute that she was a boy.

'Well, it is rather exciting, isn't it, seeing them all coming down the road,' she said apologetically. Who was that man, riding side by side with Turlough, she wondered. A young man dressed in a leather jerkin of boiled bull hide, thrown carelessly open to reveal a saffron *léine*. His face was unfamiliar to her, a very tanned face, framed by a mop of black curls. She didn't think that she had ever seen him before. As the boys came up to greet Turlough, he had stretched out a foot as a step, then reached down and hauled Cormac on to his horse, placing the boy in front of him and shouting some remark across to Turlough. Even from a distance Mara could see from Cormac's very straight back and the toss of his red-gold hair that he was thrilled and excited by the notice taken of him.

'Who is that man?' asked Mara of the steward that stood beside her.

He opened his mouth, shut it again and looked at her in a slightly strange way, she thought, almost as though he had been about to say something and then had thought better of that.

'I'm thinking that must be the MacMahon, the new young *taoiseach*, of Oriel,' he said. Mara noticed that he, like herself, was watching with interest as the curly-headed young man bent down, saying something in Cormac's ear and Cormac responded eagerly, twisting himself around and gazing up at the MacMahon.

'Himself will have been talking to you about MacMahon of Oriel,' said the steward tentatively and Mara did not reply, just inclined her head. He could take the gesture as he wished. No doubt this man featured in one of Turlough's many stories related to her about 'good fellows', but there had been nothing particular mentioned, certainly nothing about Cormac and now every maternal instinct within Mara seemed to point to the possibility that this visit, all the way from the north of Ireland, by the *taoiseach* of Oriel, had something to do with her son. The steward's tentative glances hinted at this also; these men would pick up the signs very quickly and there probably had been many muttered conversations about the king's youngest son spending so long at school and not going out in the world to receive weapons training.

'There you are, Rossa, here she is, here is Mara, what did I tell you?' The pride and excitement in Turlough's voice was so vibrant while he waved his hand in her direction, as though she were a particularly fine statue or piece of silver, that Mara felt, despite herself, the corners of her mouth lift in a suppressed smile.

'Not enough, obviously! You told me that she was fifty years old; well, that's an impossibility, for a start,' retorted Rossa MacMahon. His voice had the brisk clarity of the northern Ireland accent and it cut through the buzz of conversation and the clip-clop of the horse hoofs on the paved road outside the castle. Mara began to laugh. It was impossible to do anything else with a husband like Turlough. He was looking at her with the hopeful expression of a puppy that is not sure whether he is about to be scolded or praised for the enormous hole in the middle of a flowerbed. She allowed herself to be hugged after he leaped from his saddle with the agility of a man half his age and then drew back to greet Rossa. Cormac, she noticed, had, with a courtly air assisted him to dismount and was now holding the man's sword in one hand and the reins of the enormous coal black horse in the other, and managing to do both very adroitly. A clever boy, she thought, suppressing a sigh. He had probably had a word with his father, a month or so ago, had been given a half-promise and now, with this advent of an admired and war-like *taoiseach* from the north, had immediately drawn the conclusion that here was a mentor and a foster father for the next stage in his life.

How many foster fathers had Jesus Christ? The early Gaelic converts to Christianity had asked that of Saint Patrick, who, over from Bristol in England, had probably been taken aback at the question, but here in Ireland a boy of noble descent would commonly be furnished with many foster fathers, in ascending order of class, according to his needs and the last foster father for a war-like boy such as Cormac, son of a warrior king, would be one who could teach him war-like skills. It was, perhaps, Mara told herself, as she escorted the visitor and his train to the castle, time for him to move on. He had been trained in the law, but had shown little interest, barely scraping through his examinations at the end of each year. That training, the knowledge of the laws which each king had to swear to uphold, would now fall into its rightful place in his life; just as the knowledge of sheep farming and the ways of fishermen had been assimilated in his first seven years. Nevertheless, Mara had hoped to avoid this.

There were, already, enough contenders for the role of king of the O'Brien clan and descent was not, as in England, to the eldest son, but to the most worthy. Turlough had sons, grandsons by an earlier marriage and there were nephews and cousins – all members of the *derbhfine*, all descendants of the one great-grandfather, Turlough Beag, who had been succeeded, one after the other, by three of his six sons: Teige, the father of Turlough Donn, Conor naShrona (of the big nose) and then by another Turlough, known as the Gilladuff (the black lad). Only after the death of his last uncle had her husband Turlough succeeded to his father's place.

This waiting to fill dead men's shoes was not something that she wanted for Cormac, but he was now almost thirteen years old and he had a right to have a say in his own future.

'I look forward to talking with you and hearing all about Oriel,' she said to young Rossa MacMahon, signalling to the steward, 'but now you must refresh yourself after your journey.'

The steward, she guessed, would allocate one of the best bedrooms to this unexpected guest. There was a buzz of excitement amongst the servants and men-at-arms as Cormac walked past, solemnly carrying the huge sword.

'So, tell me all about Rossa MacMahon,' she said to her husband as soon as they were alone.

'Well, he's a very good fellow, a very nice fellow and he's got great ideas, more ideas in his little finger, than his father had in his head. He was the one responsible for winning that battle when O'Neill took it on himself to invade Oriel and do the English king's dirty work for him. Taught O'Neill a lesson that he won't forget in a hurry.'

'And you've spoken to him about Cormac?' Mara quailed inwardly at the prospect of her son's almost inevitable involvement in future teaching of the warlike kind, but she kept her voice steady. Turlough was an excellent leader himself and would be a good judge of a man. After all, she said to herself, no one is safe. A boy can fall off a horse, drown in the sea, can get some deadly illness; there were hazards in every life.

'Well,' said Turlough, 'I just thought that I'd make a few enquiries, look around me, see who would do a good job of fostering him. You see, he's like me at that age – got your brains, of course, but he does want to be out and about doing things, not just muttering Latin and learning off laws. He can always have his own Brehon. Anyway, there's no hurry about it; you can get to know Rossa and see how you like him and we'll see how Cormac gets on with him. Now, what have I done with that clean *léine*; I had it in my hand one second ago.'

And then as his head emerged from the folds of the linen, he said, with the triumphant air of one who delivers a winning argument, 'And he's got two very nice little wives for himself so the boy won't lack mothering.'

Downstairs in the Great Hall, the room with its triple mullioned windows overlooking the Atlantic Ocean and the Aran Islands, the visitors were gathering. The window casements were propped open and sea air, smelling of mineral freshness, swept into the room. And the sea itself stretched out in front of the windows, blue as harebells; the waves streaked across its ruffled surface like cream whipped to rough peaks. The colour was so intense that the sky itself paled before it and the limestone rocks were black and formless against the continuously moving water. A single-sailed Galway hooker moved swiftly towards the coast and the gulls cried and screamed overhead. The air was like wine, full of life-giving vigour. It was a perfect place for a festive gathering – a huge room with fireplaces burning tree-sized logs at both ends, a minstrels' gallery above and those magnificent large mullioned windows overlooking the Atlantic Ocean. The guests were a mixture of young and old – lots of Turlough's royal relations: his eldest son, Conor with his wife Ellice, his daughter Ragnelt, her husband, Donán O'Kennedy. There was also the king's cousin, Mauritius the bishop of Kilfenora and some of his allies from other kingdoms, such as Ulick Burke, Ulick of the Wine as he was now known. The scholars from Cahermacnaghten law school and some of their friends, young people from the kingdom of the Burren, were there also.

Cormac and Rossa MacMahon were sitting side by side on a window seat overlooking the valley of Oughtdara and from Cormac's animated face and gestures Mara guessed that the legend of the *Fár Breige* and the Morrigan was being told. She watched them for a moment, liking the interest and enthusiasm on the young man's face. Cormac was glowing with excitement, at his ease, and yet respectful and admiring. Rossa had allowed a small dagger that he had been fingering, to slip to the floor and Cormac immediately jumped to his feet, picked it up and presented it with a graceful and rather courtly bow. Mara moved away. She would talk to Rossa and to Cormac a little later, but she had a feeling that Turlough had chosen well.

Turlough himself was deep in conversation with his cousin Teige O'Brien, *taoiseach* of the O'Brien clan on the Burren; the MacNamara and the O'Connor were tasting wine together in one corner of the room and so Mara went straight towards the remaining chieftain of the kingdom.

'Well, Ardal,' she said cordially, 'now you will know how to celebrate your sixtieth birthday when it comes up, won't you?'

He looked slightly startled at her words, but then smiled. 'I was wondering whether to come here today. I almost didn't, and then I told myself that an O'Lochlainn *taoiseach* must never back away from a challenge.'

She didn't pretend to misunderstand him. 'That is all over and done with. The crime was acknowledged; the penalty paid.'

'That's just the point,' he said. 'I haven't paid the penalty. I've tried, but I can't. Aengus just will not accept it. There is no point in giving him a bag of silver; he doesn't want it. I've offered to set him up with some land, but he doesn't want that either; he doesn't want cows; he doesn't want anything. Every time that I try to talk to him, he shies away like a frightened sheep. He's even asked my steward, Danann, to get me to leave him alone. I've tried to do lots of small things, like making his place more comfortable, things like that, but it's not enough. I owe the man forty-two milch cows or forty-two pieces of silver, but how on earth am I going to get him to accept them?'

He had a look of genuine unhappiness and guilt. Mara knew that he was not going to be satisfied with a soothing assurance that he had done his best. She understood his feelings and guessed that she would share them.

'It's a difficult problem, isn't it,' she said sympathetically. 'If it were me, I could think of a dozen projects that I might use the silver for, but I can understand that he doesn't want to change his way of life. Sheep are probably very different animals to cows. He's happy with the one, but that doesn't mean that he would be happy with the other.'

'He doesn't want a house either,' said Ardal. 'He's happiest of all in one of the shepherds' huts. He asked me as a favour to allow him to stay up there. He didn't like their house in Oughtdara, and he hated Dunaunmore when Clodagh inherited it from her father. He said that she had no luck with it, these were his words.'

'I wonder whether that is why he doesn't want your money,' said Mara thoughtfully. 'After all, Clodagh's did turn out to be a fatal inheritance, didn't it? It brought her no luck, he was right there, neither luck nor happiness.' And then, because she could see how Ardal winced away from the memory of his deed, she said hastily, 'I wonder whether Aengus would like to have something done with this silver, something that he could give to the community, something that would bear his name and . . . perhaps something that would benefit children . . . he seemed very fond of Fachtnan's little daughter . . . saved her life . . .'

Mara gazed thoughtfully across the room to where Fachtnan and Nuala, both in their finest clothes, were chatting animatedly to the son of Turlough's physician, O'Hickey, who had just returned from Italy.

'Leave it with me, Ardal,' she said. 'I've got an idea in my head. Why don't you go over and talk to Fachtnan. Poor fellow; he is beginning to turn a little green. Nuala and young O'Hickey are probably discussing what human flesh looks like when it has been in the water for a few days. It would be a kindness to go and discuss the weather with him.'

She watched in satisfaction as Fachtnan turned with relief to the O'Lochlainn *taoiseach* and then went across to the window where Cormac was entertaining the MacMahon with a story about entrails being wound around an oak tree.

'Cormac,' she said with an apologetic smile at the MacMahon, 'could I ask you to get the book, *Utopia* from my satchel, it's a slim book, written in Latin . . .'

'I know it,' said Cormac. He cast a glance at her, half-defiant, half-appealing, and she nodded reassuringly. She could see his face brighten as he turned back to Rossa MacMahon, murmuring in a courtly way, 'Excuse me, for a minute, my lord.'

'Well, how do you like my son?' she said as soon as Cormac had gone through the door.

'I like him very much,' he said in a straightforward fashion that she admired. 'Clever boy, very bookish.'

'Oh,' she said, rather taken aback. 'Well, I suppose that he has been studying the law for five or six years now and . . .'

'Oh, the law, that'll be no good to him.' He dismissed the law with an impatient wave of the hand. 'It's this fellow Caesar from a way back, back in time out of mind; well, he had some interesting ideas about fighting battles and your young lad knows all about him. Good as a storyteller, he is. Must get him to tell some of those tales to my men on the long winter evenings – that's if you'll be happy for me to take him away with me, of course,' he added hastily.

'We'll have to discuss it tomorrow when all of the celebrations are over,' said Mara firmly. She got to her feet as she saw Cormac edge his way through the crowds towards them, book in hand. She knew that she was going to agree, though. She could not bear to disappoint that bright, hopeful face.

'Thank you, Cormac,' she said taking *Utopia* from him. She thought of suggesting Livy's *History of Rome* for their consideration, but decided not to tease. She rather liked this young man, she thought. His earnest and straightforward manner appealed to her; Cormac would come to no harm under his leadership. She found another window seat and beckoned to Ardal and Fachtnan and they approached her eagerly; glad to get away from medical matters, she guessed.

'Listen to this,' she said and turned the pages of *Utopia* until she found the one that she wanted. 'This was written by an Englishman, named Thomas More, about what he imagined to be an ideal state; and I must say that he has some interesting ideas. I wonder what he would think of our Brehon law if he understood it properly.'

And then she read aloud, translating the Latin text into fluent Gaelic for Ardal's benefit.

'You see,' she said triumphantly. 'All children in this state go to school, not just a few whose parents are educated and wealthy, they all go to school and as well as reading and writing, they learn the trades of their fathers and mothers, they are educated by the community. Wouldn't a school like that be a wonderful thing for the kingdom of the Burren? We could build it at a central spot, perhaps near to the judgement place at Poulnabrone and everyone would have the right to go there and everyone would contribute their knowledge and their experience to teaching the children. We will teach them to spin and weave, to dye the wool,' she went on, thinking of the young Clodagh with her colourful cloak, 'and the wheelwrights and the smiths will show their skills and those wise in the way of stone will build the school with the help of the children – they will be involved at all stages and Fachtnan, if you both agree, will be the first *ollamh* of the school.' She stopped, almost out of breath and looked at them.

'I remember you saying once, Ardal, that if Clodagh had received an education that her clever brain would have had something more constructive to do, rather than tormenting her family and her neighbours. Perhaps the school, if Aengus agrees to spend the forty-two ounces of silver on it, will not just bear his name, but will be a sort of memorial to his troubled wife also.'

And this school, she thought, as she listened to their delighted comments, and looked across the room at her husband, will also be a memorial to the golden age of King Turlough Donn O'Brien, the king who had brought peace to the three kingdoms of Thomond, Corcomroe and Burren.